KATHERINE GRAHAM

Salt Sisters

What secrets is this seaside village hiding?

QUARTZ BOOKS

First published by Quartz Books 2021

Copyright © 2021 by Katherine Graham

This novel is entirely a work of fiction. The names, characters and incidents portrayed in it are the work of the author's imagination. Any resemblance to actual persons, living or dead, events or localities is entirely coincidental.

First edition

ISBN: 978-1-8383195-0-2

*This book was professionally typeset on Reedsy.
Find out more at reedsy.com*

For Beth – my lifelong best friend from the very beginning.

And Igor, my North Star. You made it all possible.

Contents

Chapter One

We got off the plane and walked into the airport terminal, where I promptly threw up.

The river of passengers diverted as people shuffled and side-stepped around my puddle of vomit. I pressed my face against the cool of the tiled wall.

'There, there.' My best friend Adam rubbed my back, glancing nervously about.

A combination of vodka and sleeping pills had knocked me out right after take-off from Hong Kong. I'd blacked out for the entire flight, drowning in a deep sleep where I couldn't dream and couldn't wake. Couldn't picture Amy's face clearly.

The last leg of the journey was in sight and the closer we got to home, the higher the waves of nausea rose in my chest. Every so often I had to stop and rest against a seat or grab a handrail and close my eyes to avoid being sucked under the swell, taking deep breaths and riding it out until it washed away. The floor was unsteady beneath my feet.

'Just give me a moment,' I said.

Adam had taken care of everything. He had packed my suitcase while I lay on the bed, swinging between body-racking sobs and staring silently at the wall, while his husband Thierry had pulled some strings to get us two seats in business class on the next flight to Heathrow.

Was that only yesterday? It already felt like a lifetime ago. Yesterday morning, when everything had been normal, when I'd woken up and drunk my coffee like normal. I should have gone to Pilates and met friends for brunch, just like any other Saturday. Maybe spent the afternoon shopping. But then I'd checked my messages and my world had imploded.

Soon, we were in the hire car motoring up the A1, my forehead resting on the passenger window. Life was inexplicably continuing. People were making journeys, running errands, going for days out. Going on as if nothing had happened. The sun was offensively bright.

I was drowsy, and despite sleeping for twelve hours straight, I was exhausted. My head pounded and my body ached with the effort of just sitting.

We turned off the motorway and onto narrow roads bracketed by tall hedgerows, and my internal GPS flickered to life: I knew these country lanes like the lines on my hands. Adam was taking the tight corners cautiously, but I would have been whizzing through.

The sea was just coming into sight – we got a glimpse here and there as we swung around narrow bends – and I knew that under different circumstances I would have been stretching in my seat by now, craning my neck to see it. Instead, there was a quiet dread, that sick feeling in my stomach that I couldn't shake, and a heaviness that wouldn't go away.

We finally arrived at the village. Seahouses was little more than two dozen streets knotted together above a harbour that opened up onto the vast blue of the North Sea. I directed Adam to Amy's house, a detached stone cottage that had been the village post office at one time. He pulled up outside and switched off the engine, looking at me to see what was next. It was so quiet.

This was really happening. I would never see my sister again. Never speak to her, or hear her voice.

We had shared an entire life and for years, we had come strictly as a pair. Amy was the only person who had been there since the beginning, who truly knew me. But then there were all the things we'd never got to say. And now the years ahead of us, the decades stretching in front that we had taken for granted, all that time had been so abruptly and cruelly cancelled.

Everything that we would ever do together, all of it was already done. It was only me from now on.

We stood on the doorstep, and I asked Adam to give me a moment. I had to pull myself together – the last thing I wanted to do was to collapse in tears the second I saw the kids. But the longer I thought about them, just on the other side of the door, the higher my panic grew – how would they cope without their mum?

The shock was rising once more, beating in my chest and tightening its hands around my throat. I leaned against the door frame, trying to catch my breath. Adam sniffed loudly, and I knew he was trying to hold back his tears.

Eventually I raised a hand to knock, but before I could, the door opened.

'My darling girl!' Auntie Sue wailed, opening her arms for me.

I buried my face in her shoulder, weeping into her soft sweater. Her smell, the curve of her waist and the solidity of her were all so familiar. She held me out at arm's length, just to get a good look at me, then pulled me in tight again.

'And you must be Adam.' She took his hand. 'Thank you for bringing her home.'

Adam gulped.

'It's no problem at all.' His voice tightened. 'And I'm so sorry for your loss.'

I took a deep breath.

'How's Mum?'

Auntie Sue looked at me warily.

'Well, you know your mum... She's handling things in her own way.'

She turned back and ushered us through the hallway into the kitchen, where everyone was gathered.

The pain in the room hit me like a wave of despair. Amy's husband, Mike, was sitting at the table with my youngest niece, Betsy curled up to him on one side and her brother, Lucas on the other, both of them softly sobbing. Hannah, their eldest girl – how old was she now? I quickly did the arithmetic and worked out she was thirteen – was sitting across from them with her feet on the bench, hugging her knees to her chest. Their faces were raw, red, and dripping with salty tears. I wanted to throw up again.

Mum was standing at the counter, cocooned in an enormous orange cardigan. She flung herself onto me.

'Oh, Izzy darling, it's the most terrible thing!'

I looked over her shoulder and saw that she had been stirring raisins into a large mixing bowl. Smudges of flour streaked the countertop.

'Is that... a cake, Mum?'

'Yes, darling. Fruit cake – your sister's favourite. Nobody feels like eating anything, of course, but I thought if I made a nice cake, we might at least get our appetites back, and I

4

wanted to do something useful...'

'Mum,' I said softly.

She avoided my eyes.

'Amy has died, Mum. Do you understand that?'

'Izzy!' Auntie Sue hissed. 'That's quite enough!'

I sat on the bench next to Hannah and wrapped my arms around her. She wiped at her tears with her sleeve.

As Mum calmly went back to her cake, Auntie Sue put the kettle on, and she and Mike tried to fill me in on what they knew so far. As they recounted the details between them, the youngest kids started wailing again and we listened to the story through Betsy's sobs.

Mike had come back from the pub, expecting Amy to be waiting at home. Hannah had been sleeping over at a friend's and the younger kids had been upstairs watching a movie. His supper had been on the kitchen table. Amy had left her book, her reading glasses, and half a glass of wine in the living room. Her slippers had been left by the door and her car keys were gone. Mike asked the kids where she was, and they said she'd told them she had to pop out quickly, but hadn't said where she was going. They couldn't remember how long she'd been gone.

Mike didn't worry too much, not at first, assuming Amy was running an errand. Perhaps something had come up with one of her community groups, or someone had needed a nurse. It wasn't unusual for either of them to leave the kids home alone for a short while. Lucas was eleven and was a sensible boy, more than capable of keeping an eye on Betsy, who was already eight. As the night wore on, Mike tried to call Amy, but her phone went straight to voicemail. When she still hadn't called or come home by midnight, he knew something was wrong.

He called her best friend, then Auntie Sue, and even the pub to see if she had shown up there. Nobody had seen her. He then phoned the police, who told him that someone would be there shortly. Mike assumed this would be to take a report and get more details. But when an officer came to the door with his hat in his hand, he knew something awful had happened.

Amy's car had skidded off the road and crashed into a tree, on a country lane just outside the village. Nobody had seen the accident, but a motorist had arrived soon after and called 999. He'd tried in vain to give first aid to Amy as she lay there, trapped in the crumpled wreck of the car, unsure if she was still alive. When the ambulance got there, they couldn't find a pulse.

I looked around the kitchen: my sister's kitchen, in her home, with her family – all of it was hers, and all of it was her. She would walk through the door any minute now, if only I wished it hard enough...

I watched the door. Amy didn't come.

Adam parked the car outside The Ship. It was a last-minute reservation, made after I had explained to him stony-faced that we would not be staying at my mum's. Thankfully, there were two rooms available, both with a sea view.

Seahouses had two pubs – The Ship, at the top of Main Street and The Castle, out by the caravan park. Anyone desiring accommodation grander than a tin can on wheels was limited to the dozen rooms at The Ship.

We were both wired, despite our exhaustion, and decided to have a scotch in the bar after dumping our bags. It had been after 11 p.m. by the time we had left Amy's, when all three children had finally gone to bed and Mike had insisted, red-eyed, that we should go and get some rest.

The Ship was a traditional pub, perched above the harbour and decorated with antique equipment and memorabilia from the local fishing trade. Every inch of wall space in the bar displayed an array of brass dials, gauges, and maritime gear. It was the closest pub to our house, and Dad had always insisted it attracted a better class of clientele. Most of the regulars were fishermen. He used to bring us here when Mum had evening classes, and sometimes on Sundays for lunch if nobody wanted to cook. It was the pub where Amy and I – and every other local teenager – had ordered our first drinks, getting sloppy drunk on pints of snakebite.

I didn't recognise the woman behind the bar, but I knew Seahouses people and I knew she would be a talker, so I sent Adam up to order. She was quite taken with the handsome out-of-towner, smiling and flicking her hair. I heard her ask where he was from and what brought him to Northumberland, and when Adam explained quietly that we were here because a family member had sadly died, I saw a flash of understanding on her face. News of Amy's accident had spread quickly.

I necked two whiskies and took a third up to bed with me. Adam tucked me in, and I cried fresh tears at how lucky I was to have him.

'Are you sure you don't want to stay at your mum's? I don't know what happened between you two...'

He folded the duvet down around me, just like my dad used to do. I closed my eyes.

'You have no idea.' I barely got the words out before sleep finally came.

That night, I woke countless times. Every time I dozed off, I was yanked cruelly back to the surface. The same nightmare came to me again and again – Amy was there, but I couldn't see her face clearly; she was right in front of me, but I couldn't touch her; she was talking to me, but her words were muffled, as if she was underwater. Amy. My Salt Sister, now lost forever.

Chapter Two

A knock at my door woke me. The bed looked like a fight scene: I was face-down on the pillow with the duvet knotted around my legs.

Adam brought me a coffee and a bacon roll before heading out to explore. My appetite hadn't returned, but the caffeine was much needed. The bags under my eyes were as big as my matching luggage.

My phone pinged. There were messages of sympathy from some of the Hong Kong group, who had heard the bad news from Thierry.

I scrolled back to the last message I'd had from Amy. She'd tried to call me on Friday night, just as I'd been arriving at the bar. I'd already been running late – the traffic had been terrible – so I'd let her call go to voicemail and sent a text:

Sorry! Can't talk now, I'm out. Everything OK?

She'd replied: *No worries. I had a quiet half-hour and just thought I'd try you. Enjoy your night and talk soon?*

I'd texted back: *Sounds good. Speak tomorrow xo*

Nothing out of the ordinary – we were both busy, and the time difference made it difficult to find occasions when it was convenient for both of us to talk.

When I'd first moved to Hong Kong from Zurich, before I'd

met the people who would eventually become my friends and while I'd still been settling in at work, Amy and I had had a regular standing call. Every Friday night, I'd phone her when I got back to my quiet little apartment in that new and strange city. I'd tell her about my job – my big promotion at the bank that had been too good an opportunity to turn down, even though it meant moving to the other side of the world – and she would tell me about her day at the hospital and how the kids were doing.

But then I'd made friends and started going out more, and work had become so much busier, and then Amy's shifts had changed and she'd had to work on Friday afternoons. We'd never set a new time for our regular catch-up and had tried instead to snatch conversations in the small gaps of our equally hectic schedules.

Hong Kong had seemed so superficial at first, impossible to crack – I thought I'd never fit in, never be one of the it-crowd. I'd come so far and still had not quite made it. But then I met Adam, and he introduced me to Chiara, the Italian glamazon, and Mathilde, a kind-hearted Parisian cool-girl, who took me out and introduced me to more people. And one day, when I looked around and saw the life that I'd made for myself so far away, I realised I'd found what I'd been searching for.

But had it pulled me away from Amy?

I caressed her name on the screen. How had we not found the time to talk? What had we both been so busy doing all the time?

Out of habit, or longing, or disbelief, I sent her a message: *Sorry we missed each other. I wish we could talk now xo*

The icon stayed grey. Undelivered. Unread. Amy would never see it.

The rest of my messages were in a new group chat:

*Mum added you to the group: **We love Amy***

Mum: *Darlings – we are all waking up this morning and remembering our loss. Just understand that this is the saddest you will feel. The pain will never go away but it will not, cannot get worse than this.*

Mum: *I invite you to a shared simple meditative experience: take the sitting lotus position, hold the memory of Amy in your left hand and place your right hand to your heart centre. Take ten deep, cleansing breaths.*

Mum: *The embodied soul is eternal in existence, indestructible, and infinite, only the material body is factually perishable (Krishna, Bhagavad Gita).*

Mike: *Thanks Anne. We will certainly need some deep breathing to get us through this.*

Hannah: *But meditating won't bring Mum back*

Auntie Sue: *Meditation isn't for everyone! The most important thing is that we are all here for each other. Love Auntie Sue. x*

Mum: *Actually, studies show that mindfulness and practising meditation can improve mental well-being after traumatic experiences by two thirds.*

Mum: *I'll do an energy cleansing today. There's so much sadness in the house and some crystals will help.*

Auntie Sue: *Anne! I told you it's not for everyone! Love Sue. x*

Mike: *Maybe it can wait until tomorrow? The police are here.*

I pulled on yesterday's outfit and ran over to Amy's house. Mike was in the kitchen with two police officers – a woman who looked like she should be serving in a canteen rather than fighting crime, and an unfeasibly young-looking man who was possibly on work experience. They stopped talking as I came in, and Mike introduced me.

The dinner-lady-policewoman explained that although Amy had drunk a glass or two of wine, it almost certainly hadn't put her over the limit. There would be a post-mortem to confirm it and check that there were no other substances or health issues that could have impaired her driving. There would also be forensic tests of the car and the scene of the accident, but in cases like this, she said, the post-mortem usually revealed the whole story.

I sat listening to her with my head in my hands and bile rising in my throat. The room was closing in on me and I desperately needed some air. I excused myself and stepped into the hallway. Lucas was sitting on the floor outside the kitchen door, his knees tucked up to his chest. He'd clearly been listening in on the conversation.

I led him outside and we sat side by side on the front doorstep. I pulled him in close, watching my tears dripping onto the top of his head.

'They said a *post-mortem*. That means they're going to cut Mummy up into pieces!'

'It doesn't. They just have to do some more tests, like they would if me or you went to a doctor. I'm sure it's not as bad as you imagine.' I wasn't sure who I was trying to convince – Lucas or myself. 'And anyway, your dad didn't want you to hear that. He's trying to protect you and make this as easy as possible.'

'I just want Mummy to be here!' he wailed.

'I know, my love, I do too.'

I led him back into the living room, where Auntie Sue was sitting in the armchair with a cup of tea and Betsy was asleep curled into Hannah on the sofa. Hannah glanced up with red-rimmed eyes, her arm draped protectively around her little sister, and offered a weak smile before going back to her phone. There was no sign of Mum.

'Where is she?'

Auntie Sue pinched the bridge of her nose.

'Your mother's at home. I told you, she's dealing with this the only way she can.'

'Maybe she could put down the burning sage and provide some actual comfort to her grandchildren, don't you think?'

'Give her time. You know how hard this is for her.'

It would take something stronger than tea to get me through this. I texted Adam:

Do me a favour pls: buy a bottle of the best vodka you can find (supermarket on Main Street) and fill up my hip flask. It should be in the inside pocket of my hold-all.

Adam replied: *I would totally judge you under normal circum-stances but giving you a pass for now. Coming up ASAP xo*

I ran a fingertip over the engraved initials on my silver hip flask: *E. M.*

It was my father's, a gift from my grandparents when he'd qualified as a doctor. He'd taken it everywhere with him, from beach walks to family weddings. He would insist there wasn't any occasion a nip of good whisky couldn't improve.

Thinking of him made me smile, and I wondered what he would be doing now if he were still with us. He was always the strong one, and had been the centre of the universe for me, Amy and Mum. I still missed him every day and I would have given my annual bonus just to have another hour with him. It wasn't fair that Amy's kids would now have to live with the same pain that we did.

It took half a hip flask of Grey Goose to get me through lunch.

As I was clearing away the half-eaten plates of microwave macaroni cheese, the front door opened. I assumed it was Mum until a woman walked into the kitchen. It took me a second to recognise Rachel, Amy's best friend. I had a vague recollection that she worked with Amy at the hospital. We had only met once before, at the pub on Christmas eve. Was that three years ago? Or four? She had been a redhead the last time I saw her, and now had light brown hair.

'Auntie Rachel!' Betsy jumped up, wrapping her arms around her.

In fact, all three kids leapt on her, showing far more enthusiasm and affection than they had for me when I'd arrived yesterday. Betsy and Lucas started wailing again.

'Auntie' Rachel held her arms out to hug me.

'Oh my god, Izzy, what are we going to do?' She sobbed on to my shoulder and I gingerly patted her back.

Rachel put me down and swooped down onto Mike, kissing the top of his head.

A tall man in blue mechanic's overalls followed her into the kitchen carrying two large plastic bags, shuffling and mumbling hellos. He flashed a shy smile at me, and his eyes filled with tears.

The bags were full of home-cooked meals that Rachel had made and boxed up in Tupperware, which she instructed the tall man – her husband, Phil – to load into the freezer in the garage. My heart surged in appreciation.

She took over the washing up, looking pitifully at the remnants of our lunch. She had been in touch with the school to get time off for the kids, if they wanted it, and had asked the vicar to come over the following day to explain how to organise a funeral. Rachel had thought of everything, it seemed, and was a reassuring presence – even I felt calmer.

I tried to fight the thought, but reluctantly had to admit to myself that she was much better at this than me. By the time she and Phil left, Rachel had tidied the kitchen and set out meals for the next three days. Most crucially, the kids were no longer crying. It was progress, but I felt like I'd just lost a game I'd never agreed to play.

Mum didn't show up all day – according to Auntie Sue, after her burst of energy in the morning she'd taken to her bed, asking to not be disturbed.

After helping Mike and Auntie Sue put the kids to bed, I walked back to the pub to find Adam. He'd sent me texts throughout the afternoon, telling me to stay strong and to cry when I needed to.

I was expecting to find him up in his room, but when I popped into the bar to get the key, there he was – cosying up in the corner with two women. He waved me over.

'This is Izzy, everyone. So apparently, you already know Carrie,' he said, giving me a look that told me to pretend if I had to, 'and this is Gina, who runs the pub.'

Carrie jumped up and pulled me into a hug as I struggled to work out how we might have known each other. I hadn't showered all day and didn't feel like making new friends or pretending to remember old ones.

'I am so, so devastated.' She blew her nose into a tissue. 'I just can't believe it, and them poor bairns!'

'Now, now,' said Adam, patting her arm. 'You girls promised me you would hold it together for Izzy. And this is not' – he wagged a finger at her – 'what I would call stoicism.'

'I'm sorry, but it's been a long day. My bed is calling.'

I left them to it and made my way upstairs.

There was a new message on my phone:

It's nice having you here. Night night. Hannah xo

Smiling, I texted back: *I'll always be here for you. Love you all to the moon and back. Now get some zzz xo*

My eldest niece had barely said two words to me since I'd arrived, and getting a text felt like a breakthrough. I turned the phone to silent before going to sit at the window.

Beyond the lights of the harbour, the sea was an immense stretch of black, with the moon clipping the tops of the waves as they broke against the sea wall. I rested my forehead against the cool glass and closed my eyes.

When we were little, I would make up stories for Amy about sea monsters and mermaids, and all the fantastical creatures that lived under the waves. She was only eighteen months younger than me and a ready-made, always-on friend. Although Seahouses came alive with day-trippers on the weekends, there weren't many other kids to play with most of the time. We were used to being our own entertainment. We had vast imaginations and a playground that stretched over miles of sand – we didn't need anyone else.

I opened the window and lay back on the bed. When Dad had died, Amy and I had dragged her bed into my room so we could be closer. We would sleep with the window open so we could hear the sea. We used to lie opposite each other, sobbing into our pillows, holding hands across the gap between the beds.

The pillow was cold against my face and it was soothing. I slowed my breathing to match the rhythm of the waves and drifted off into a sleep punctuated by weird dreams. Amy was playing on the beach, wading into the sea, as a little girl – then she dived under the surface, and when she came up for air, she was a woman. She went under again, and on the next breath she was a mermaid, waving to me left behind on the shore. A cloud of briny white foam came crashing over her, and I saw a slip of a tail before she disappeared into the deep.

Chapter Three

I woke with a start: the wind was howling at the window and I was hot and sticky. It was still dark outside, but I knew I wouldn't sleep. I picked up my phone and read Amy's messages again.

When was the last time we had spoken properly? I couldn't recall the last words we had said out loud to each other, and it suddenly felt very important to remember them. Why hadn't we made more time for each other? How could I have been too busy to speak to my own sister? When had we last said 'I love you'?

I sent her a message:

I love you. I always loved you. Sorry we were always so busy. xo

The text blurred as I blinked back tears. I opened Facebook on my laptop and scrolled through Amy's profile. Photos of her with the kids, of Amy and Mike, Amy with Rachel, and of some other friends I didn't recognise. Amy with Mum and Auntie Sue at Christmas. Amy in fancy dress at The Ship. Her entire life, here in posts and pictures, and I was nowhere to be seen.

I decided I was going to be better today, I was going to do better for the kids, for Mike, and I was going to be calm and patient with Mum. I was going to be the Izzy that Amy needed right now. I just had to figure out where to start.

Rachel was already at the house by the time I arrived. She had been grocery shopping after noticing yesterday that we were running low on a few things and had made sausage sandwiches for everyone's breakfast. She had done one load of laundry and as I walked in, she was delicately suggesting to Lucas that he take a shower – something that hadn't even crossed my mind. I added the kids' personal hygiene to my growing list of things to worry about.

I watched Rachel move around the kitchen like it was her own, unpacking the dishwasher and knowing exactly where everything belonged. She was at ease with Mike and the kids, and I said a silent prayer of thanks for her. Trust Amy to have found an amazing friend.

On the upstairs landing, I fished a sweater of Amy's out of the laundry basket and held it up to my nose. The smell was so clearly her, it was as if she had just walked in. I slumped to the floor, my face buried in the wool, my tears wetting the collar.

'What are you doing?'

Betsy appeared from nowhere.

'Sorry, love – I didn't see you there.' I tried to compose myself. 'But this jumper smells just like Mummy and it made me sad.'

She climbed onto my lap and sniffed at the sweater, curling up like a cat with her cheek resting against it.

'Auntie Izzy, what's going to happen to Mummy now?'

I struggled for an answer that would make sense to her.

'Well, most people believe that when someone dies, they go to a better place. Some people call it heaven, or paradise – it has lots of names, but it all means the same thing. And then

19

they wait there, and look down on the people they love, until they follow them to heaven, too.'

'Will she be a ghost?'

'I don't believe in ghosts. Not the kind you're probably thinking of. But when someone you love dies, it sometimes feels like they are still here. You can smell them, or see or hear something that reminds you of them. Our memories keep them alive.'

'Is that what happened when your daddy died?'

I stroked the nape of her neck, the delicate paleness where her hair was still baby-soft.

'Your mummy and I were very sad when our daddy died, and we used to think about him every day. We still do. I still do' – I corrected myself – 'and I miss him. But as long as I love him, his memory stays alive.'

'Was Nanny very sad when your daddy died?'

Betsy looked up at me, her eyes the same as Amy's, blue-grey with gold flecks. The same as mine.

'Of course she was,' I said quickly. 'We all were, just like we're all sad now. That's why we have to help each other. Especially you, Lucas and Hannah.'

'Hannah doesn't talk to me very much,' Betsy sighed. 'Mummy says she needs to put that phone down and have some real human conversations for a change.'

I laughed at her parroting of Amy.

'Well, we shall just have to find something worth talking about, won't we?'

Back at The Ship that evening, I found Adam in the bar again with Carrie and Gina. He was three gin and tonics in, and I decided to catch up.

Adam discretely recapped for my benefit – Carrie had been in primary school with me and Amy, but had gone to secondary school in Berwick, while we had headed off to St Helen's in Alnwick. Carrie insisted that Amy had been one of her best friends, and she simply didn't know how she was going to cope without her. She wiped away a tear with a finger tipped with a long acrylic nail.

Gina dived straight in with her life story, and I tuned her out pretty quickly, my ears only pricking up when she got to the part about how she knew my sister. She had befriended Amy and Mike after slipping on the pub's icy steps one night. Amy had taken her home and bandaged her up.

Eventually someone asked me what I did in Hong Kong, and I explained that I was a client relationship manager at one of the world's biggest banks. I rearranged my Celine bag on the seat beside me so they would get a better view of it, but neither of them commented. They probably didn't know what it was. Adam flashed me a side-eye.

I couldn't imagine how he found anything in common with these small-town girls. He must have been so bored these past couple of days, despite insisting that he was loving the fresh air and daily beach walks. There wasn't much for him to do now apart from wait for the funeral. I supposed I should be thankful that he had made himself a couple of friends.

The girls hung on Adam's every word, and I doubted they'd ever met anyone so cosmopolitan – both of them were fawning over him. Gross. They were fishing for gossip, too: Carrie told me there were rumours circulating that Amy had been drink-driving. She tapped an acrylic claw against the table, waiting for me to answer.

There was a hush in the pub as the chatter dimmed. I glanced around – everyone had stopped talking. A fisherman sat at the bar in a faded Aran jumper, a hand as big as a bear's paw on his pint glass. He was staring at his beer, pretending he wasn't listening.

The anger inside me hardened, a little stone in my stomach. Adam must have seen it, and before I could say anything, he whisked me out of the bar and up the stairs to bed.

I was grateful for the early night. Tomorrow, we were meeting with Amy and Mike's solicitor, and I wanted to be as sharp as possible. The vodka in my hip flask was still cold and I finished it off, praying it would help me find sleep quickly. But the little stone in my stomach grew, and my simmering resentment kept me awake.

That was the worst thing about a village. Everyone made it their business to be intimately acquainted with everyone else's entire lives. There was no escape from it, no matter how far you ran or how long you stayed away. No matter how high you climbed in life, there would always be people who remembered your darkest moments.

Welcome home, Izzy. Seahouses – where everyone knows everyone's business, and nobody can keep a secret except the sea.

Charles Moore Jr. eased his ample frame into the chair at the head of the kitchen table and took some papers out of his briefcase. The wooden seat groaned under his weight. He peered over the top of his glasses at the various members of the Morton and Sanders families assembled around him.

'First of all, I must say how sorry I am for your loss. This is a particularly sad case, but I believe that Mrs Sanders has made some provisions in her will that may help to ease the burden

22

on you all at this time.'

His top lip glistened. Was I imagining it, or was he avoiding eye contact with me?

'This is the last will and testament of Mrs Amy Helena Sanders, it revokes any earlier wills, and is dated November 14, 2018.'

'*What?*' Mike's eyes were wide and spots of colour appeared on his cheeks. He shook his head. 'No. Amy and I wrote our wills together. We did it eight years ago, right after Betsy was born.'

'I regret that this is coming as a surprise to you, Mr Sanders, but I can confirm that Mrs Sanders wrote a new will in November last year. This voids any earlier versions.' Charles adjusted his collar. 'Is everyone clear on that?'

We all nodded. My throat scratched when I swallowed.

'Mrs Sanders had a *very* generous life insurance policy. She requested that the entirety of any payment, estimated to be around £1.2 million...'

Auntie Sue gasped and we exchanged a wide-eyed glance – why the hell was Amy's life insurance so high?

Charles cleared his throat.

'Mrs Sanders's policy directs the insurance be held in a trust and shared equally among her three children – the sole beneficiaries – when they reach the age of twenty-one.'

'No!' Mike slammed his palm against the table. 'That was *not* what we agreed. She can't change it without telling me, can she?'

Charles responded with silence. He pushed his glasses higher up his nose.

'Mrs Sanders has also stipulated that her savings, approximately £65,000, be allocated to a hardship fund – hardships to be qualified and determined by Moore, Moore & Ridley as the executor of her estate – for her mother, aunt, spouse and children.'

The spots of colour had vanished, and Mike was pale. He shook his head and then smirked, like this was all a practical joke and the punchline was about to be revealed.

'With regards to the care of her children, Mrs Sanders made a... somewhat unorthodox request.'

Charles stared down at the paper in front of him. I glanced at Auntie Sue, who gave a barely perceptible shrug in response.

'Mrs Sanders requested that legal guardianship and care of her children be divided equally between her husband, Mr Michael Sanders, and her sister, Miss Isabelle Morton.'

Charles glanced up and met my eyes. I was still processing his words – something about legal and dividing... He spoke slowly, carefully enunciating every word.

'Furthermore, Mrs Sanders requested that her sister, Miss Isabelle Morton, make a permanent residence in Seahouses to facilitate her sharing joint responsibility for the children until the youngest, Elizabeth Sanders, reaches eighteen years of age.'

There was a loud gasp, and it took a second before I realised it came from me.

Everyone stared, waiting for a response that I couldn't give. The room started to spin, and I spread my palms on the table to steady myself. In the corner of my eye, I saw Mike bury his face in his hands.

'That's...' I stuttered. 'I mean, er, perhaps you can explain?'

'Mrs Sanders predicted such a reaction from you, Miss Morton,' Charles said, almost with a chuckle. 'She left a letter for you by way of explanation. I advise you to read it carefully.'

24

Mike's mouth was set in a tight, hard line and Auntie Sue looked like she needed a lie-down. I sensed the shocked stares of the children on me.

Mum's eyes were glistening.

'But that's wonderful news, Izzy. Now you can come home.'

I flopped onto Lucas's bed. When Mike and Amy had first bought their house, this had been the guest room. It was the room I had stayed in whenever I'd visited, until Lucas had arrived and the floral wallpaper was replaced with a spaceship decal and bunk beds.

I took the hip flask from my pocket and had a swig. Amy's letter was in a sealed envelope and she had written my name on the front. I traced the lines of her handwriting. Why had Amy replaced her will behind Mike's back? And shouldn't she have asked me if I would mind babysitting her kids for the next ten years?

No way could I move back to Seahouses. My entire life – my career, my friends – everything was in Hong Kong. What had Amy been thinking? Surely, she must have known I could never come back here. I would make an appointment with another solicitor and check the legality of it. There must be some way to politely decline.

And I wouldn't be any help anyway – I didn't know the first thing about kids. Amy might have made it look easy, but the past few days had reminded me why I had chosen a child-free existence. Mike could manage on his own, especially with Rachel on hand and Mum and Auntie Sue living around the corner. Auntie Sue had been our rock after Dad had died and Mum left.

I couldn't think about that right now. Too many upsetting

thoughts in one afternoon. I fired off a text to Amy:

What have you done???

Amy had also made some provisions for the funeral, so there wasn't much for us to do. Rachel seemed almost disappointed that the hard work of organizing had been done for her.

Adam brought fish and chips over for dinner, and having a fresh face broke some of the tension. After the meal, with Rachel busy washing up and Adam holding court in the living room, I slipped out into the back garden for some fresh air.

Mike was sitting on the step, smoking. He eyed my drink.

'Is that whisky?'

'Depends. Is that a cigarette?'

He shrugged. 'I haven't smoked in years. Amy made me quit when she was pregnant with Hannah.'

'We all need something to take the edge off today.'

I handed him my glass and he took a sip.

'I don't understand, Izzy. Why would she do this? Did she say anything to you?'

'Is this the face of someone who was prepared?'

Mike laughed – a sad chuckle. 'We can challenge it, you know. At least find out what our options are.'

'I was thinking the same. Let's speak to Charles, see what he suggests.'

Back at The Ship, I took a scotch up to my room and steeled myself to read Amy's letter. I used my nail scissors to carefully slice the envelope open.

Dear Iz,

I'm writing this in the hope that you will never have to read it – so if you are, I am truly sorry for what you're going through.

26

Although I hope it never comes to this, I want to be prepared. It seems extreme, but we never know what curveballs life has in store for us. We learned that the hard way, you and I. Just in case anything ever happens to me, I'm making sure there's a plan.

By now you will know that my lasting wish is for you to come home and raise my children. I hope you didn't swear in front of them. I warned Big Charlie that you might have to be revived with smelling salts.

I wanted to discuss this with you, but I am running out of time. There never seems to be the right moment, or the right mood, and it is important that I get this sorted.

It matters to me, Iz, and I hope you understand that. But I cannot force you to do anything you don't want to do. I'm writing this letter to explain my reasons, in the hope that you will understand and agree.

When Dad died, our world imploded. Everything went to pieces. Remember how we started sleeping in the same room? We never wanted to be apart. You were the only person who understood what I was feeling, and you fixed me. If it weren't for you, I wouldn't have got through it.

I have never known pain like it. And the pain never disappeared – not even after all these years. It just got easier to deal with.

I can't bear the thought of my kids having to be without me. Knowing the same loss that we did. So, here's the thing: if I'm not here, I want them to have the closest thing to me – and that's you.

Mike does his best and he's a great dad. But the children need more than he can give them.

Me and you, we're cut from the same cloth. We chose different paths and our lives are worlds apart, but you know me inside out: you know me better than anyone. You know best what I would want for the children.

You will have loads of help – Auntie Sue will be there for you, too.

Mum is what she is. Please give her a chance, Izzy. We all make mistakes, and nobody is perfect. None of us can say for sure how we would react in her situation. She'll be a big help, just let her do things her way.

I don't have answers for the big questions. I can't tell you where to live or what to do about work. All I know is that if I'm not there, I want you to raise my children, the way I would.

Please Izzy, I hope you understand and you find some way to grant me this wish.

I love you forever, no matter what.

Your sister,

Amy

The next morning, I asked Adam to drive me up to Alnwick. I still felt too shaken to get behind the wheel. Amy's request was weighing on my mind and I'd lain awake for most of the night, tossing the idea around. There was no way it could work. Hopefully Charles Moore Jr. could explain my options.

Moore, Moore & Ridley Solicitors was in an old building opposite the market square. I was greeted by a lone secretary sitting at a huge desk inlaid with worn green leather.

'I'm sorry, but Mr Moore is in court this morning.'

Damn it, I thought, realising I should have made an appointment.

'Is there anyone else I could talk to?'

With a kind smile, the secretary led me into one of the offices and told me that another partner would be along soon.

The room was like travelling back in time – everything was

28

brass and varnished wood and smelt of old books, with large windows overlooking the riverside. I was admiring the view when the door creaked open behind me.

A tall, dark-haired man walked in and promptly tripped over, falling to his knees and scattering his papers everywhere. I resisted a giggle as he scooped them back up, muttering to himself. He was about my age and had that whole Hugh Grant bumbling-hottie vibe nailed, complete with floppy hair streaked with grey. Out of habit, I checked for a wedding ring. His hand was bare.

'Sorry about that.' He pushed his glasses back up his nose. 'Jake Ridley.'

Jake offered a handshake.

Always look someone in the eye when you shake their hand, Dad used to say – *you'll know right away what kind of person they are.* Jake had brown eyes framed by thick dark eyelashes, and I caught myself looking into them a little too long.

He explained he was the newest partner in the firm, but assured me that he was aware of the particulars of my sister's case, and offered to give me the same advice he and Charles had given Mr Sanders about the process of contesting Amy's will.

'What do you mean, the advice you've given Mike? When?'

'Mr Sanders came by earlier this morning. He indicated that the family intends to challenge the will, and we explained that there are very poor grounds for doing so. Contesting a will is a serious business and shouldn't be undertaken lightly. Your sister was in a sound state of mind and knew what she was doing.'

Blimey, Mike was keen. He really wanted to make sure I wouldn't be sticking around.

'Well... actually... we haven't decided for certain that we'll contest it. I just want to understand what my options are on the legal guardianship thing. It's quite difficult for me to consider moving back here. I know it's what my sister wanted, but she never actually asked me...'

The words lodged in my throat. Jake's eyebrows knotted into a frown.

'Mr Sanders – er, Mike – suggested the family's main concern is the life insurance being held in trust. He didn't mention the issue of guardianship.'

That was weird. Mike and I hadn't even discussed the trust fund. It was a huge amount of money and to me, it seemed like a wise move to put it away until the kids were old enough to spend it sensibly. I thought the problem was Amy appointing me as a guardian.

Jake registered my confusion.

'Can I suggest that you speak with your brother-in-law about the family's financial situation? That seems to be the main concern of Mr Sanders.' He gave me a sympathetic smile. 'As for guardianship, well, that's really up to you. Nobody can force you to do anything. It was your sister's wish, but she understood that it would be your choice.'

I thanked Jake for his advice and he told me to call him if I had any further questions. He gave me his business card and by reflex, I gave him one of mine in return. He insisted on seeing me out, but struggled to open the door and shake my hand at the same time, prompting an awkward dance between us on the threshold. I blushed as we finally said goodbye.

I walked along Market Street, my head spinning. Why was Mike so concerned about the money? He had a good job, and he and Amy owned their house outright.

Surely the real issue was that my sister had asked me to euthanise my career and kill my every chance of future happiness by confining me to lifelong spinsterhood back in the village I had done everything to escape?

I found Adam in Barter Books, sipping a mug of steaming coffee while flicking through a hardback of vintage fashion adverts.

The bookshop had always been a favourite place of mine and Amy's. We would go after school for tea and a scone, then take the late bus back to Seahouses. Books were our window to the world and we were avid readers as children, devouring anything that conjured up far-away places and exotic characters. We kept a detailed list of all the places we wanted to visit, and frequently debated where we would eventually live. Our imaginations took us far from Northumberland. My dream was to move first to New York, then relocate later to Paris. Amy wanted to have a villa somewhere warm, where she would grow her own lemons and olives and where she could swim in the sea all year round.

We had a mutual understanding that there was nothing for us in Seahouses and we would leave as soon as we were old enough. Even Newcastle was too provincial for us. We had grander plans.

Then, when Dad died and Mum left, there was nothing worth staying for.

Both of us went away to university – me to Edinburgh, and Amy to Leeds. But we found the distance between us too great and she joined me in Scotland after her first year. That was when she met Mike, and from that moment on, her priorities started to shift.

I'd been working at *The Scotsman* as a trainee reporter in my first year after graduating from my English degree, waiting for Amy to finish. Our bigger plan had been to move to London together, but first we intended to have an adventure: we were going to fly to Sicily, then spend three weeks making our way by ferry and train up the west coast of Italy and into France, staying in hostels and cheap B&Bs. We had our inheritance from Dad, but we wouldn't need much cash. And after everything we had been through, we felt we deserved a summer of fun.

But then Amy had met Mike, and her enthusiasm for the trip dampened. She decided she wanted to spend the summer in Edinburgh, enjoying more time with him and their friends after graduation, before everyone left to become proper grown-ups. The Italy trip wasn't cancelled, merely postponed – we figured we had many summers ahead of us to do it.

In the beginning, I hadn't thought Amy and Mike would last. He was uncultured, a bit loud, and I felt she could do better. He had studied something pointless and vague with 'administration' in his degree title, whereas Amy was on track to be a high-flyer in nursing.

Then she took him to Seahouses for the weekend and he loved the place. Before I knew it, they were talking about buying a house in the village to renovate. I ended up moving to London on my own. Mike became the centre of Amy's universe, and I shifted into her orbit.

We spoke almost every day at first, sometimes for hours, both of us taking special deals on our landline because mobile calls were too expensive back then. But gradually, our calls trickled out to twice a week, then even less frequently. Our lives had been completely intertwined for so long, but the rope eventually started to pull apart.

Mike set up his own business, a consultancy or something, and it seemed to do well, so maybe that degree wasn't a complete waste of time. Before I knew it, Amy was settling back in Seahouses for good, and I was off on my own adventure. It turned out we were two different people after all.

So why did she want to pull me back now?

Adam and I headed back to the car, him with a bag of books that would definitely not fit in his suitcase.

'Did that help to clear things up?'

I sighed.

'I think I have more questions now than when we started.'

Chapter Four

My laptop purred to life and I stretched my neck. This was good – work was something I could control. A few blissful hours of distraction. But my assistant, Bethany, had already set up an out of office reply on my behalf, and my inbox was not as full as I had hoped. There was a message from my boss, Toby, the Vice President of my department, expressing sympathy and telling me to take it easy, and another from HR reminding me that the bereavement policy allowed two weeks off following the death of a sibling. As if I could afford to take it.

Annabelle Taylor – that bitch – had sent an email saying I should take as long as I needed, offering to handle my clients while I was away. I clenched my jaw. The vultures were already circling, ready to take advantage.

I hadn't had a holiday yet this year, and I hadn't used my full allowance last year either – I'd only agreed to take a few days off when Toby had threatened to fire me if I didn't. I'd checked in to a women-only wellness retreat in Bali and tried to focus on the yoga and massages and not my accounts, but my mind had kept flitting back to my portfolios.

I called Bethany and told her not to let Annabelle anywhere near my clients. She was to tell everyone that I was dealing with a family issue and working remotely for one week only. Possibly two. Bethany reluctantly agreed.

Rachel had already taken care of breakfast by the time I got to Amy's house. She was brushing Betsy's hair while Hannah scrolled her phone absent-mindedly. Mike had gone out, so I couldn't ask him about his visit yesterday to Moore, Moore & Ridley and his plan to contest the will. The funeral director was coming later to run through the plans, but there was nothing for me to do in the meantime.

My mobile phone rang and I stepped outside to answer it, expecting it to be from work. Instead, I got a stammered greeting from Jake Ridley.

'Yes, hello, Mrs Morton – um, *Miss* Morton, er...'

'Please, just call me Isabelle. Er, I mean Izzy.'

He was making me flustered.

'I just wondered how you were holding up. After the coroner's update.'

I hesitated for a beat, frowning. 'We haven't had an update.'

There was a pause on the line before Jake spoke again. 'Er... actually... That's a good point. It's Mr Sanders that they would have contacted. He's Amy's next of kin. Forgive me, I assumed he had already updated the family.'

My jaw tightened. 'It must have slipped Mike's mind. What did they tell him?'

'The good news is that the body has been released. The funeral can go ahead.'

Great. I could be on a plane home by next weekend. If I wanted to.

'There are... er, one or two issues that are unresolved. Some questions outstanding, that the police will now look in to.'

I froze to the spot, eyes wide.

Jake stuttered. 'I'm sorry, I thought you knew this from your brother-in-law... That's why I was calling, really, to see how you were.'

'What questions?' I leaned against the wall to steady myself.

He paused and took a deep breath. 'Mrs Sanders – er, your sister – had unidentified substances in her blood. They're running some further tests on the samples. But more significantly, there seems to have been a problem with the car - some damage to the front wheel. The police believe that possibly caused the crash.'

Was I hearing this right? My pulse pounded in my ears.

'What kind of damage to the wheel? What does that even mean?'

'Those are questions for the police to answer. They'll pass any evidence back to the coroner, who will decide if an inquest is needed.'

'I don't understand - they think it might not have been an accident?'

And what did *that* mean? I shuddered.

'Please don't jump to any conclusions. It just means that there are some questions to be answered. They're ruling out all possibilities.'

My mouth was dry. 'Do me a favour please,' I said in a quiet voice. 'If you hear anything else, please let me know. Just in case Mike forgets to tell me something important.'

I thanked him and put the phone down, my head pounding. The sky was starting to cloud over and a threat of dark grey rain was creeping in from the horizon. I tried to dislodge the idea that Amy's death might have been anything more complicated than a tragic accident.

After Dad died, Auntie Sue used to take us for long walks on the beach. I decided now that we needed a change of scenery and some fresh air before the rain started.

Adam had pulled together some inspired outfits while packing my suitcase, but he hadn't included much outdoor gear. I went up to Amy's room to search for warmer clothes and came back downstairs in her sweater, fleecy jacket, Barbour coat and walking boots.

'Oh my.' Rachel's eyes glistened as she saw me. 'For a moment, I thought it was Amy.'

We walked through the village to the top of the coastal path that ran down to the wide, sandy beach. The tide was out, and we had a huge stretch of golden sand between us and the water. I dug my hands deep into the pockets of Amy's coat, reaching for some warmth and shelter from the cold wind.

The beach was empty apart from a few dog walkers, and we set off towards Bamburgh Castle. Betsy held Rachel's hand and I wished she'd chosen me, even though I knew Rachel was more of an aunt to Amy's children than I had ever been.

When Mike and Amy decided to start their family, I was still working in London and making the long trip up north every couple of months. I would leave after work on a Friday, driving up the A1 in my Corsa and getting to Seahouses just in time for last orders.

The first time Amy was pregnant, I knew right away. There was something different about her, nothing obvious, just like she had a secret and was keeping it to herself. She hadn't even told Mike at that point, and when I pulled her aside to ask, she just laughed.

A week later, she called me in tears – she'd miscarried at six weeks. Totally normal, she said. Happens all the time. Nothing anyone could do. Just wasn't meant to be.

I got straight in the car and came to her. She stayed in bed for three days. When she eventually got up, she wanted to draw a line under it and move on. Three months later, she called to tell me that she was pregnant again. I was going to be an auntie.

Amy was made to be a mum. As a little girl, she'd had a collection of baby dolls that she lovingly cared for, bathing and feeding them in complex little routines and putting them to bed each night in their cribs. We were both committed tomboys and loved playing outdoors, but Amy would usually bring a doll in her backpack to join us on whatever adventure we had imagined. I had no interest in dolls but I would tolerate them for her sake.

Mike took a while to adapt to parenthood, but for Amy, being a mum came naturally. She took everything in her stride and for the most part, made it look easy. She and Mike would argue occasionally, especially in the early days when the shock of their new responsibility and lack of sleep would drive them to the edge of patience. But they were loving, and they worked well together as a team.

The babies bored me silly in the early years, and Amy found it hilarious. I never tried to hide my disinterest and it would drive Mum and Auntie Sue mad. They gradually became more interactive, the seeds of their individual personalities beginning to grow. But I moved further away, and more time passed between my visits home, and the children and I barely knew each other.

I watched Hannah now, as she walked silently alongside me on the beach, looking down at her shoes. Lucas was picking up stones and hurling them out into the vast expanse of the sea, his little body contorting with the effort.

Why hadn't Amy spoken to me about her will? Asking someone to be your kids' guardian had to be worth a phone call. Even a conversation by email would have been better than leaving a note.

And why was Mike questioning her plan to put the insurance money in a trust fund? That was the only part of Amy's will that made any sense to me.

And where the hell was Mum? She'd always insisted how sorry she was about last time, but here she was, doing the same thing again. Why was it falling on me to pick up the pieces? Did my life not count for anything? The anger smouldered inside me. I balled my hands into tight, hard fists.

It wasn't fair, none of it was fair. Amy should have been there.

I took deep a breath of the cold salty air and let out a belly-rumbling scream.

Hannah jumped, startled by the sudden noise. Rachel snapped to a stop and spun to face me, instinctively grabbing Betsy's hand. A smile spread across Lucas's face. He turned to face the sea, and screamed too.

Within seconds, all five of us were standing in a line on the sand, screaming out at the tameless, thrashing surf. The wind carried our cries out towards the horizon.

The sea air and exercise lifted everyone's mood. We bought fresh rolls from Clarke's bakery on the way home and Rachel microwaved another Tupperware of her home-made soup.

Later that afternoon we sat down with the funeral director and put the finishing touches to the plan. Mike was back, but the house was too full to get him on his own for a quiet chat. My questions about his intention to challenge the will would

39

have to wait.

Amy had made some requests – instead of flowers, we would ask for donations to the Royal National Lifeboat Institution, and everyone was under strict instructions to wear bright colours. She'd even picked the music for the service, and had asked to be buried next to Dad in St Cuthbert's churchyard.

Each of the children had a poem or dedication they wanted to give to their mother, and every time one of them shared an idea I was reminded what caring, thoughtful kids my sister had raised. Rachel was a big help, making suggestions and giving the children prompts without pushing her own ideas or opinions. Mike was still raw, barely keeping his head above fresh waves of grief.

It was an exhausting evening and after clearing up the dishes, Rachel left us to it. Betsy shyly asked me if I would put her to bed, and I almost burst with happiness.

It was hours later that Mike woke me up. I had fallen asleep next to Betsy on her bed, her story book in my hand and her nightlight still on. We went downstairs and he poured us each a whisky. He had lit a fire and it cast a flickering glow on the room.

I took a sip of scotch for courage. 'I need to ask you – are you serious about contesting the will?'

Mike shrugged and sighed. 'I have no idea what I'm doing these days. I know Amy wanted what's best for the kids. And the trust fund might seem like a great idea. But without an aggressive investment plan, the money could just sit there, doing nothing.' The ice cubes clinked in his glass. 'It's a lot today, but by the time Betsy is twenty-one, what will it be worth?'

I bit my lip – I had been too quick to doubt him. But it was

Amy's request – it felt strange to be questioning what she had decided was best. Apart from the fact she had decided that me giving up my life was a good idea. I was entitled to question that. But the money? It was hers, after all. Mike was clearly still in shock. I was sure he would see reason sooner or later.

I wanted to talk about the possibility that Amy's death wasn't an accident – but the thought was so ugly, so terrible, that I wasn't sure where to begin. We sat in silence, listening to the crackle of the fire.

'Can I ask you something?' Mike didn't look at me, keeping his gaze fixed firmly on his glass. 'What did Amy say in her letter?'

I squirmed, struggling to think of a way of explaining it to him, of conveying the message Amy had known only I would understand. 'She knew more than anyone how hard it is with only one parent. She thought it would be easier on the kids if I could help.'

'Did she think I was a bad father?' His eyes started to fill.

'No, goodness, no! Don't ever think that.' I moved to sit next to him on the sofa. He smelled like he hadn't showered. 'She definitely, specifically said: Mike is a great dad. Quote-unquote.'

He smiled.

I took a gulp of whisky. 'I haven't decided what I'm going to do, yet.'

The words came out before I'd thought them through.

Mike shrugged. 'You shouldn't do anything you don't want to. She wouldn't want you to be unhappy.'

We clinked glasses in a toast to Amy and sat in silence, watching the flames flicker down to the embers.

It was past midnight when I left for the short walk back to

the pub, my footsteps echoing down the empty street. In Hong Kong, the noise never stops – the buzz of millions of engines, animals, and humans packed together. You can be alone but never lonely, permanently insulated by strangers. I missed being amidst that sheer volume of people.

The night air was crisp and it was a cloudless sky. In Hong Kong, you couldn't see the stars – in Seahouses, there were too many to count. I tipsily gazed up at an eternity of lights and wondered which one was Amy. I wished she could help me decide what to do.

My phone pinged. It was Hannah:

Thanks for today. I needed a good scream. I'm glad you're here

I texted back: *We all needed it. Same again tomorrow?*

Then I sent a message to Amy.

I miss you. We all miss you. xo

The next few days were shapeless, without form except for the ticking of the hours, the passage of day to night, and the certainty of the tide. Daily beach walks became the foundation of what little routine we were able to construct and the only thing that buoyed our spirits. Adam, Mum, and Auntie Sue came too, and we showed them our trick of screaming at the water. It relieved some tension, although Auntie Sue was sure the police would give us all ASBOs if anyone heard. One step at a time, putting one foot in front of the other and screaming at the waves became our way of coping with grief.

With the funeral only a day away, we needed a distraction. Mike had shut himself up in his office again, leaving me to watch the kids, and I decided everyone would benefit from another dose of salt air. We covered miles, making it all the way to Bamburgh and back again.

After lunch, we crowded into the living room to watch one of Amy's favourite films – *The Little Mermaid* – and Adam and Rachel cajoled everyone into a singalong. It was a grey and drizzly afternoon, perfect for snuggling up together under blankets and throws. Amy would have loved it.

The mood darkened at bedtime. The children were coping so well, but choosing their funeral outfits led to questions about what their mum would have wanted them to wear, and the tears came again.

Between me, Rachel, and Mike, we helped each of them pick out their clothes, with Mum and Auntie Sue on hand for extra hugs when needed. We rallied each other, and I couldn't help thinking that Amy would be proud.

I walked back to The Ship with Adam and we headed straight up to my room. I bought another bottle of Grey Goose – the first two had gone so fast – and he took some ice from the bar. I started to weep as I climbed into bed. It was cathartic. I realised I'd been bottling it up all day, and it was a release to let it out.

Adam reached for the box of tissues by my bed and handed me one.

'I'm so proud of you. And if your sister could see you now, she'd be proud too. No matter what happens, you were there for the kids when they needed you.'

I bawled, letting the tears flow freely. 'I don't know how we'll get through tomorrow. It's just so hard. When Dad died, I remember feeling how bloody unfair it was. And this is ten times worse.'

We sat like that for a while, me choking on sobs while Adam rubbed my back. Eventually, I managed to calm down enough to breathe properly. I downed the rest of my vodka.

The phone pinged twice. The first message was from Hannah:

Can't sleep. Can't stop thinking about Mum. I miss her.

I miss her too. Try and get some rest, I texted back, the screen blurring beyond my tears.

The second message was from Mum:

I'm doing my best, Izzy. I don't always get it right, but I won't let you down this time.

I sighed. How many times had I heard that?

The windows were frosted with condensation and it was still dark outside when I woke up. I figured I could squeeze in an hour of work – just checking in – before I'd have to start getting ready for the funeral. But Bethany was all over my inbox and there were disappointingly few emails that needed my urgent attention. I picked at a cuticle.

Adam had helped me to select an outfit, and I knew it was perfect. Amy's favourite colour was purple, and by coincidence, Adam had packed some violet wool trousers that I quite honestly had forgotten I owned. He'd paired them with a silver sequinned long-sleeved top from Amy's wardrobe, which I vaguely remembered her wearing on Christmas day several years ago.

I blow-dried and curled my hair, wanting to look my best for my sister, and finished the look with oversized Dior sunglasses.

The sun was just starting to rise as I walked down the lane towards Amy's house. I took a nip of vodka from my hip flask before letting myself in.

Mike was asleep in the chair in the living room in yesterday's clothes, an empty bottle at his feet. He reeked of whisky, and his eyes were red and puffy. I ushered him upstairs to shower and shave before the kids could see him.

I sent a message to Hannah, as she seemed much more comfortable communicating by text than actually talking. Hey, whatever worked.

Good morning, rise and shine. I'm downstairs. Do you want a cup of tea?

She replied right away:

Thanks, but I've been awake since 4 a.m., and already had tea.
P.S. I don't think I can do this.

I tiptoed upstairs. Hannah was sitting up in bed, her cheeks streaked with sticky tears and a shoebox of photos on her lap. She shuffled along to make space for me. The battered shoebox was familiar. Amy never threw photos away, and any that didn't make it to a frame or album were all in here.

There were pictures from when we were kids, Mum and Dad almost unrecognisable as thirty-something-year-olds. Group shots of school trips and sleepovers with teenage girls who were grown women now. People from university whose faces I recognised, but whose names I had long forgotten. Amy and Mike on a beach. Separate photos of them at the same table of a Greek taverna, long before selfies existed, back when people used to take it in turns to take pictures of each other.

I picked out a photo of me and Amy. She was laughing, a full toothy cackle, her head tossed back and her hair in wild curls. The familiarity of her features – the shape of her nose, her teeth, the colour of her eyes – made me want to climb in to the photo and touch her. I knew every freckle on that face.

There were hundreds of photos, and I wanted to take my time and devour every single one. But first, we had a funeral to get through.

In her room across the landing, Betsy was still sound asleep and breathing in delicious snuffling snores. She was so peaceful, and I didn't want to imagine what the next few hours had in store for her. If I could have left her sleeping and come back for her when it was all over, I would have gladly done it. I stroked her shoulder, singing her name. She slowly blinked awake and there was a flicker, precious seconds before she remembered and reality hit. I held her tight, inhaling the scent of her hair, permanently perfumed with sea air.

I walked into Lucas's room and found him curled up on his bottom bunk, contorted by great body-wracking sobs that made no sound. My heart broke and I collapsed onto my knees beside him.

'I don't want to... don't make me go!'

He pressed his face into my neck, his hot tears rolling down my collar. I wrapped my arms around him, pulling him as close as possible, wishing that I could absorb his pain. I wasn't prepared for this. Was I supposed to force the kids go to their mum's funeral, even if they refused?

Mercifully, Rachel had arrived and come upstairs to find me. She stuck her head around Lucas's door. I turned to her, silently begging for an answer. She joined me at the foot of the bed.

'You know what, Lucas? Me and Auntie Izzy were just saying yesterday how proud your mum would be of you. Of all of you. And she would hate to see how much you're hurting.'

Lucas snivelled.

'And if you don't want to go to the funeral, you don't have to. You don't have to do anything you don't want to do. This is just a chance to say goodbye to Mum and celebrate her life, but there will be plenty more chances. You don't need to do it

46

today, or in church. We can celebrate and remember her every day for the rest of our lives.'

Rachel looked at me, her eyes wet with tears.

Lucas bravely nodded and shuffled to the edge of the bed. Rachel put a hand on his knee and talked to him softly.

'Why don't you get ready, and then see how you feel? You still have time to decide. Now, would you like some help, or can you manage on your own?'

I breathed a sigh of relief as Lucas traipsed off to the bathroom. 'Thanks for that,' I said to Rachel. 'I don't know what I would do without you. In fact, I don't know how we would manage any of this without you.' My lip started to tremble.

'You're doing great. And I'm so glad you're here.' She wiped away a tear. 'I just miss her so much.'

Mum and Auntie Sue were waiting downstairs. Auntie Sue's face was red and puffy and her eyes shone wet. Mum was moving slowly, and her speech was a little slurred. I wondered what she had taken.

Not that I could blame Mum for self-medicating on a day like this, I thought, as I popped to the downstairs bathroom for a few sips of vodka.

St Cuthbert's had been our parish church for as far back as we could trace the Morton family history. It was the church that everyone got married in, where Amy and Mike had their wedding, and for a long time, I had imagined I'd get married there too. Amy and I, and all her children had been christened here. It had formed the backdrop to life events and hundreds of ordinary moments – nativity plays, harvest festivals and carol services.

And on one of the hardest days of my life, we had come here to say goodbye to Dad.

I couldn't believe we were back here so soon to bury Amy.

The churchyard was already packed by the time we arrived. Hundreds of faces turned towards us, but I kept my sunglasses on and my head down. I didn't want to make eye contact, let alone small-talk with these people. I just had to focus on the kids and getting us through the next few hours.

In her list of requests, Amy had explicitly forbidden a funeral procession, believing it would be too upsetting for the children, so we had made our way to the church on foot. Adam was waiting for us by the entrance, smart in a blue wool suit with a purple cravat. I led the family inside.

At the front of the church, an oak coffin was drenched in peonies – Amy's favourite flower. The vicar, whose name I had already forgotten, greeted us in a soft voice. I looked the other way while he held Mum's hand and whispered blessings on the children.

This wasn't the same vicar who had been here when Dad had died. That day had been bitterly cold, and I remembered I'd been worried the ground would be frozen when they lowered Dad into it. Me, Amy and Mum had sat at the front of the church, clutching onto one another, Mum staring vacantly ahead.

I allowed myself a peek at the crowd that had filed in behind us. The church was a riot of colour – underneath their dark coats, everyone was dressed brightly as requested, with flashes of purple everywhere.

Some of the nurses from Amy's hospital were in uniform, and members of the RNLI were in formal dress, complete with medals and caps tucked under their arms. They had run out of space on the pews and people were packed into the back and down the sides of the church.

I tried not to think about the coffin. How could a whole life fit into such a small box? The finality of it hit me. There was no more time, no more Amy. She was really gone, and now I had to say goodbye.

Mike, Rachel and I sat with the kids in between us. I put my hand on Hannah's shoulder. I didn't want her to have to grow up as fast as we had after Dad died. I wanted, as much as possible, to cocoon her from the heartache of losing a parent, only to inherit so much of their responsibilities. I looked over at Mum. She had her arm around Lucas, who was weeping softly. I wondered how much of the aftermath of Dad dying she remembered. Did she even understand the pain she had caused? Was Amy right – had she turned over a new leaf?

Betsy snuggled into Rachel, sucking her thumb, a habit that Amy had been trying desperately to break the last time I'd visited home. It had also been a habit of Amy's when she was little, and Betsy looked so much like her. I flashed an appreciative smile at Rachel, and Adam gave my shoulder a little squeeze from his seat on the row behind.

I had said no to doing any kind of reading – that was completely beyond me. Mum had wanted to do something, but Mike had diplomatically talked her out of it. With Mum, you never knew which way it might go.

I just about held it together until the kids went up to the front. Hearing them reading the messages they had written to their mum was almost too much to bear. Hannah had written a particularly poignant poem, and I dabbed at my tears under my sunglasses as muffled sobs echoed around the church. Mum was in pieces, with Auntie Sue and Adam trying to prop her

49

up, and I wished in that moment that the gulf between us was smaller. I reached across to her and held her hand.

Outside the church, a strong sea wind whipped at us as we stood huddled together around the freshly dug grave, watching Amy's coffin being lowered in to the ground. A lone gull cried out above us. We had asked for this part of the service to be private, and so it was just us – the family, plus Adam, along with Rachel and her husband Phil, who clung to each other, both crying. Even Adam had given up trying to hold himself together. I said my silent goodbye to my sister, salty tears streaking my cheeks. The wind carried away the sounds of our sobbing.

I wasn't sure the children would want to go to the wake, but they pulled through and once again amazed me with their resilience. We had chosen to hold it at The Castle, because The Ship didn't have a big enough function room, and besides, we didn't want to spoil the happy memories we had there.

As soon as we got to the pub, Adam and I stole away to a quiet corner for a whisky – I had two – which blurred the edges of my pain and numbed me just enough to shake a few hands and accept some condolences.

Rachel introduced me to Betsy's headteacher – I immediately forgot his name and would have forgotten him entirely, except that he held my hand for just a little too long. He had deep, blue eyes, and looked like he might burst into tears. I pulled myself away and move on to the next well-wisher.

I hadn't seen Mum for a while, so I went looking for her. She was sitting on a bench with Auntie Sue, not in the sheltered beer garden at the back, but on the side of the pub that faced out to sea, staring down the lashing wind. I sat down and looped my arm around Mum's shoulder. She looked up at me with red, wet eyes and the three of us stayed like that for a while, watching the frenzied sea, saying nothing. Two sisters who were inseparable, and one who had just lost her other half.

I saw then the gulf that Amy had left behind – a huge void, much bigger than one person, and more than I could ever fill. But I had to try. The stuff I thought was important – my job, my friends, the life I had built for myself – was miniscule next to the vacuum left by my sister. Right now, this was where I was needed. I had to come home.

I sent a message to Amy:

You'd have been so proud of the kids today.

And a second:

I can't stay forever, but I'll stay for now xo

Chapter Five

The funeral had brought none of the comfort or closure that I might have hoped for. The enormity of our loss remained entirely undiminished in the days that followed, and reaffirmed my decision to stay – for a while, at least.

I opened my computer and started a spreadsheet. I had to work out the financial impact of taking a short-term sabbatical from my life. Putting it all down on the screen forced me to consider the harsh reality.

There were far fewer options to spend money here than in Hong Kong, with all its temptations. There wasn't a shoe shop for miles, and I could forget about eating out. For the next few months, I'd be swapping fusion dim-sum and gourmet cocktails at pop-up restaurants for home-cooked Sunday dinners, fish and chips, and nights at the pub. I sighed, already missing it.

My bank balance was in pretty good shape. It would be easy to negotiate unpaid leave from work, and I could sublet my apartment in Hong Kong for three months – or however long I ended up staying. The rent was a huge chunk of my outgoings, and I could comfortably lease a place in Seahouses without making a dent in my savings. The village was full of holiday lets and I was hopeful that I could get a good deal out of peak season. In fact, I could probably get a three-month rental in Seahouses for what I sometimes spent in one weekend in Hong Kong.

Adam and I bought a bag of chips and found a bench at the corner of the harbour, and I told him about my plan. An enormous seagull eyeballed us greedily.

'And what about work?'

I sighed. 'I don't know. I've been so swept up in it for so long, and now that this has happened...'

'It's good. You've got new priorities.'

I nodded. A fishing boat pulled into the harbour. 'Being here, and remembering after everything that happened with Dad, then Mum... I can't let Hannah, Lucas, and Betsy go through that.'

'What happened with your mum?'

I looked the seagull right in eye and held its amber glare as I told Adam the story.

'Dad was the anchor of our family, the big personality. Dr Edward Morton. Always playing games and the first to spot any opportunity for fun. Mum came alive when she was with him; she just sparkled in a way that she didn't when he wasn't there. Maybe we all did.

'He loved nothing more than spending evenings sitting at the bar of The Ship, cheerfully dispensing medical advice to men who spent their days at sea and had no time to see a GP. A doctor can treat an ailment, but don't forget who puts food on the table, he used to say. Old Salt does dangerous work, risking his life so that we can eat.

'That's what he called them – Old Salt – it's what fishermen call each other. I can't even remember how or when it happened, but one day, Amy called me Salt Sister and it stuck. We became the Salt Sisters.' I smiled at the memory of Dad encouraging our new nicknames.

'Dad was fit and healthy. At least that's what we all thought. He never gave us any reason to suspect otherwise. Maybe he knew something was wrong and ignored it. Or maybe he knew that whatever he had was incurable, and he wanted to live his fullest life until the end. We never found out.

'We had finished Sunday lunch and he was trying to round us all up to go for a walk along the beach. I was fifteen. Amy and I'd had some stupid row – I can't even remember what we were fighting about – and I was sulking. I didn't want to go on a family walk, so I said I had exam revision to do. Amy said if I wasn't going, then she wasn't either. We stayed at home, sulking in our bedrooms, ignoring each other. So Mum and Dad went off, just the two of them.'

I could still picture that day perfectly. There had been an easterly wind, the one that blows straight in off the sea, smearing soapy foam across the sand and leaving your lips with a taste of salt. The beach was quiet, with only a few hardy souls out walking.

'Nobody heard Mum scream when Dad collapsed. She had to leave him there on the sand, clutching his chest, while she ran back up the path and flagged down a car on the main road.

'The first thing we heard were the sirens of the ambulance. We all assumed it was a heart attack at first, even the paramedics. They took him to hospital and helped him to breathe, pumping air in and out of his lungs. But it turned out he had cancer. The doctors couldn't even tell where it had started, but it had spread like wild weeds and taken over his body from the inside.'

That was how I had pictured him when they explained it – his insides like a sprawling, overgrown garden.

'He never woke up again, and after three days there was nothing more anyone could do. That laugh, all that charm and brightness, just vanished - like a switch being flicked off. He looked like he was sleeping. There was still sand in his hair from where he had fallen. I kissed him goodbye.

'We had stayed by his bedside the whole time and came home together, the three of us and Auntie Sue, to a house that was now empty. Mum went straight to bed, and Amy and I took it in turns to bring her cups of tea and meals, or to climb under the covers and lie curled up next to her as she stared out into space.

'Amy and I took over the housework and chores – that was nothing, and it felt good to keep busy. Auntie Sue stayed for a couple of weeks, until we were back on our feet. Except Mum didn't get back up. She stayed in bed for weeks, only getting out when we hauled her into the bathroom for a shower and when we needed to change the bedding. She kept the curtains closed, and the room was overpowered by a strange smell that was new to me, but I soon learned was sadness.'

I shuddered at the thought of that peculiar combination of damp, sweat and unwashed laundry that I couldn't ever forget.

'Mum was lost without him. And then one day, she was gone.'

I paused then, and Adam put an arm around me and wiped a tear from my cheek that I hadn't realised was there.

'Come on. You don't have to tell me the whole story now. Besides, we've got to find you a home.'

I took fish and chips over for Mike and the kids for lunch. I wanted to check in on them and let them know I would be sticking around for a while. Rachel was already at the house and was sorting laundry in the kitchen, so I told her first.

'That's... good news, I suppose.' She didn't take her eyes off the basket of socks as she spoke.

'I thought you'd be... a bit more pleased?' I blushed. I thought Rachel liked me and we were getting on so well. Had I imagined it?

'I am pleased, really – I think it's great.' She put down the laundry and looked at me. 'It's just... well, what comes next? You stay here for a few months and then you leave again?'

'Well yes, that's the idea.'

She rubbed her eye with the heel of her hand. 'These kids have just lost their mum. What they need now is consistency and stability. Not to get close to someone, only to lose them too.'

I crumpled, my balloon burst. I hadn't thought about it that way.

'I can't just drop everything and come back forever,' I said. 'I have my own life, the life that I chose, just like Amy chose to stay here and have three kids.' I waved my arm around the kitchen, as if that was the sum of my sister's life choices.

Too late, I noticed that Lucas was standing in the doorway, listening to everything. He bolted and ran back up the stairs.

Could I get anything right today?

I followed him to his room and knocked timidly on the door. He was lying on the bottom bunk, his head twisted to face the wall. I stroked his hair.

'Please don't be cross with me. I'm going to stay for a while – I thought you guys would be happy?'

'But you don't want to stay with us. You're only staying with us because Mummy said you have to!'

'That's not true. Of course I want to be here. We're going to stick together and look after each other, like we promised. It's just that I can't stay forever, like Mummy wanted. It would be too complicated for me.'

'We have a spare room here. Or you could come and live with Nanny. It's not that complicated.'

If only life was as simple as the perspective of an eleven-year-old.

Mike looked rough. His skin was grey, with puffy blue bags under bloodshot eyes, and his hair was greasy. I wanted to run him a hot bubble bath.

I offered to take the kids out for a few hours so he could get some rest. Adam had already lined up some properties for me to see that afternoon, so I told them they could come along and hang out at the amusement arcade between viewings.

We called in at Mum and Auntie Sue's first for some tea and cake. Mum was still in her dressing gown but didn't seem to be embarrassed to have unexpected visitors. Without make-up, she looked so much older. I told her I would be staying in Seahouses for three months and her expression didn't change.

'I'll make up the small bedroom for you,' said Auntie Sue. 'It's probably not what you're used to, but your suitcase can go in the loft, and if you need more storage, there's half a wardrobe in my room...'

'Thanks,' I said quickly, 'but I think it's better if I have my own place. It might be a bit much for all of us, squeezed in here.'

Mum gazed out the window, her attention suddenly captured by a blackbird on the garden fence.

Adam had arranged three viewings. The first address was on Swallow Street, just around the corner from Mike and Amy's house. I must have walked down that lane thousands of times, but I struggled to picture it until I arrived.

The location was perfect. It was a row of old fishermen's houses perched at the top of the hill above the harbour, accessed by the back lane which was sheltered from the wind despite the height. A narrow footpath ran along the front of the row, putting just a few feet and some ornate iron railings between the front doors of the cottages and the dizzying drop down to the harbour.

Each house was painted a different colour. Puffin Cottage, the one I was viewing, was pale pink and had a tiny, pebbled back yard. Climbing honeysuckle framed a pale green door with a big silver knocker. It was absolutely beautiful.

The owner, a weather-worn woman in her late fifties, was there to give us the tour. She introduced herself as Sandra and started chatting to Adam while I took in the cottage.

Everything was small, scaled-down like a hobbit hole. The back door opened right into the kitchen-dining room which was no more than a few metres wide – serving would be a very short walk. The kitchen was gloriously retro, with little embroidered curtains covering the bottom units instead of cupboard doors, and a stove that had probably been there since gas was first installed. The dining table would seat four at a pinch and took up half of the room. I gazed admiringly at the patterned floor tiles.

The living room was a little bigger, with a two-seater sofa along one wall and a couple of armchairs snuggled into the bay window. It had an open fireplace with a brick surround, and bookshelves built into the recesses on either side of the chimney breast. The room smelled smoky and I could imagine how cosy it would feel with a roaring fire.

A narrow staircase led to the top floor, which was dominated by a surprisingly spacious main bedroom. It was also very old-fashioned, with a forest green carpet and crocheted bed cover, but the height of the house and the elevation of the hill gave it the most incredible views out to sea. I pulled back the lace curtain to get a better look.

I could see for miles, from up here – as far as Bamburgh to the north. Years of salty wind had beaten the glass and distorted it in patches, warping the fishing boats in the harbour far below. *Amy would have loved this,* I thought to myself.

The green carpet should have been a warning sign – the bathroom next door contained the kitschiest avocado suite. The room was also facing to sea, and I could picture myself enjoying a soak in the green tub while enjoying the views from the beautiful big window. Adam clapped his hands in delight and Sandra let out a sigh of relief.

'I was nervous to let you see this! I thought you'd find it painfully uncool. Shows how much I know about what's hip these days!'

She headed back downstairs, shaking her head and chuckling to herself. Adam and I smiled at each other as Betsy wrinkled her nose up.

'Gross,' she whispered.

Adam insisted that I view all three properties before making a decision, but I knew Puffin Cottage was the one, and I told Sandra to go ahead and arrange the contract. Adam and I had arrived in Seahouses with just a suitcase each, so he called Thierry and asked him to urgently airfreight some of my clothes and personal belongings.

We went to kill some time in the amusement arcade. Amy and I used to hang out there as teenagers and most of the year it was a sorry story, a place for rain-soaked day-trippers to dry out and curse the British weather as they counted down the hours until their bus home. But in the summer, when the village swelled with holidaymakers and the population quadrupled, the arcade had been a great spot to meet boys.

Today it was empty, apart from a couple of old ladies at slot machines. I happily changed a twenty-pound note into pound coins for the kids, congratulating myself on finding a way to keep them amused and entertained.

'Legal guardianship' – it sounded so official, so serious. As much as I wanted to fulfil Amy's wishes, perhaps it didn't need to be a full-time gig. Mike was more than capable of looking after the children on his own, especially with Rachel, Mum, and Auntie Sue right on the doorstep. What more could I add? Perhaps I could come home every month or two for a few days, just to check in on them and be the fun aunt. Puffin Cottage could be my home away from home.

Adam must have read my mind.

'You're pretty good at this, you know. Better than you realise. And they clearly like having you around. Who knows – after three months, you might decide to make it a more permanent arrangement?'

'And what about that small matter of my own life? Not to mention my career?'

He sighed. 'There are other careers, you know. You would find some other way to fill your days.'

Betsy came and climbed onto my lap, clutching her tummy. 'Auntie Izzy, I feel sick. I want to go home.'

We trudged back up Main Street, past The Ship and along the road to their house, determined to make it back before Betsy threw up and ruined my winning streak.

With Adam returning the hire car to the airport before he flew back to Hong Kong, I needed some wheels, too. Rachel suggested we pay a visit to Phil's garage to see if he had any cars that were between owners and available for hire.

The garage was at the end of a side street, out towards the caravan park. It was a modest business, and the space was scarcely big enough to hold two cars, with three more parked outside. The door was open when we got there, and a pair of long legs were sticking out from underneath a rusting Vauxhall. I coughed loudly and the rest of Phil appeared.

He only had a Mini, but that was perfect – I wasn't planning any long trips. As long as the children could comfortably fit inside, that would do. Phil offered a discount on a long-term rental if I paid in cash, and I agreed to come back once I'd been to the bank. Once again, he looked like he was about to cry just at the sight of me. I was clearly radiating sadness these days.

With new digs and a new set of wheels, we had achieved a lot in one day. Now I just needed to persuade my boss to give me extended bereavement leave – figuring out how to resuscitate my career was a problem for three months down the line. I fired off an email to Toby, officially requesting a short sabbatical.

Adam had been my rock, and I was dreading saying goodbye to him. We decided to spend our last night together in the pub. Auntie Sue was taking care of dinner for Mike and the children, and we called at the house first so Adam could say goodbye to them. Mum was worryingly chipper, playing with Betsy and asking Hannah if she wanted her hair plaited. She wrapped Adam in a tight cuddle and thanked him for everything. Auntie Sue pulled her off to help peel vegetables and gave me a knowing look.

Back at The Ship, Adam packed his case and came to meet me in the bar. We shared a steak pie at our usual corner table and I started to drown my sorrows.

Adam eyed me as I poured a third glass of wine. 'Easy, tiger. You're not in Honkers anymore.'

Gina was serving behind the bar, dressed in a low-cut leopard print blouse and big hoop earrings, and not even in an ironic way. Adam caught me watching her. 'You know, you will need some friends around here once I've gone. She's a nice girl, which you would know if you gave her half a chance.'

We went up to my room to do a face mask before bed. Adam was leaving early in the morning, so we had decided to do our goodbyes the night before – I always handled the emotional stuff better when alcohol was involved. He'd promised to come for a visit at the end of next month, but that was an eternity away.

'So, what's next?'

I sighed. 'I don't know. Surviving one day at a time seems to be a reasonable goal right now.'

'You'll be great. Just remember – your sister wouldn't have asked for your help if she didn't think you could do it.'

He had way more confidence in my ability than I did. What had made Amy so sure I'd be any good at this?

'Thank you for everything. You were a true friend when I most needed one.' I started to cry, unable to stop myself.

'Now listen here: I've seen you do a lifetime of crying these past couple of weeks. But you're strong, Izzy. You're stronger than you know.'

For the last time, Adam tucked me in. From now on, I was flying solo.

Chapter Six

Adam had left by the time I woke up the following morning. My head pounded and my mouth was dry – that had been a bigger night than I'd realised. I drank a whole bottle of water and followed it with a swig from my hip flask, just to soften the sharp edges that were poking in my brain.

I checked out of The Ship and made my way to Puffin Cottage, wheeling my single suitcase noisily down the back lane. Sandra was waiting to meet me at the gate to the yard. She boiled the kettle for tea as I looked over the rental agreement. I noticed the name on the contract: Wheeler. The name of my favourite schoolteacher.

'Are you related to Mrs Wheeler, by any chance? I mean, er, Diana Wheeler?'

'Yes, she's my mother. This is her house.'

'She taught me and my sister at St Helen's. She always... Let's just say, I was very fond of her. Please tell her I said hello. It would be lovely to see her, if she ever wants to stop by.'

Sandra shook her head. 'She's not doing great, I'm afraid. Losing her touch, a bit.' She tapped a finger to her head.

I felt a pang of sadness for the woman who had once played such a big role in my life. 'Sorry to hear that. She was a wonderful teacher.' *And had fabulous taste in interior design*, I thought to myself as I admired the kitchen cupboard curtains again.

As soon as Sandra had left, I sent a message to the family chat:

Hello from Puffin Cottage! Do you want to come over for tea and biscuits?

The responses came quickly:

Hannah: *Yes, would love to. See you soon*

Auntie Sue: *Me and your mum will come. Love Auntie Sue.* x

Auntie Sue: *Do you need us to bring anything?* x

I smiled, replying:

Yes please! Tea bags, milk, sugar and biscuits...

Hannah: *LOL*

Rachel: *I'm in too – extra biscuits coming right up! xxx*

I selected an eclectic mix of tea-cups and saucers from the cupboards in preparation for my guests' arrival. After welcoming them and giving the grand tour, we raised our teas in a toast my new home. Mum looked uneasy.

'Is everything all right, Mum?'

She shook her head.

'The feng shui in here is way off. We should rebalance it or you'll be wallowing in negative energy.'

I resisted rolling my eyes. This was exactly why I wasn't moving in with her and Auntie Sue. I desperately tried to think of some way to change the subject, but was saved by a knock at the door.

It was Gina, holding an enormous bouquet of red roses.

'Gina, you really didn't have to...'

'They're not from me,' she blurted. 'They were delivered to the pub this morning, after you left. I think there's a card in there.'

I opened the small envelope and read aloud: *'To Isabelle. Sorry for your loss. Glad to hear you're staying in Seahouses for a while.* But no name. That's strange...'

Mum clapped her hands in delight. 'Looks like you have a secret admirer – how romantic!'

I shook my head, frowning. That was odd – who could they be from? Obviously, the whole village knew by now that I was staying for a while – these people had nothing better to talk about. But why not leave a name? Was Mum right – did I have a secret admirer?

A tiny part of me hoped that maybe they were from Jake Ridley, and the thought caught me off-guard. Really, this was not the time for romantic aspirations. Besides, it was probably just someone trying to be friendly. It would be weird to woo a girl right after her sister had died.

I hunted through the cupboards for a vase – the best I could find was a large ceramic jug. I tried to arrange the roses in the jug, but they were too tall, and leaned awkwardly. I looked around for somewhere to display it, and then had a better idea.

'Come on, everyone. I know just the place for these.'

Amy's grave was still a brown mound of freshly dug soil, with grass seeds scattered on top that would take months to root. The air smelled of new earth, and a light drizzling of rain dusted us in droplets of water.

We gathered around the grave, holding on to one another. It hurt to be here, but it was a necessary pain. I didn't know what I was doing, but I wanted to be closer to Amy, and I wanted the kids to form a connection with this place. Or was it too much? Maybe we should have let them heal in their own time and grieve in their own space.

I pushed my doubts aside. This felt like the right thing to do, and I had to go with my instincts. We scattered the roses onto the hill where Amy was sleeping, red petals tumbling in the wind across the graveyard.

It was my turn to make dinner for the family. I hadn't cooked in years, and I couldn't remember having prepared anything more complicated than a salad in Hong Kong. It was too easy there to go out to eat, or have food delivered, and I had been spoiled for choice with so many places on my doorstep. Seahouses – that was a different story.

I decided it was best to start simple, so I boiled a bag of dry pasta that I found at the back of the cupboard. When it was cooked, I stirred in tins of tuna and sweetcorn with some mayonnaise. I surveyed and sampled my efforts – not too bad for a first attempt.

'That smells great,' said Mike with sincerity.

The kids were less excited.

'I don't think Mummy ever made this,' said Betsy. 'Except maybe for barbecue days. It's very nice though. It's like eating party food for tea!'

Hannah smiled as her sister tripped over the attempt at a compliment.

Amy had been a good cook. She'd started when Mum left, and as we'd found our way into our new routine, cooking had become her thing. As the family ate, I vowed to look online that night for some simple recipes and make a proper go of it tomorrow, with fresh ingredients and everything.

After dinner I was left to clear up – that was when I really noticed Rachel's absence. Perhaps she was trying to give us some space to find our feet.

Mike had been quiet for most of the meal, and left the table as soon as he finished eating. He hadn't said anything else about contesting Amy's will, and I hoped he had changed his mind. The idea just didn't feel right, and I couldn't see how we could do it without putting more strain on the children. I loaded the dishwasher and went upstairs to find him.

As I came up the stairs to his office, I heard him on the phone.

'Listen, it's under control – you'll get your money back. I'm working on it. I'm going to go and see him, and I'll tell him myself.'

Mike was speaking quietly, but I could hear the tension in his voice.

I stood statue-still at the top of the stairs, half of me wanting to stay and the other half wanting to run. Who was he on the phone to? Was this about his business, or something else? And was this why he was so anxious to get the insurance money? One thing I knew for certain – Mike would not want me listening in on this.

I crept slowly, carefully, silently down the stairs and slipped back to the living room where the children were watching TV. I squeezed in next to Betsy, who was sucking her thumb again, and she curled into me. I just hoped she wouldn't hear how hard my heart was pounding.

Mike came in some moments later. He was calm and cool, like nothing had happened.

'Listen, kids – and Izzy – I have to go away for a few days.'

'No! You can't!' Lucas wailed.

'Sorry mate, but we have bills to pay and it's my job that pays them. That's why Auntie Izzy is here, to look after you lot so that I can carry on working.'

What the actual...? I raised a quizzical eyebrow at Mike, but he missed it.

Hannah was outraged. 'Dad, you promised you wouldn't leave us!'

'I'll be back in five days.'

'But that's practically a whole week!'

He raised his hands, palms towards her. 'It's only Amsterdam and I'll be home by the weekend.' Mike sighed. 'I'm sorry, sweetheart. I know the timing's not great, but they didn't give me any choice.'

That was weird – because just minutes ago, I'd heard Mike insisting on going. And he worked for himself. Who was this 'they' that he was talking about?

I followed him into the kitchen. 'Couldn't you have let me know first? Shouldn't we discuss these things?'

'Sorry, it's just that – well, that is why you're here, isn't it? To help look after the kids?'

'Still... don't you think you should ask me first?' I tried to keep the anger from the edges of my voice.

'Right, sorry...' Mike's lip started to tremble.

I found myself relenting a little. Perhaps I shouldn't have snapped at him. 'I mean, I'm happy to help and everything – but just let me know, OK? Let's work together on this.'

His eyes filled. 'It's just... I miss her so much.'

I looked down, shuffling my weight from foot to foot. Looking anywhere except at Mike.

'Clearly, I'm not the parenting expert here, but don't you think the kids need you right now?'

He shook his head. 'I wouldn't go if I could avoid it. But this is work, it's my business – I can't take time off.'

I thought back to the days after Dad died, when Mum started

69

to slip away from us too.

Mike knew what I was thinking. 'Look, if I keep working, I'll keep sane. I want to be there for them – of course I'm going to be there for them. I just need to do this as well. For me.'

I had to sympathise – I would have loved a distraction right then, too. Looking after three grieving kids was a lot of work. But I couldn't shake my suspicions about the phone conversation I'd heard.

'You are all right for money, aren't you?'

'I'm fine.'

'Because if you need cash—'

'We are fine.' There was an edge to his voice that told me to back down.

We were facing each other across the galley of the kitchen and I could feel my heart thundering in my chest. Mike's face was red. He turned his back to me to search for something inside the cupboard, and I slipped away to join the children.

So much for settling into a new routine, I thought as I unpacked my overnight bag in Amy's spare room. This would be the third bed I'd slept in this week.

Mike had gone to the airport early that morning, and the day stretched ahead – terrifyingly long and empty. How to fill it? Rachel was coming over after her shift and it was Mum's turn to help with dinner, but that was hours away.

I suggested to Hannah that we go through some of her mum's things with her brother and sister, starting with the box of photos she had found. After Dad died, we'd put off sorting his stuff, believing it would be too painful. But when we'd finally started, we'd found the opposite – it was like having him back with us. Amy and I had spent weeks on it, savouring the process for an hour or two each evening. I fingered his hip flask in my pocket now, running my thumb over the grooves of the inscription.

Hannah, Lucas and Betsy each picked out a photograph to have framed, and I took a couple for Puffin Cottage – one of me and Amy on the beach, and one of us from Edinburgh. In the Edinburgh photo, we were at a party in the kitchen of a house I couldn't remember, and she had her arms around my shoulders in a protective hold. We were both smiling brightly at the camera with wide, toothy grins.

And suddenly I remembered a fragment of a conversation I'd had with someone that night – a guy in a bucket hat and anorak. He'd asked who was the older sister, because it was hard to tell who was looking after who.

My phone rang, snapping me back to the moment: Jake Ridley. I went out onto the landing to answer it, making sure the children wouldn't be able to hear.

'You asked me to let you know if I heard any news on Amy's case?'

'Yes.' My voice was a thin croak. I sat on the stairs, biting my lip and digging my fingernails into the palm of my free hand.

'Only, I was speaking to a contact in the coroner's office. Apparently Amy's blood tests showed high levels of benzodi-azepines. It's a type of medication prescribed to patients with anxiety disorders. When it's taken with alcohol, it can have psychoactive effects.'

Amy had been on anxiety meds? This was the first I'd heard of it. And she'd had a glass of wine the night of the accident. I gripped the phone.

'So what happens now?'

'The police have spoken to Mike and it was news to him, unfortunately. So they'll speak with her GP to find out if she had a prescription. Do you know if she was taking anything?'

'I... I... Sorry. I have no idea.'

How could I not have known this? I ached for my sister – for what she must have been going through, and the gulf between us widened. What had she been unable to tell me?

Jake told me not to worry, and that the police would check it out. He was cushioning my feelings, but it didn't lessen my guilt.

I thanked Jake and went back to the children. Sorting through Amy's belongings was a great way to start conversations about her, and the children were happy to talk – once we started, it was hard to get them to stop. Their stories didn't point to Amy being stressed, or upset – in fact, quite the opposite. She was busy, very engaged in village life, and physically active. They told me that Amy had started going for long runs along the coast road. She said it was her 'mum time' and her way of unwinding.

God knows, I could do with that. I put my hand under my sweater – my tummy felt soft, and I could pinch an inch I swore hadn't been there back in Hong Kong. I was missing my weekly Pilates and Muay Thai sessions. Maybe running could help me keep in shape and preserve my sanity at the same time. I asked Hannah to show me where Amy kept her running gear.

By the time Rachel arrived, I was wrapped up and ready to go, eager to see what all the fuss was about. Anything that would help me feel what Amy felt.

It was bitterly cold – the kind that bites at your ears. I pulled

Amy's hat as far down as it would go and tugged at the collar of her fleece jacket until it covered my chin. It was years since I had run anywhere, and it hurt – the cold air burning my lungs while the wind whipped at my face. The kids had said that Amy used to run to Bamburgh Castle and back again. I didn't think I'd make her full route, but I decided to try and see how far I could get.

I jogged along the back streets and past the harbour carpark, keeping my pace steady and wondering how soon I could stop for a break without it being embarrassing. I passed the last houses on the coast road – including our old house – and kept my gaze firmly ahead, not wanting distractions from the past. My thighs itched from the cold and my fingers were on icy fire despite the gloves. But something about it seemed right. This was what Amy had done. I could feel her in the clothes, the shape of her feet in her trainers, and I pressed myself against the empty outline of my sister. Tears blew across my cheeks.

I got part-way down the road before a stitch got the better of me, so I headed back, crossing over to walk beside the houses, in case that was any warmer than the beach side. At the third house, a man was standing at his garden gate, and as I approached, he called out to me.

'Isabelle?'

He was about my age, but dressed like a much older man in a tank top and chequered wool trousers. I noticed his blue eyes. He looked familiar, but I struggled to place him.

'I'm so sorry, but I saw you running by just now and I thought – just for a moment – the craziest thing, but you look just like your sister. I thought it was Amy.' He wiped away a tear. 'Gosh, I'm so stupid! Sorry, my goodness – what a thing to say. I'm Richard Pringle... Mr Pringle?' He said it

73

like the name should mean something to me, and offered me his hand to shake. When I looked confused, he elaborated: 'The headteacher at North Sunderland Primary School? We met at the service... for your sister.'

That's where I knew him from – Amy's funeral. He had a kind, but tired face, and he seemed genuinely upset by the mistaken identity. He invited me in, and I found the prospect of getting warm and being able to talk about Amy was too tempting.

Richard's house was just a few doors down from the house we had grown up in. It wasn't as large as our old place, but it had identical sea views, and seeing them again from this vantage point was like hearing an old song. He brought in a tray with a pot of tea, two cups and a plate of biscuits.

It turned out that Richard had known Amy quite well – she had been chair of the PTA and had regularly organised fundraising events for the school. I'd seen pictures of these things on Facebook, but I hadn't bothered to understand that Amy was actually organising them. How much did I not know about my sister?

'So', said Richard, leaning forward in his chair. 'How are you coping?'

I thought about where to start, trying my hardest not to cry. 'It's been tough,' I finally said in a small voice. I took a deep breath. 'To be perfectly honest, it's terrifying. Just the responsibility, you know?'

Richard smiled. 'I know that feeling – every teacher does. It's perfectly normal.'

'All the questions they have, and all the things you need to think about – and the rules! My goodness, the rules... I seem to make them up as I go along.'

'The key is to sound like you mean it,' he said with a chuckle.

'I don't know,' I sighed. 'I hadn't planned for this.'

'You'll find your stride. We all go through the same learning curve.'

We sat in silence, sipping our tea. I mulled over Richard's words. Maybe I was being too hard on myself? After all, this was just like any new job – it was just a case of learning the ropes.

Richard set his cup down on the tray. 'You know, Amy was a very dear friend of mine, and I was very fond of her. If there's anything at all I can do - even if it's just providing tea and biscuits, you only have to ask.'

He held out the plate and I gratefully took a custard cream. I glanced at my watch, suddenly realising that I'd been gone for almost an hour. Some guardian I was – I'd left Rachel to do the work and forgotten all about her. I reluctantly said goodbye to Richard, telling him to call at Puffin Cottage any time.

Mum had arrived by the time I got back and was cooking in the kitchen. She hugged me hello, and for the first time in as long as I could remember, I let myself melt into her. Maybe running had been a good idea after all. I offered to help with dinner, and she showed me how to roll up the lentil and herb mix she was working on into little balls.

Rachel and the kids were in the living room, giving me a chance to speak to Mum privately.

'Was Amy having any problems, Mum?'

'Like what, dear?'

'Was anything stressing her out? Was she anxious about something, before the accident?'

'I don't think so. If something was troubling her, she didn't tell me.' She stopped and put the spoon down. 'Perhaps you'd be better off asking your Auntie Sue about things like that...' Her bottom lip started to tremble.

I shifted my weight from foot to foot. 'Sorry. I didn't mean to upset you.'

'I haven't been much of a mother to you girls, I know that. I never got the chance to properly make up for it. And now I never will with Amy.' She blew her nose with a tissue from her pocket.

I shrugged. 'What's done is done. And it was a long time ago. There's no point dwelling on it.'

I wondered if I meant that.

'If I'd been better, if I hadn't messed up, you wouldn't have moved to the other side of the world and you wouldn't be in such a rush to get back there. You should be staying with me – not in a cottage down the road. We should be together now, as a family.'

I thought carefully about how to explain without hurting her feelings. 'I just need my own space, Mum. It's already a lot to deal with, and I need room to breathe.'

She gave a sad sigh. 'I know what that's like. I suppose if anyone can empathise, it should be me. Sometimes we need to go away in order to find our way home...'

She trailed off, gazing out the window at the sky, which was turning inky as dusk fell. The moment was over.

I pulled out my phone and sent a message to Amy:

I'm doing my best here Ames, but this is so hard. I miss you every day. xo

Chapter Seven

The children were finally going back to school, and as much as I thought it would be good for them to get back into a routine, I also selfishly couldn't wait to have the day to myself. That was, until I checked my morning messages, and found one from Hannah:

I don't want to do this.

I growled into the pillow and pressed snooze on my phone. Monday mornings had always been a struggle for me, but I was determined to get this right. I'd insisted to Mum and Auntie Sue that I didn't need extra help – I wanted to handle the morning routine on my own. I told them it was important for the children's sake to keep it as fuss-free as possible, but deep down I wanted to prove to everyone – including myself – that I could do it.

It took some arm-twisting to convince Hannah that she'd have to go back to school sooner or later – and later meant she'd have more catching up to do. We had done ourselves a big favour by laying out uniforms, packing bags and making packed lunches the evening before, but there were endless last-minute tasks that I hadn't foreseen – from plaiting Betsy's hair to helping Lucas find his missing library book. He and Hannah had to run for the school bus. I knew they were trying their best, but the whole experience was wearying.

By the time I got back from dropping Betsy off, I wanted to go back to bed. I poured myself an orange juice and topped it up with vodka.

I needed to pull myself together: I had digging to do. There was something about the suggestion Amy was on anxiety medication that just didn't sound right to me – Amy had herself together.

On the other hand, if she and Mike had been experiencing money problems... That might explain why she had been on edge, and why she was taking something for it. But would she have been drinking, too? And would she have got into the car like that? Amy was a nurse, she would have known better.

Rachel was coming over for lunch, which gave me the whole morning to rummage around. I went up to the office on the first floor and surveyed the scene.

It was officially Mike's study – the hub where he ran his business, whatever that was, but it was by no means off limits to the rest of the family.

The room was dominated by a desk, on top of which sat a computer monitor surrounded by several stacks of files and loose papers. The back wall was covered in bookcase units, with cupboards underneath that screamed IKEA. There was a nod to a nautical theme, with a couple of model ships on the shelves and some seashells lined up along the windowsill. The shelves were full of files. A lone post-it served as a reminder of the Wi-Fi password: I traced a finger along the black loops of Amy's handwriting.

I started at the top of the first pile and moved my way through each folder systematically, looking for anything interesting. They kept everything – appointment confirmation letters from the dentist, permission notes for school trips, PTA agendas. I had forgotten Amy's mild hoarder tendency. It had first kicked in when we'd had to sort through Dad's stuff and ever since, she'd disliked throwing things away.

There was a family medical file, with letters from the GP and confirmations of hospital appointments. There were a few prescriptions inside, but I couldn't see anything about benzodiazepines or anxiety. In fact, it looked like the last time Amy had seen a doctor was for an ear infection three years ago.

Mike's business was something to do with innovation. From the looks of things, it was nothing more complicated than pairing start-ups with investors or helping them access public funding, and I wondered how Mike made any real money from it when he was just the middleman. There were some sidelines too, such as training workshops for innovator-entrepreneurs and some invoices for consultancy services, which might have meant anything. He had even done some Amazon selling, although I couldn't figure out what the products were.

Then the interesting stuff: bank statements for their joint account, for Amy's account and her credit card. I could see that Mike was putting money into the joint account each month, and all the outgoings seemed to be bills. Amy's account showed her salary coming in, and it gave me a jolt of guilt when I realised how little she took home from her job as a district nurse. Still, she wasn't spending much from her salary. In fact, she was putting almost all of it into a savings account. *Good for you*, I thought.

I couldn't find Mike's bank statements, or the business accounts, which was strange, because the invoicing paperwork was all here. He must have filed them somewhere else. I turned to open the cupboard behind the desk, but it was locked. The other cupboards were all open. Where was the key?

I was digging through the desk drawer when the clatter of the front door shattered through the quiet house, startling me. I put my hand to my chest, my heart pounding against my palm. Rachel called out from the hallway below and I breathed a sigh of relief.

Where had the morning gone? I had completely lost track of time. I quickly pushed the piles of papers back to their original positions and went to meet her downstairs.

She had made us lunch of quinoa and feta cheese salad with pumpkin soup, and my dearly departed Pilates body thanked her for it. As she set out plates and bowls, I wondered how to broach the subject of Amy and Mike's finances without making it awkward.

'Amy told you everything, right?'

Rachel nodded. 'We were best friends.' She hesitated, looking concerned. 'And you can trust me, too. Is something on your mind?'

'I'm fine. I'm just wondering though... I mean, how do you think they were doing, financially?'

'They do quite well, I think.' She waved a spoon, gesturing to the kitchen. 'Just look at this place. It's one of the nicest houses in the village. Way nicer than mine!'

'So Amy didn't mention anything about money worries, or anything else that might have been troubling her?'

'Nothing. Why? What's going on?'

'I'm just trying to work out if there was more too it. When she crashed her car that night. Was she stressed or worried about something?'

Rachel thought about it. 'She had a lot going on, you know – three kids isn't easy. And although she was only working part-time, the hours are always longer than they're meant to be, plus the stuff with the school, and then the fundraising, community projects... But she liked to be busy.'

'So she wasn't taking anxiety meds...?'

Rachel stopped stirring the soup and turned off the hob. She was standing with her back to me, and I wished I could see her face. She ladled the soup into two bowls. 'Where did you get that idea from?'

I rubbed my thumb over the engraving on the hipflask in my pocket. 'You mustn't tell anyone.'

'Cross my heart.'

I sat down at the table. 'The coroner. Apparently Amy's blood tests showed she was on medication, one of those types that you're not supposed to mix with alcohol. But she had drunk a glass of wine that night, and got behind the wheel. It all just seems... so unlike her.'

Rachel frowned. She placed the bowls on the table and folded herself into the chair opposite me.

'I don't think she was on anything, no. Not that she told me. But between you and me... and don't take this the wrong way' – Rachel slowly stirred her steaming bowl of soup – 'I'm not sure that she was always happy.'

'You mean with Mike? Why, what did he do to her?'

'Nothing! I mean, really, nothing. I think it was her. Sometimes... sometimes it just seemed as if this wasn't enough. Like she wanted more.'

As soon as Rachel left, I went back to my search of the study. That cupboard was bugging me, and I couldn't find a key anywhere. Nor did I see anything to suggest that Amy hadn't been happy. Anyone looking at her life would have said she had it all.

The Amy who had longed to get away from here and travel the world with me, she was a shadow in the memory of this woman. Had she simply buried those ideas because real life had worked out differently? It looked like Seahouses and village life – Mike and her family – all of that had become enough for her.

Or had the memory of young Amy haunted her? Had she regretted giving up her dreams?

I decided to take a walk to the harbour to clear my head.

Seahouses was perched on top of a very gentle slope, one of the highest points on that stretch of coastline. It was a clear sunny day, and on the horizon, I could clearly make out the rocky protrusions of the Farne Islands. When the wind was high, it was possible to hear the shrieks of the million birds that nested there.

I walked down towards the harbour, resisting the smell of chips from the takeaway van parked at the top of the bank. I had no idea how Amy and I had stayed so skinny as teenagers, considering how many of those damn things we'd eaten. We would get a bag between us, load them with salt and vinegar and eat them from the paper while they were steaming hot.

The sea was a rich navy blue, broken only by the occasional line of white wave. A great day for going out on the water. Indeed, as I turned the corner into the harbour, I saw that it was almost empty – anyone who could be, would be at sea. The fishing boats would be back by early evening, hauling fresh catches of herring, haddock and a few cod if they were lucky. I scanned the row of fishermen's cottages at the crest of the harbour hill – the sea houses that gave the village its name – for the blush pink of Puffin Cottage. I couldn't wait for Mike to get home so that I could get back to my new bed.

Still, it was useful to have Amy's place to myself. Where could the key for that cupboard be? I took a nip from my hip flask to help me focus.

Back at the house, I looked at the study with fresh eyes. With all the crap on the desk, it would be easy for a small key to get lost. I wondered if Mike took it with him when he travelled, but that seemed risky. He might have hidden it somewhere, somewhere it wouldn't be easily found, but not a place where he was likely to lose it. I scanned the bookcase. The model boats were replicas of cobles, the type used by the local fishermen. I picked up the miniature *Farthing* and shook it – and there was the distinctive rattle of metal on wood. I peered through the tiny porthole and saw the glint of a small silver key inside. I ran my thumb along the hull until I found the join of the seam and prised it open, the key falling onto the floor below.

The cupboard opened with a creak. Finally, the business accounts. I had a couple of hours before the kids got home and about three years of bank statements, invoices and purchase orders to go through. I poured a small vodka. Time to get to work.

Business had been good. At one time, it seemed that Mike's company had been bringing in around ten thousand pounds each month. That was from a variety of streams, including the Amazon selling. He had received a few big payments from a German company, the year before last. But as I got to the most recent statements, the numbers told a different story. There was much less coming in, but the same amount going out monthly to Mike's personal account – presumably, what he allowed for his salary. There were monthly payments to a credit card too. I scanned the numbers, searching for clues.

It looked like he had loaned money to other companies and had lost it when they had failed to take off. He had paid twenty-five thousand pounds for shares in a start-up that had gone bankrupt before it turned a profit. There were letters from investors too; creditors sending final payment notices and demands for overdue invoices. He had even taken out a small loan against the house, and although it seemed like he had managed to pay it back, I got the impression that Mike was only just keeping his head above water. I wondered how much Amy had known.

I took photos on my phone of some of Mike's bank statements and the letters. I wasn't sure what it all meant, but it didn't look good, and this was clearly why he wanted the money. That felt wrong to me – Amy had wanted any life insurance to set up the kids for the future, not to pay back Mike's bad business decisions. Hopefully Jake could help me understand all this better, and maybe I could use it to fight Mike's challenge on the will, if he went ahead with it. I sent Jake a message:

I think Mike is in financial difficulty, and I want to learn more. Can I come to see you tomorrow?

He replied promptly: *Yes, of course you can pop by. I'm free all morning.*

I sent another message to Amy:

Were you worried about money? Or did Mike hide it from you?

The timer on my phone buzzed – I had about ten minutes before the kids got home. I quickly packed everything back up and put the key away in its hiding place, then went downstairs to make a start on dinner.

I absent-mindedly peeled the carrots, letting my mind

84

wander. The strangest part of being on sabbatical from work was the lack of emails. The uncomfortable silence from the office was making me anxious, and I was annoyed at them for treating me like this – like I was weak. I was missing my friends, and my social life, too. After the initial waves of sympathy messages, the texts and phone calls had ebbed away. Adam had been in touch daily to check in on me, but I hadn't heard from most of my friends since before the funeral. I sighed. Out of sight, out of mind. Besides, I was hardly the life and soul of the party these days. I had nothing to share except misery.

Still, it was giving me the space and the time to focus on my family, and on getting some answers. The thought that Amy's death might not have been an accident was a terrifyingly deep and dark hole that I didn't want to fall into, but my gut was telling me something wasn't right. Mike's finances and the way he had reacted to Amy's will would give anyone cause for concern. I didn't want to link the two, but I couldn't shake the dark cloud of dread.

I poured another vodka. I longed for my sister in that moment – for all the moments we had missed, and all the moments we would never have.

What was troubling you? I texted her. *What was so bad that you couldn't tell me?*

I thought about who might know more, and who I could trust. If Amy hadn't been able to talk to me, I doubt she would have confided in Auntie Sue. Still, it was worth a try. Then there was Rachel – she had been a rock to me. She knew my sister better than anyone and could probably give me the clearest picture about what was going on in Amy's life.

I was also curious about Richard Pringle. He and Amy

seemed to have been good friends, and I wondered how well he had got on with Mike.

I was jolted out of my thoughts by the front door opening. The kids trooped in – Betsy's face was tear-stained and Hannah looked weary, while Lucas stormed straight up the stairs without even saying hello.

Betsy gave me a long, garbled explanation about some boy who had said something mean, and they'd had what sounded like a pretty vicious argument. I did my best to follow the story, but I was trying to chop vegetables and follow the recipe book at the same time, and I kept missing bits. Hannah sat at the kitchen table with her head in her hands, and only offered me a grunt when I asked her how her day had been.

I was quite proud of the shepherd's pie I made for dinner – not bad for a first attempt. It had taken way longer than I'd realised it would, and everyone was starving by the time we eventually sat down to eat. But Hannah just pushed it around her plate and Lucas couldn't even pretend to enjoy it.

'Is there anything else for tea? I don't like this. It's got lumps in it.'

The back of my neck was getting hot and itchy.

'Me either,' said Betsy. 'I want sausages.'

I took a deep breath and was thinking about my next move when the front door opened.

'Only me!' Auntie Sue cried out from the hall as she took her boots off. 'Just thought I'd see how everyone was doing after the first day back.'

She bustled into the kitchen, tossing her coat and scarf to one side and sliding up to Lucas. 'Ooh, that looks delicious!'

'It's lumpy. And it doesn't taste like Mummy's,' he said again, for Auntie Sue's benefit.

My patience was stretched to a fine thread.

Auntie Sue caught my eye. 'Listen you lot, we're all trying here – nobody harder than your Auntie Izzy. Remember what we were saying about being patient and kind to one another? We all miss your mum, but sometimes we're going to have to do things that are a bit different, just while we get the hang of things. And that starts with eating your dinner, right now.'

How did she always know what to say? I banked her lines for later use.

By some miracle, the kids ate most of their dinner, and I ignored the grumbling and downcast faces as I watched the food on their plates slowly disappear.

'Thought you might need this.' Auntie Sue pulled a bottle of wine from her bag as I loaded the dishwasher. It was a crappy Rioja, but I couldn't have been happier if it was a bottle of champagne. I had to suppress tears of joy as she opened it and poured me a glass.

'Are you OK?'

I took a gulp of wine.

'It's just been a long day. Make that a long week, actually. I've no idea what I'm doing with the kids, my mum is typically useless, my career is on life-support and most of all, I just miss my sister!' I wailed onto Auntie Sue's shoulder.

'Come on now,' she said, rubbing my back. 'You're doing a great job. Our Amy would be so proud. Let's just take one day at a time.'

I smiled at her weakly. Right now, one day at a time was the best plan I had.

Chapter Eight

With that morning's chores completed, I got in the Mini and headed up to Alnwick. It was another clear, bright day, and I took the coast road to appreciate the views at their finest. I had forgotten quite how lovely this corner of the world could be.

At the offices of Moore, Moore & Ridley, Jake poured me a cup of tea from a pot while I told him what I'd seen from Mike's accounts and the conversation I had overheard before his mysterious last-minute business trip. He agreed that it sounded a bit fishy and promised he would look into it. I AirDropped him copies of the documents from my phone.

By the time we were done, it was 12.30 p.m. and Jake suggested going for lunch. We walked across the street to a cute little Italian place and I had a vague memory of going there with Amy, Mum and Dad after a school show or something. Normally I would have ordered a glass of wine, but I had the drive home, and that just didn't seem right after what happened to Amy. Knowing I had to drive that day, I'd even skipped my morning special of vodka and orange juice.

Jake fidgeted with his cutlery.

'I hope I'm not about to overstep the line here. But your sister's life insurance policy... it's enormous.'

'Isn't that a good thing?'

He swallowed. 'Most people don't take out policies that size. It would have been very expensive. And it's completely disproportionate to her income, assets and debts.'

'But presumably Amy and Mike had their reasons for doing it,' I said, thinking out loud.

'Absolutely, I'm sure they did. Although it's very strange that Mike wasn't aware his wife had changed hers. If it does turn out that there were suspicious circumstances surrounding her death, a huge life insurance policy would be a red flag. And of course, the insurance company will wait until the coroner's final report before paying anything.'

I could imagine exactly why Amy would take out decent life insurance – after what we had gone through, she would have wanted to make sure her kids would be well taken care of if anything happened to her or Mike.

Absentmindedly, I reached for my glass of water and took a sip. Jake blinked at me, spots of pink appearing on his cheeks.

'That's mine,' he said, a shy smile dancing on his lips.

'Oh my goodness, I'm so sorry!'

Now it was my turn to blush. I wiped the edge of Jake's glass with my napkin and sheepishly handed it back to him. His fingers brushed mine as he took the glass from me and there was a spark of something, almost like a shiver of electricity.

Was I seriously getting a crush on the senior partner of the family's solicitor firm? What was wrong with me? I shook it off and quickly turned back to polite conversation. Jake seemed equally happy to move the discussion along.

It turned out that the Ridley in Moore, Moore & Ridley was actually Jake's father, who had been a school friend and university classmate of Charles Moore Sr. The elder Moore and

Ridley had shared lifelong passions for grouse-hunting, golf, vintage brandy, and the law. They had forced these pursuits onto their sons from a young age, but Ridley junior had shown no interest in any of it apart from a legal career. And even that was a stretch – Jake had hoped to travel the world as a crime writer, until his father had convinced him that the best route to literary success was to write as a sideline, once he was well-established in the legal profession.

I laughed as Jake told me he came from a long line of decreasingly distinguished law-makers, which he could trace back through the Ridley family archives through to his great-great-great-grandfather, a Sheriff of Northumberland. When his father had died, Jake's inheritance had been tied with the practice and he had finally resigned himself to fate. Writing fiction would have to wait.

He asked me about growing up in Seahouses, and I told him all about Amy, entertaining him with the stories of how we used to keep each other amused. Jake was a good listener and was very easy to talk to. Besides, he had already seen my family – or what was left of it – at our worst. I just hoped he wasn't about to see us sink to a new level of despair.

Back at the village, I called in on Mum and Auntie Sue. Auntie Sue answered the door in an apron and I followed her back into the kitchen. There was a strong smell of incense coming from the living room.

'Does she ever stop burning the herbs?' I asked.

'Hush now, you know that's just how she's dealing with Amy,' she said, whispering over the washing up.

I went to join Mum in the living room. She had laid a circle of candles around a yoga mat in the middle of the floor and was burning joss sticks, while soft bongo music pitter-pattered from an ancient CD player.

'Izzy – come and meditate with me.'

For once, I didn't feel the normal surge of anger that rose like a wave whenever Mum was doing her hippy thing. I simply didn't have the energy to fight her on it anymore.

'Fine. Where do you want me to sit?'

Mum positioned me sitting cross-legged at the centre of the mat and arranged my hands on my knees so that my palms were facing up. She told me to close my eyes, and then re-positioned my head, first turning it gently to the left and right, then forwards and backwards, then released me so slowly that it was hard to tell how high my head was lifted.

'Just breathe,' she said in a weird, soft voice. 'Feel your breath. Feel your body. Just focus on you, and nothing but breathing.'

I took a deep inhale and let it out slowly. How far away were those candles? Burning the place down would be such a Mum thing to do. With my eyes closed, I could hear the bongo music more clearly, and noticed a new noise – the gentle tinkling of running water. Where was that coming from?

'Mum, do you have a leak or something? Why can I hear water?'

'Ssshhh, don't break your focus!'

I ignored her and looked in the direction of the noise. 'Is that a fountain?' My attention was drawn to a bubbling rock decoration on the TV stand.

'Izzy! I told you to concentrate!'

I snapped my head forward again, eyes closed, trying not to giggle.

Mum took a deep breath. 'It's a miniature indoor fountain.

Having water in a room is essential for a good balance of elements, and if you must know, that one has a peace crystal at the centre to promote the well-being of everyone who comes in this house. It's all about the feng shui.'

OK, now I really was going to get the giggles. If only Amy had been here to see this.

But she must have seen it. Surely that would have been worth a quick text to her sister? I tried to imagine a scenario in which Amy would have discovered that our mother had installed a universal-healing indoor water feature in her living room and not thought it merited sending a laughing emoji my way. How had we grown so far apart that she wouldn't have shared this with me, the person she once shared a whole world with?

'Now, the only important thing is your breathing. All of these other thoughts, competing for your attention – they're the distractions you face, every hour, every day. Meditation is rising above the distractions and empowering yourself to focus on what really matters.'

Mum was doing her stupid yogi voice again, but what she was saying actually made sense. I did have a lot of distractions right now and needed to remember what was important.

'Channel the energy from the elements, from the earth, from inside your body. You have everything you need to overcome any challenge; it's already within you. You are stronger than you ever knew. You just need to get past the distractions and rise above the noise...'

I felt stupid, but also strangely serene. Just sitting still and doing some deep breathing was making me feel more relaxed than I had been in weeks – yet, at the same time, strong.

'Sorry, Mum,' I said, reluctant to break the spell. 'But that water thing – it's really making me need the loo.'

Meditation session and toilet break over, Mum cleared away the candles and yoga mat while Auntie Sue prepared a pot of tea and biscuits. Auntie Sue switched off the water feature at the socket and I caught her eye briefly before she looked away, hiding a smirk. She dragged the coffee table back into the middle of the room and I began to pour.

I took a deep breath. 'While I've got you both here, I need to ask: was everything OK with Amy? Did she and Mike have problems?' I glanced up from the teapot. Auntie Sue frowned anxiously at Mum, who was facing the window and had become captivated by something outside. 'It's just... Mike's acting a bit weird about the life insurance thing,' I continued. 'Probably nothing to worry about...'

Neither of them was giving me anything.

'But it would raise eyebrows, don't you think?' I persevered. 'A woman is killed in an unfortunate accident and the husband thinks he is going to get a pay day from the insurance...'

'Enough, Izzy!' Mum snapped, glaring at me with wide eyes. 'Don't say things like that unless you mean them.'

'I'm sorry,' I said, realising I'd pushed it too far. 'It's just that I have a few questions about what was going on with Amy before she died, and we need to answer them – for all our sakes.'

'What questions? Sweetheart, I know it is hard to accept, and it makes no sense, but Amy is gone. The universe took her from us. There was no reason for it and there's nothing we can do about it. We could ask our whys for a thousand years and drive ourselves mad in the process and still be none the wiser.'

I held my head in my hands. 'Mum – you guys saw her every week. You spent time with her and Mike. All I'm saying is that we should think hard about what we might have seen or heard. Anything that might help us understand or get some answers...'

'My darling girl,' Mum said, her eyes becoming watery pools and her hands trembling as she folded them over mine. 'When somebody dies, there are no answers.'

Auntie Sue stood up. 'I think perhaps that's enough excitement for your Mum for now,' she said, ushering me out of the room. 'Maybe you can pop back over later?'

She grabbed her coat from the back of the door and followed me out into the street. I took long, purposeful strides so that she had to jog to keep up.

'Come on, Izzy. You know that's just her way...'

'Yes, her way of dealing with things.' I twirled back to face her. 'So you keep saying. But you know what? I'm tired of hearing it. How about if she gave some useful advice for once instead of energy crystals and that ohm shanti crap?'

Auntie Sue was panting to catch her breath. 'She's trying her hardest. And your questions are way out of order. There was nothing weird going on with Amy, or between her and Mike. If there was, I'd have known.'

'What if there was something going on and they were hiding it from us? Like if his business was in trouble, or they had money worries or something?'

Auntie Sue took a deep breath. 'It takes ten minutes to walk from one end of this village to the other. None of us have secrets.'

I walked back to Amy's, chewing over Auntie Sue's words. The wind was blowing up from the south, a mild but strong wind that would trace fossil-like patterns over miles of sand dunes.

'Oh Amy,' I whispered to her on the breeze. 'What was troubling you?'

I hadn't been back for long when the door clanged open and the house was suddenly full of noise – school bags flung down in the hallway, stockinged feet thundering up the stairs, the chatter of three distinct voices shouting over one another. It was only 4 p.m. There were at least another five hours until bedtime and my stomach lurched as I wondered how we were going to fill them. Rachel had stressed the importance of maintaining their routine, but I had no idea what their routine actually was. I needed help.

I yelled up the stairs: 'OK kids, I'm calling a meeting.'

I set a plate of biscuits in the middle of the table and they came down and gathered around, looking from me to one another, bemused.

'Only one agenda item: re-establishment of the routine. I think it would help us all if we agreed a timetable for our days. We need to know where we're supposed to be and what we're supposed to be doing.'

Blank stares.

'For example, what time do you like to eat dinner?'

'Do you mean tea?' said Betsy.

Lucas giggled. 'She's just being fancy.'

Hannah rolled her eyes.

Lucas helped himself to another biscuit. 'Well, Mum normally – Mum used to do tea at half six, and a bit later on weekends. If one of us is out, then we get tea before or after everyone else. And sometimes if Dad isn't home in time, they would eat together later,' he said, bumbling his tenses. My heart broke for him.

'Great – super helpful, Lucas. So, if we eat at half six, what are you guys doing for the rest of the evening?'

'Depends what day it is. Everyone has different activities on different evenings. It's all on the calendar.'

I peered around the kitchen – I hadn't seen a calendar anywhere.

'Not down here.' Betsy rolled her eyes. 'On the computer!'

We crowded around the computer in the study and Lucas logged on. Within a few clicks he had opened a very elaborate, colour-coded monstrosity of a spreadsheet.

'There. We each have a colour, and this tells us where we're supposed to be and when. See there' – he tapped the screen – 'I'm green. And this shows that I have computer club on Wednesday evenings.'

All the colours, the randomly-placed blocks of time, the overlapping appointments – it was enough to make me dizzy.

'So, how do you keep up with all of these activities?' My mouth was dry.

'Well, it was Mum mostly keeping the calendar up to date,' said Hannah. 'She gets emails from our schools and all our clubs, and she puts the dates in.'

As Hannah said this, an idea came to me. Auntie Sue was right – it was impossible to keep something secret in Seahouses. But what if Amy had confided in someone outside the village? Someone at work, or one of her university friends? The answer would be in her emails or on her social media. I just needed to access it.

'Do any of you know how to log in to your mum's email account?'

It turned out that the email address linked to the calendar was shared by the entire family. Definitely not somewhere

Amy would have kept private correspondence. The password was the first line of their address – not a great secret. While the kids were occupied with their homework, I did some digging around on the computer. I tried the same password for Amy's personal email account, but it was incorrect, not surprisingly. Nor did it work for Facebook.

How could I get her password? Mike might know it, but obviously I couldn't ask him without making him suspicious. I could ask the kids for help, but they would be unlikely to have it. Rachel – perhaps she could give me a clue. If anyone could guess at Amy's password, her best friend seemed like a good place to start. I sent her a message:

Do you know Amy's email or Facebook password by any chance?

By 6.45 p.m. I had served up a dinner of fish fingers with jacket potatoes and baked beans. Only fifteen minutes behind schedule and a good balance of protein, carbs and fibre, but the kids were less than impressed. Hannah pushed it around her plate and Betsy didn't even touch her beans.

Lucas's lip jutted in a sulk.

'This tastes different to Mum's jacket potatoes.'

I sighed. *Here we go again.*

'Hers has more flavour,' he said.

My jaw clenched, locking in the angry thoughts I didn't want to say out loud. We ate the rest of the meal in silence, the burden of loss hanging over us like thick sea fog.

After dinner, the kids dispersed to various corners of the house to do their own thing. I half-thought about checking that they were playing nicely, but I had just opened a bottle of wine and the first glass was going down very well.

Rachel hadn't replied to my message, so there was no more snooping to be done that night. I idly scrolled through

Instagram, flicking through pictures of my Hong Kong friends partying and eating out. There was one I lingered over: Chiara and Mathilde with Adam and Thierry, posing at the beach. I should have been there, too. That was everything I'd ever wanted, everything I'd worked for. Why should I have to give it up? I sighed. I missed my real life.

The doorbell rang, startling me out of my daydream.

An elderly lady was standing on the doorstep, the hood of her coat pulled up over her head, wisps of white hair blown in a halo around her face. Her face was criss-crossed with lines in every direction and her eyes were sparkling blue.

'Isabelle Morton – how lovely to see you.'

The musical chime of her voice sounded strangely familiar.

'I'm sorry, but... I'm not good with faces.'

There was something about the way she said my name, but I couldn't think where I knew her from. Undeterred, the visitor squeezed past me into the hall and started unbuttoning her coat.

'Really, Isabelle? I'm disappointed, I'd have expected more from my star pupil,' she said, removing her hood.

I squealed. 'Mrs Wheeler! Oh my god!'

She gave me a light slap on the wrist. 'Less of that 'god' stuff please, young lady. And try not to look so surprised to see me – you did invite me over.'

'So I did,' I smiled, thinking back to the conversation I'd had with Sandra. I followed her obediently into Amy's kitchen.

Diana Wheeler must have been well into her eighties, not that I dared to ask. And despite Sandra suggesting that her mother was past her best, Mrs Wheeler seemed as sharp as ever. She had been the Head of English at St Helen's, where she was a firm favourite of many pupils. It was Mrs Wheeler who had nurtured my love of reading and taught me that books were a passport to the world, inspiring my ambition to travel. She ran the drama club and the school newspaper, so I'd spent plenty of my lunchtimes and evenings in her company.

She lived at Amble, just a couple of miles down the coast, and had known our parents well. Right after Dad died, Mrs Wheeler had come to call on me, Mum and Amy, bringing home-cooked meals and making sure we were able to keep up with schoolwork while also having the space to grieve. When Mum had disappeared, Mrs Wheeler had been one of the first to notice something wasn't quite right. It was probably thanks to her that we'd got the help we needed and weren't taken into care. But she never made a fuss about it, and always left us feeling like we were in charge.

I chose my words carefully. 'Forgive my surprise, but your daughter said that you don't get out so much these days.'

'That bloody woman!' Mrs Wheeler exclaimed with a surprising strength. 'She's full of rubbish. I ask her to help me out from time to time and she thinks I can't do anything for myself. Utter nonsense!'

I bit my lip to suppress a giggle. Mrs Wheeler was in fine form.

'Let me assure you, Isabelle: I lead a very full and active life. It's true that I no longer have the physical capacity for life's more arduous tasks, but I am one hundred percent *compos mentis*!'

She took a seat and gestured for me to sit beside her.

'So tell me,' she said, squeezing my hand with cold, thin fingers. 'Are you working at *Vogue* magazine?'

I cringed – the teenage me had vowed to be covering Paris and New York Fashion Weeks for the style bible. Where had

99

that dream gone wrong?

'Not quite, but I do work in communications. Sort of. Client relationship management. Marketing for a wealth services provider...' My shoulders sank as I heard for myself how uninspiring that sounded.

Mrs Wheeler chuckled. 'Don't worry, dear, I'm only teasing. I've kept up quite well with your career over the years. Amy told me how well you were doing at the bank.'

Hearing her say Amy's name was a punch to my stomach. 'You... you spoke to my sister? Recently?' My breath came in small gulps.

Mrs Wheeler beamed. 'But of course! We were both on the school governing body and the Lifeboat Institution committee, and then she and I would meet up in our spare time to gossip about the rest of them!' She gave a wicked cackle. 'We saw each other for coffee every Tuesday.'

I realised once again that I knew so little about my sister's life.

'And Amy spoke about me?' I almost choked on her name.

Mrs Wheeler looked at me with her kind, glistening eyes. 'All the time, Isabelle. She was enormously proud of you.'

I couldn't hold back my tears any longer.

Mrs Wheeler dabbed at her own eyes with a cotton handkerchief. 'You two were always so close. As thick as thieves! The Salt Sisters, that was what you called yourselves, wasn't it? Closer than any other sisters I know. It was to be expected, after everything you went through. It's all very sad, dear. Very sad.' She put her arm around my shoulder and pulled me towards her tiny bird-like frame. 'But Amy would want you to hear it from me: she adored you. And even though you weren't living in each other's pockets, you were always in her thoughts.'

I wept onto Mrs Wheeler's shoulder. 'Was – was – she happy?' I blurted out between convulsing sobs.

She pulled me around by my shoulders so that I was facing her. 'Oh yes,' she said, smiling through her tears. 'Amy had everything she'd ever wanted.'

Chapter Nine

I woke up still raw after the visit from Mrs Wheeler. Her words had been comforting but had dug up fresh guilt. How had I let such a gulf grow between me and Amy? Sisters who could once read each other's minds, and yet in the end we couldn't even make time for a weekly phone call?

I sent Amy a text:

Sorry we drifted apart, and sorry I didn't realise it until too late. But you're always in my thoughts too. xo

It was also tough to square Mrs Wheeler's perspective of Amy's happiness with what Rachel had said about her wanting more. Although I wanted to believe Mrs Wheeler, I knew who was closer to Amy and who knew her best.

The morning routine was getting slightly easier with each day and things were finally starting to go more smoothly – the older kids had left on time for the third day in a row and Auntie Sue had offered to walk with Betsy. *Maybe this child care lark is easier than everyone makes out*, I thought to myself as I put my feet up and sank back into the armchair with a cup of tea.

A moment later, the peace was shattered by the front door bursting open and the thunder of boots up the stairs. It caught me completely off-guard and I spilled my tea onto the armchair, only getting a glimpse of a figure hurtling around the bannister. Seconds later, Lucas reappeared, running back down the stairs two at a time.

'I forgot my trainers!'

I glanced at my watch: three minutes until the bus came.

'You're not going to make it now.' I grabbed the keys to the Mini. 'Come on. I'll drive you.'

I made a mental note for the future to not relax until after 9 a.m.

As I was in Alnwick already, I decided to call in on Jake Ridley, telling myself that it was strictly to see if he had any news on Amy's case.

I called at Costa on the way and took two coffees to go. Jake was on the phone when I arrived, and as I sat waiting for him to finish, I regretted my messy top-knot and no-make-up look.

He welcomed me into his office with a smile and gratefully took his latte.

'I have got something for you, actually.' He opened a folder. 'First of all – Mike's business. It's a private limited company, and he had some outside investment at the start – shareholders that he'd have to pay back if it went belly-up. And you're right – it does seem that he has run into some difficulties.'

If Amy had been aware of Mike's problems, that might explain why she had kept her finances separate from his. It made sense, but an alarm had started ringing in my temples. I focused firmly on Jake.

'Secondly, the life insurance. Both Amy and Mike took out very large policies two years ago. According to the insurance company, the reason they gave for wanting the additional insurance was to cover their joint debts and to secure the financial well-being of their children – all perfectly normal, except that we know their debts were nowhere near that size.' Jake shrugged.

My heart was pounding.

Jake closed the folder and folded his hands in his lap. 'There was one more thing. I had a chat with the coroner's office. This is all off the record, you understand. And under the circumstances, it might make sense to keep this to yourself for now.'

I nodded and took a long, deep, breath.

'There was a problem with the car, as you know. There's no reason for this, given its age and service history. Apparently one of the front wheels was missing several nuts, and the police suspect that they could have been loosened deliberately.'

My hand flew to my mouth and I suppressed an urge to scream.

'Are you OK?'

I shook my head, saying nothing.

Jake poured me a glass of water. 'This is very upsetting, I know, but there are now some reasons to suspect that Amy's death was perhaps not an accident after all.'

I sat paralysed in my chair.

'The police are looking into it, and we should pass every-thing you have to them,' Jake said slowly. 'They need to know that Mike is in financial difficulty, and his response to the life insurance policy.'

'Do you think he did it?' I threw the question at him.

Jake sighed. 'With the majority of murders the perpetrator

is usually known to the victim. A spouse would be an obvious place to look. But let's not get ahead of ourselves.'

Oh my god, the kids, I thought. What would this do to them?

'So what happens now?' My hands were shaking. I held them together in my lap so that Jake wouldn't see.

'I'll pass this on,' Jake said, closing the folder. 'They'll probably talk to Mike, maybe take him in for questioning. They might wait to gather more evidence first. I'm sure they'll need to speak to you, at some point.'

I nodded glumly, weighed down by the feeling that before things got any better, they would get far worse.

I took the coast road home. I needed the space and the view of the open sea to help me think. Even though the evidence pointed to Mike, I couldn't work out how he could have done it – he had been in the pub the night of the accident and had spent the whole evening there. I tried to imagine how he might have sabotaged Amy's car, drugged her then convinced her to drive, but I couldn't make the pieces fit together. He would be home at the end of the week. I had to find some answers before he got back.

My instinct was that whatever I was looking for would be buried somewhere in Amy's online life. If she had been anxious, depressed or suspicious of Mike, there must be some proof of it somewhere. I knew my sister wouldn't keep something like that bottled up. She hadn't said anything to me, but she must have confided in someone.

The police still had her phone, and I needed a chance to go through it before Mike got his hands on it. Come to think of it, they had been keeping it for quite a while now.

I pulled over and called Jake. 'Me again. Could you do me a

favour and ask the police when will they be releasing Amy's phone? I could pick it up today if they'll let me take it?'

Jake paused. 'The police don't have Amy's phone. All of her valuables were signed over to the family.'

'So where is it now?' I asked, genuinely puzzled.

'It was handed over with the rest of her things to her next of kin.' He hesitated for a second. 'You could ask Mike what he has done with it.'

Back at the house I began a new search, this time for the phone. I was certain that it wasn't in the office, so I started to look in other places. It felt like a betrayal of Amy to be searching through the bedroom that she shared with Mike, but I had to make sure he wasn't hiding it somewhere. I couldn't decide if I suspected him or not – I just knew I needed to find that phone. I even tried calling Amy's number in case it was switched on and I might hear it ringing. It was like looking for a needle in a haystack.

Suspicion, guilt, grief – what was I supposed to be feeling right now? My head was pulling me in a hundred different directions. I slumped back against the bedroom wall and took a sip of vodka from my flask, wiping the tears from my face with the back of my hand.

Downstairs, I heard the front door open and Rachel's familiar voice called out. Snapped back into the moment, I went down to find her in Amy's kitchen.

'Hello, stranger,' she said, pulling me into a hug. 'How are you doing?'

The note of concern in her voice made me realise how bad I looked. I still hadn't got around to putting my make-up on. What was the point?

'Well... I'm still here...' I shrugged.

Rachel heated up soup and unwrapped home-made sand-wiches onto plates while I debated how much to tell her. Jake had cautioned me to keep it to myself, but I was sure that Rachel would have the answers to some of my questions. She passed me a spoon and a napkin.

'So truly, how is it all going?'

I thought about where to start. 'Well, it seems that Amy's accident... maybe it wasn't so straightforward after all,' I said, choosing my words carefully. 'There are a couple of... outstanding questions.'

'Anything I can help with?'

I stirred my soup. I so badly wanted to confide in her. Maybe she knew something that she didn't realise was important?

'Are you sure Amy didn't say anything about Mike having money worries? Like, financial problems with the business?'

She considered this, then frowned and shook her head slowly.

'It's just that he's been really weird about Amy's will, and the whole trust fund thing. I'm starting to think that maybe' – I choked on the idea – 'maybe... her death wasn't an accident. And Mike might have been responsible.'

Rachel gasped. 'No.' She shook her head, her eyes wide. 'He couldn't have. No way.'

I nodded glumly. 'It's starting to look that way.'

'I can't believe that, not from Mike. There must be some mistake.'

'Do not say anything to him,' I said, sternly. 'The police are looking into it.'

'But why would they think that?'

I wanted to tell her, to talk about how the car might have

been deliberately damaged, but I couldn't see how I could without betraying Jake's confidence. Instead, I shrugged.

She took my hand in hers.

'I'm sure it was nothing more than a horrible accident. The police are just crossing the t's and what have you.' Her eyebrows knotted together in a determined frown. 'What can I do to help in the meantime?'

'Nothing – not unless you've seen Amy's phone.'

'What for? Don't the police have it already?'

'Apparently, they already returned it to the family. But if Amy and Mike had been fighting, maybe she told someone, or maybe there's something on the phone that might help us understand if he did it—'

'Or clear him.'

I nodded. 'Or clear him.'

Rachel leaned back in her chair and let out a long exhalation, folding her hands together in a prayer. 'I know this is hard,' she sniffed. 'It's been tough for me too – and I only lost my best friend. I can't imagine what you're going through, losing your sister and being stuck here. But you need to stay strong. Don't make it harder on yourself. Focus on the children and your mum, and let the police do their job.'

I saw myself through her eyes – paranoid, grieving. A hot mess. I hadn't even showered yet. What must Rachel think of me? What had Jake made of me when I showed up at his office that morning? Clearly, from the outside it didn't look like I was doing well.

'I know what you need,' said Rachel, 'a girls' night!'

That did sound appealing. I missed having a social life.

After Rachel left, I decided to squeeze in a couple of hours of self-care. I ran myself a steaming hot bath, adding Epsom salts and essential oil that I found in the bathroom cupboard, lit a scented candle, and climbed in.

Had Amy lain here, just like this, when she needed a break? When she had been stressed about Mike's financial problems? I pushed the image from my mind. If I closed my eyes and took deep breaths, I could almost forget where I was and what I had been looking for.

That evening, I was washing up after another disaster of a dinner and trying my hardest not to cry, when the doorbell rang. I sighed. Who was it now?

I was still drying my hands on the tea towel as I opened the door to Richard Pringle. I didn't do a good job of hiding my surprise, nor my delight that he was holding a bottle of red wine. The kids were scattered in various corners of the house. Perhaps a little social visit could distract me from my misery?

I led Richard to the kitchen and poured two glasses of wine. He fingered the stem of his glass, glancing down the hall to check that the children were out of earshot.

'We'd normally call parents into the school to talk about this, but I thought under the circumstances, it would be more relaxed for me to see you at home.'

'Oh god. What's happened?'

'It's nothing' – he held up a hand – 'it's nothing to panic about. But Betsy is... Well, she's grieving, and I'm concerned that she's lashing out. While this is quite normal after such a trauma, we can't let incidents of violence go unpunished.'

I pictured the eight-year-old who couldn't resist a snuggle and had started sucking her thumb again.

'What incidents?'

'She's had a number of scrapes, since she came back. This

afternoon, she slapped a boy's thigh so hard that she left a handprint. I'm sorry to have to tell you this, but Betsy is now on her final warning before a suspension.'

My heart sank. There was me thinking I was making progress with the kids. Richard read my thoughts.

'It must be so hard - I can only imagine what you're all going through. And whatever you need, I'm here to support you. We're all feeling your loss.'

I winced, aching for my sister. 'You and Amy were close, right? You spent a lot of time with her?'

He nodded sadly. 'We were good friends. I miss her a lot.'

'And Mike?'

Richard looked unsure. 'Not so much. It's Amy that I'm closest to. *Was* closest to...'

'Was everything OK between them?'

He frowned. 'You're asking me if everything was OK between your sister and her husband? Like, if they had relationship problems, or money worries or something?'

So he did know something. I leaned in. 'Tell me everything.'

'It's nothing like that...' He waved his hands in denial. 'I don't know anything. I just always got the impression...' He hesitated, his voice softening. 'This is bad, but...'

I stiffened, willing him to continue. The clock ticked loudly on the wall.

'I always felt like Amy could have done better than Mike.'

'What do you mean—'

The phone rang behind me, making me jump. 'Hold that thought,' I said to Richard as I stood to answer it.

'Izzy?' Mike sounded far away.

'Mike, hi.' I watched as Richard stiffened at the mention of Mike's name. 'Where are you? When are you coming home?'

Richard stood, moving his chair carefully so as to not make any sound. I gestured to him to sit back down.

'Sorry, but I've been held up for a couple more days. I'll be home on Sunday evening. Can I speak to the kids?'

Richard was shrugging on his coat.

'What? But you said... Actually, now's not a great time. Could you call back in five minutes?'

Stay, I mouthed to Richard. But he waved his hand, tapping his watch and miming that he had to go. Shaking his head as he inched towards the hallway. I'd missed my chance and knew that I might not get another.

I sighed. 'Never mind. Let me get them for you.'

What had Richard been about to tell me?

It rained all of Saturday and each of my attempts to entertain the kids fell flat. Lucas moped, not wanting to do anything, but Betsy was angry, even lashing out at me a couple of times. Hannah stayed glued to her phone.

Lucas sidled up to me at the stove. 'What's for dinner?'

I took a deep breath and forced myself to smile. 'I'm making lasagne.'

We had invited Mum and Auntie Sue over, and lasagne had seemed to me like a simple way of feeding six of us.

'Will you put broccoli in it?'

'No, of course I won't – don't worry, silly.' I ruffled his blond hair.

'Mummy always puts broccoli in lasagne,' he said in a small voice.

I was about to answer back when a memory started to form. It was so long ago that I had almost forgotten, but suddenly I could see me and Amy, in the days not long after Mum left, sitting in the kitchen eating dinner. Amy had made jacket potatoes... but with a secret ingredient. She had beamed as she told me what she'd added. What was it?

'Marmite!' I yelled, as the memory hit me like sunlight bursting through clouds, making Lucas jump. 'That's how she did jacket potatoes!'

It was one of the 'Amy Specialities' that she'd invented after Mum left and before Auntie Sue swooped in. I had completely forgotten her fondness for putting a twist on recipes, like adding broccoli to lasagne.

Suddenly I could picture her, aged thirteen, proudly presenting a shepherd's pie made with banana mixed into the mashed potato. I had asked her what had inspired it. She'd replied that we had bananas left over that she didn't want to waste and there were no grown-ups to stop us. I heard Amy speaking to me from across the years and I traced her words in my mind.

'Who says you can't put bananas in shepherd's pie...' I mumbled.

'Exactly!' Lucas clapped his hands. 'That's exactly what Mum says!'

Perhaps I'd assumed she had outgrown her penchant for experimental cooking. At some point she must surely have decided it was safer to stick to the recipe books? But judging by Lucas's enthusiasm, it was a tradition Amy had not only continued but had passed on to her kids.

There were so many things we'd had to learn that year. With no parents and no money, we had been forced to take a crash course in adulting. It had been in the days before you could ask the internet how to do stuff, so we had worked everything out for ourselves – from operating the washing machine to lighting the fire and paying the phone bill.

We had been afraid of anyone finding out that Mum had gone and had been convinced that social services would come and take us away, with me still six months away from my sixteenth birthday. I'd been sure that Mum would come back soon, and we just had to hold on for another day. That was what I used to tell Amy – just another day – but mostly, I was convincing myself.

We simply told everyone that she was sick. Somehow, Mrs Wheeler had figured out that there was more to it, but she allowed us the dignity of maintaining the pretence. Once a week, she would bring a home-cooked meal boxed up in Tupperware and tell us to pass her regards to our mother. Other people had known too – I could tell from the way they looked at us. But as long as we were clean, healthy and going to school each day, nobody seemed to think there was any need to raise an alarm.

Auntie Sue was horrified when she eventually got there. Fed up with her calls to her sister going unanswered and her nieces making increasingly crap excuses for their mother's inability to come to the phone, she got in her car and drove down from Aberdeen. We tried to pretend Mum was out for the evening, but she knew straight away that something wasn't right. There was no discussion – shortly afterwards, she simply moved all of her stuff in.

It had been such a relief to me to finally have an adult around again, if only to have some authority assume the decision-making. I hadn't realised how exhausted I had been until the weekend after Auntie Sue arrived, when I slept for almost two days straight. It had been four months since Mum had left, but when you're drowning, any time at all is eternity and finally, here was our lifeboat.

Auntie Sue had allowed us to keep the routine we had grown used to, assuring us that we'd been doing remarkably well and that she could learn a thing or two from us – like Amy's recipes. That's why Amy had kept on cooking.

And now here was Lucas, sharing his mother's passion for throwing out the rules of the recipe book. If he wanted to keep on cooking, I would encourage it.

I offered him the spoon and he took a taste from the mixture in the pan, knotting his eyebrows in concentration.

'You know what this needs? A good dollop of honey!'

I sent a message to my sister:

Banana in shepherd's pie. You were one in a million xo

Chapter Ten

I t was quite possibly the longest weekend of my life. I found myself wishing for a crisis at work, something with one of the clients that they would absolutely need my urgent help with, but nothing came. The hours dragged by so slowly that I could practically see the minutes and seconds stretching out in front of me. By the time Sunday afternoon rolled around, I was convinced there must be something wrong with the clock.

I went for a quick run after lunch to clear my head. The tide was out, so I ran along the sand, imagining that I could just keep going, leaving my problems behind and seeing where the beach led me.

A stitch in my side forced me to stop. I got my breath back, greedily gulping the crisp, salty air. I'd forgotten how relaxing it was to simply watch the sea. It was a reassuring presence, and just being so close to the water made me feel calmer.

How was I going to tackle Mike about my suspicions without accusing him of something horrific? I played out the conversation in my head, watching as the white foam lapped greedily at the sand.

I was making dinner with Lucas when we heard a car pull up

out front.

'Dad's home!' he yelled to his sisters.

Betsy and Lucas jumped onto Mike in the hallway while Hannah hung back, leaning shyly against the radiator. As Mike swooped his eldest daughter into a hug and kissed the top of her head, I saw that he had tears in his eyes. It was clear he had missed them.

He came towards me, and his arms widened reflexively. Was he about to hug me, too? I mumbled a hello and he caught himself, looking down at his feet, gluing his hands back to his sides. I busied myself at the stove.

'So, did everyone behave for Auntie Izzy?' He ruffled Lucas's hair.

'They were as good as gold,' I replied.

Mike peered over to see what we were cooking. Lucas had reminded me of Amy's egg and mushroom pie, another classic I was pleased to see she had kept up.

'I'm thinking of handing over all responsibility for cooking to Lucas,' I said.

Lucas beamed.

Mike opened a bottle of wine, and over dinner, told the kids about his trip. He'd brought back nothing more exciting than liquorice sweets and Dutch wafer biscuits, but the kids seemed thrilled with their airport-bought souvenirs. He looked like he'd aged ten years since Amy's death. There were bags under his eyes and crows' feet stretching towards his temples, and I could have sworn he had more grey hairs. I could probably say the same for me.

As we cleared up, I got ready to say my piece. I'd built up the courage during my run along the beach – now I just needed to get Mike alone. I made sure the kids were out of earshot and took a deep breath. He was standing at the sink with his back to me.

'Listen, Mike – we need to talk about the findings from the coroner's office. Amy's blood tests and the problems with the car...'

He stopped washing, hesitated, then started again. 'I was going to tell you all, I was just waiting until they'd finished the report. It's not final yet, you know. No point upsetting everyone in the meantime.'

He didn't ask me how I'd found out.

'Don't you think it's strange that there were drugs in Amy's system, stuff that would have slowed down her response times if taken with alcohol? Medication that we can't find a prescription for?'

'I'm sure they'll work it out. There has to be some explanation.' He kept his back to me.

'And her front wheel was loose. Possibly damaged on purpose. What if her death wasn't an accident?'

There, I'd said it. Mike stopped washing and slowly twisted the cloth to squeeze out the water. He said nothing.

For all Mike knew, the police had spoken to me. It was time to get creative with how much I knew. 'They're worried Amy might have been upset about something. Can you think of any reason why she was distressed?'

He turned to face me, his lips pressed together, transforming his mouth into a small white line. 'She wasn't worried about anything, I told the police that already.'

'They think that she could have been stressed about money.' I kept my eyes on him. 'They seem to think that the two of you were having financial difficulties. Are they on to something... ?'

Mike's hands balled into fists at his sides. 'The business hasn't been doing great, but nothing to worry about.'

'Did Amy know you were in trouble?'

'I wouldn't call it "trouble". I don't know what the police said, not that they have any right to share my company's financial performance with my wife's family, but it's just a short-term cash-flow issue, really – it's not a big deal.' His face was getting red and he exhaled, a hiss of steam, as he eased himself into a chair.

'How much are you talking about?'

'*Excuse me?* Do you really think that's any of your business?'

'It is my business when my sister has died in mysterious circumstances and lo and behold, there's a huge insurance payout that nobody knew about—'

'How dare you!' Mike slammed his fist on the table. 'How dare you speak to me like that in my own home!'

'What are you hiding, Mike? What are you worried they'll find out about?'

His eyes narrowed and his fists balled so tightly that his knuckles turned white.

I held his gaze, my arms crossed tightly in front of my chest to hide my shaking hands. My breath was coming in short, sharp gulps and it took all my strength to hold my stance.

For a moment, I thought he was going to hit me. Then he crumbled into tears, burying his face in his hands.

'Mike, stop – the kids will hear,' I said, edging cautiously towards him.

'I'm sorry, Izzy, I'm sorry about everything,' he sobbed.

I desperately wanted him to quiet down. I needed for us to not be interrupted. 'What is it, Mike? What have you got to be sorry about?'

He sat back and took a deep breath.

'There have been some problems,' he said, in a shaky voice. 'I owe some investors, but I have nothing left to give them. After what happened with Amy, I figured I could at least use the insurance to settle our debts and get the business back on track, but when I realised that she'd tied up the money, I freaked out. I'm sorry. I'm trying my best to fix it.'

'But why did you guys have such a big insurance policy in the first place?'

'A few years back, I took a couple of gambles and lost. I messed up. At one point, we even had to remortgage the house... When Amy found out what I'd done, she hit the roof. I got to a low point, Izzy. Really low. Amy was worried that something might happen to me, or that I might do something stupid. Like, *really* stupid.' He collapsed, sobbing into his hands.

Amy had been worried that Mike was suicidal?

'So the insurance was her idea?

'Yes!' he wailed. 'She was worried about how much I'd borrowed and how much I owed, and that she wouldn't be able to pay it back on her own if I wasn't there.'

'But why did she have such a big policy on her life, too? If it was you that she was worried about?'

'I don't know, it just made sense at the time. All our assets are shared, anyway.'

Something still didn't quite make sense. The payout was way more than they had ever borrowed. And why had she changed her will without telling him?

'You don't think I... did something to hurt Amy, do you?' He looked up at me with red-rimmed eyes and I saw his terror.

'No, of course I don't,' I said, unconvincingly.

'Because I would never hurt her. I would never hurt Amy, you should know that.'

I knew no such thing. Mike's financial problems and the insurance payout were huge red flags to me. But he looked exhausted, and his devastation was plain to see. I would have to give him the benefit of the doubt for now, even if I knew I still wasn't getting the whole story.

'That's why I had to go to Amsterdam,' he continued. 'I'm talking to one of our project's creditors about holding off the repayments for a while. I've got a deal that will pay out soon, and then I'll be back on track.' His words were hollow.

'I want to help you. We're in this together. But please, don't hide things, you have to be honest with me,' I said, not believing that he would.

'I know,' he said, sniffing as he poured himself a glass of water. 'I promise, I'll do better from now on.'

'Oh, there was one more thing,' I said, trying to sound casual. 'Apparently the police signed over Amy's personal belongings to you. I was wondering if I could take a look? I don't think I've seen them yet...'

Mike looked confused and then remembered something.

'Yeah, they did give us a box of things. Two days after the accident. I was too upset to open it. Your mum took it home with her.'

It was a chilly evening, but the cold was invigorating, so I walked the long way home to make the most of the fresh air. It was just beginning to get dark and I caught a flash of the lighthouse perched on top of the Farnes.

Walking back into Puffin Cottage was like coming home. I raced upstairs and changed straightaway into my grey cashmere pyjamas. With the fire lit, I poured myself a glass of wine. My phone pinged. Hannah:

Thanks for looking after us this week. It's nice having you here. H

Why couldn't she have said that to me tonight? I found it tough to match up the sullen teenager who was absorbed by her phone with the sweet girl who sent me the loveliest texts.

After finishing the bottle, I climbed the stairs to bed. That night, I had horrible dreams. I was sitting beside Amy in her car, with her asleep at the wheel. The tyres screeched around a bend and the engine burst into flames, and the shadow of an enormous tree loomed towards us through the smoke. Amy slept on as I screamed.

I woke in a cold sweat, panting, and whispered a silent prayer that Amy had felt neither pain nor fear. I sobbed myself back to sleep.

It was already light outside by the time I woke up. I grabbed my phone and pulled the duvet back over my head, planning on half an hour of catching up with social media – but I had a text from Mum:

Auntie Sue baked bread this morning. We'll be over at 9.30 for breakfast.

It was already ten past. *There goes my idle scrolling,* I thought, rushing to get ready.

When they arrived, Auntie Sue made a pot of tea as I set the table with a mishmash of some of the fabulous vintage crockery I'd found in the cupboard. The bread was still warm and steaming as I unwrapped it from the cloth Auntie Sue had carried it in.

After we'd eaten, Mum started to fumble about in her

handbag, finally retrieving an incense burner and pack of joss sticks.

'Oh Mum, seriously?' I said in protest.

'It's just a quick meditation, dear. I thought it did you some good last week and you could use a little more practice,' she said, her eyes pleading.

'Go on,' Auntie Sue said as she nudged me. 'I'll wash the dishes while you can go and do your ohm-shanti-whatevers.'

Mum elegantly folded herself into a sitting lotus position and motioned for me to do the same opposite her. Despite my regular Saturday morning Power Pilates sessions and her being thirty years older than me, she was way more flexible. I grumbled as my joints refused to bend any further and huffed as my knees made worrying cracking noises.

She guided me through a breathing exercise and I began to relax. It was true that my mind was racing these days, my questions about Amy keeping me awake at night, and this did help to quiet the voices in my head. It pained me to say Mum was right, but meditation was doing me some good. By the time we finished, I felt almost serene.

As Mum packed away her props – including a tiny drum that I didn't want to know the backstory to – I asked her about Amy's possessions from the police.

'Yes, they did give us a box. It's at home.'

I was anxious to get Amy's phone, but didn't want to sound desperate – the last thing Mum needed was a slice of my anxiety. 'Mind if I come over to take a look?'

I waved off Mum and Auntie Sue, after making arrangements for me to call over mid-afternoon. Rachel was coming over for our girls' night, and I wanted to impress her with something fancy. I had just enough time to squeeze in a beach run before shopping for the ingredients.

I got dressed and threw Amy's fleece on. I instinctively sniffed the collar for any trace of my sister but all I could smell was fabric softener.

Before I reached the end of the street, my phone started ringing.

'Isabelle? It's Richard Pringle here.'

He was doing his serious, I'm-the-headteacher voice.

'Sorry to bother you, but I'm unable to get hold of Mike. We've had an issue at the school with Betsy. Can you come and pick her up please?'

'Oh my god! Is she all right?'

'Betsy is fine. But Mrs Neeply will need her blouse to be replaced and Katie McGee – well, let's just say I'll have some explaining to do to her mother. Betsy can tell you all about it during her three-day suspension.'

'You're suspending her? What am I supposed to do with her?' The panic was rising in my chest.

Richard cleared his throat. 'You can bring her back to school on Friday,' he said, before adding, 'I'm so sorry.'

I clicked off the phone and ran back to the house to grab my car keys.

Betsy sulked the entire way home, insisting that she had been set up and that Katie had consented to having a moustache and glasses drawn on her face. It wasn't quite the same version of the story I'd heard from Richard, nor from Mrs Neeply – the teacher that Betsy had attacked with a felt-tip pen when she'd tried to pull the fighting girls apart.

Betsy didn't strike me as a bully, just a very angry little girl. I didn't want to be too lenient with her, but she had just lost her mum and probably felt that the world was against her right now. Richard had given her homework and had promised to email me more stuff for her to do tomorrow. Great – so everyone just automatically assumed I'd be the one to watch her.

By the time I'd collected her, there was just enough time to dash to Mum's and do the shopping for that evening's dinner. We pulled up outside the house.

'You wait here. And stay quiet.'

I shuffled on the doorstep, refusing to come in and fighting off Auntie Sue's questions about why Betsy had been sent home from school. Mum finally handed me the small brown cardboard box of Amy's things and I tucked it under my arm. I'd have to deal with Betsy and dinner first, but hopefully I'd have a chance to look through it before Rachel arrived. Between her and the phone, I was sure that I'd have answers by the end of the evening.

Betsy sulked around the supermarket, trailing behind me like an annoying shadow as my blood pressure crept up by the second. The supper I had imagined wasn't going to plan – I'd found a recipe for miso mushroom polenta with a side of steamed kale, but the store was tiny and I struggled to find any of my main ingredients. When I asked the cashier if they sold polenta, all she could offer was a blank stare.

Making the best of a challenging situation, I picked up some broccoli, some blue cheese and sliced ham. Maybe one of Amy's special recipes could save the day.

I'd left Mike a message to let him know what happened. Hopefully he wouldn't be too hard on Betsy. She did her work at the kitchen table while I made a start on supper, keeping one eye on the clock and counting down the time until Mike would arrive to collect her – and until I could take the nice bottle of wine out the fridge.

By the time Rachel arrived at seven, dinner was in the oven and I was already one glass of wine in. She was quite dressed up in a knitted dress and knee-high boots, and I felt lousy – I'd gone for a cosy-night-in look. I blushed, hoping that my casual outfit of jeans and cashmere sweater didn't give the impression I didn't care.

Rachel had brought a bottle of wine with her too, which instantly sent her soaring in my estimation. Dad always said you should never turn up at someone's house empty-handed, and it was a lesson that had stayed with me my whole life.

I was certain that Rachel knew more than she was letting on, probably from some misguided loyalty to Mike, or to protect my feelings. My plan was to get her drunk and see if it loosened her up. It wasn't the most sophisticated plan, but it was the only one I had.

It was no mushroom polenta, but my Amy special of blue-cheese broccoli had turned out well. Rachel and I raised a glass to her memory. I'd lit candles that cast us both in warm glow, and the wine softened the sharp edges of our loss.

We reminisced over Amy, swapping stories of the woman we had both loved. Rachel had known a different Amy to mine, or at least another side of her, and for hours we traded anecdotes, talking about nothing else. It felt deliciously indulgent, and for once, I didn't drown under a wave of sadness at the mere mention of Amy's name.

I refilled our glasses with the last of the bottle. The candles had burned down to flickering pools of molten wax.

'So that day when you said that Amy might not have been

happy... What exactly did you mean?'

Rachel's shoulders sank. 'We've been over this. I just said, sometimes it was like she wanted more—'

I cut her off. 'Because Richard agrees with you. He thinks that something was troubling Amy. Something to do with Mike.' That wasn't exactly what he had said, but I was entitled to some artistic license.

Rachel raised an eyebrow. 'Richard Pringle? What did he say?'

'He thinks that Amy could have done better than Mike. Maybe that's got something to do with whatever was bothering her...?'

'And how would he have an opinion on a thing like that?'

'He and Amy... They were good friends.'

Rachel swirled the wine in her glass, then sighed and took a sip. 'Your sister was a kind person, you know that. Maybe Richard *thought* she was his friend. I'm just saying, I don't think Amy saw it in quite the same way. Sometimes, to be frank, I find him a bit creepy. But maybe that's just me.'

Had I misunderstood Richard?

'My god, look at the time! I should get home, I'm on the early shift tomorrow.' Rachel stood up to leave.

'Don't go yet, please stay.' I could hear the desperation in my voice. 'Are you sure Amy said nothing about being unhappy, or stressed?'

Rachel looked at me with pity in her eyes. 'She had everything. Her and Mike – they had it all. I just worried sometimes that she was missing something or wanted more. You know, like we all do from time to time.'

She gave me a hug, thanking me for supper and promising to call me tomorrow, and left.

So, that had got me nowhere. At least she was gone, and I could finally go through Amy's phone. Her best friend might not have answers, but there had to be some clues in her messages.

I dug into my bag and set the box of Amy's possessions on the table, taking a deep breath as I opened it.

There was no phone.

Chapter Eleven

Where was Amy's phone? It was meant to be here! I frantically raked among the stuff in the box – definitely no phone. I'd have to follow the trail back again, starting with Mum – someone else must have had access to Amy's things before I'd been able to get them.

My mind was racing and I needed space to think clearly. Mike must have taken the phone, but when would he have had a chance to do it? He hadn't been over to Mum's since he got back, as far as I knew. And if not Mike, then who? And on top of all this, Rachel's view of Richard was confusing me. He'd seemed so nice. How had I got him so wrong?

As much as I wanted to prioritise finding Amy's phone, my first point of call the next morning was to collect Betsy. Mike had given her hell the night before, and she was much more sheepish than she'd been yesterday afternoon.

She was mature for her eight years, but I could still see glimpses of the little girl who adored her mum and loved to be tucked up in bed or have snuggles in the sofa. I knew it was the hardest thing to suddenly lose a parent, and Betsy was so young – it broke my heart and took all my strength not to cry over it in front of her. I prayed she could stay innocent for as long as possible and I wanted to do everything in my power to make that happen.

Her teacher had been quite sympathetic, but rules were rules, and the school couldn't be too lenient with her. I decided that it wasn't my job to discipline her. I just had to keep her occupied and safe.

We called in on Mum and Auntie Sue and I was determined to keep the visit brief and to the point. Auntie Sue gave Betsy a bit of a telling off, but Mum sent her straight to the biscuit tin – we were anything but consistent. I fidgeted while the two of them fussed around her. Was the phone in here somewhere?

'About that box of Amy's things...'

'I gave it to you yesterday,' Mum said, with a puzzled expression.

'I know, it's just that Amy's phone should have been there – only it's not.'

Now she really looked confused. 'There was definitely a phone in there before.'

'Yes, an iPhone,' said Auntie Sue.

Mum shook her head. 'No, it was one of those other ones. With a silver case.'

'Are you sure it was silver?'

'No, you're right. Hannah's has a silver case.'

Auntie Sue bit her lip. 'Come to think of it, I'm not certain I do remember a phone.'

Mum shook her head. 'Now you mention it...'

'Okay.' I held up a hand to stop them. 'The phone is not there now. Could anyone have taken it from the box?'

'No,' said Mum, at the same time as Auntie Sue said, 'Possibly.'

'Oh dear.' Mum looked anxiously at the ceiling. 'I hope Amy

129

won't be cross with me.'

I'd figured there were fewer distractions for Betsy at Puffin Cottage, so I took her home with me and set her off on her homework assignment. She stretched out on her tummy on the living room floor and spread her books out in a fan around her.

We needed something for lunch but I didn't have anything in the fridge, so I told Betsy to not move while I popped out to the shop. I opened the front door and almost fell on Mrs Wheeler holding an enormous basket.

'Are you going somewhere, dear?' She smiled up at me.

'I was just popping out on an errand,' I said, as she stepped past me into the kitchen and set the basket on the table. 'I guess that plan is shelved, for now...' I muttered under my breath.

'What on earth is going on here?' Mrs Wheeler asked, motioning to Betsy.

Betsy looked down and hid from her gaze. I wondered which of us looked more sheepish.

'Betsy was naughty at school, Mrs Wheeler. She got in a bit of trouble and she has been sent home to think about how she can behave better in future.'

'Not to worry, dear,' Mrs Wheeler said, patting Betsy's head. 'We all make mistakes, it's how we make them right that counts.'

Mrs Wheeler had brought quite a spread, with pea and ham soup, home-made scotch eggs and doorstop cheddar sandwiches, with a Victoria sponge for dessert. Betsy licked her lips and I sighed, wondering if I'd ever see my abs again.

'I'll have a tea please, Isabelle,' Mrs Wheeler said, her blue eyes twinkling mischievously.

'Gosh, right – yes, sorry, coming right up.'

I brought out three of the prettiest plates I'd found in the cupboard, with a pink and gold ribbon design around the edge, and set down some of the green cut-glass wine glasses that I thought were just adorable.

'Do you mind if I take a photograph?' I said, whipping out my iPhone.

'Not at all.' Mrs Wheeler draped her arm around Betsy and smiled for a portrait.

'Sorry,' I laughed, 'but I meant a photo of the table.'

She looked at me like I was speaking another language. 'Why would you take a photograph of the table? It's not for that Instagram, is it?'

'Mrs Wheeler, I'm impressed!' I chuckled.

'I am well aware of the concept of social media, although I can't help thinking it's all a dreadful waste of time. I see my friends in real life; I don't need to see them on the screen. What does one hope to achieve by publishing a photograph of one's lunch?'

'It's beautiful,' I said, stroking the green glass. 'I find it very aesthetically pleasing, and so will thousands of people around the world.'

Mrs Wheeler couldn't hide her glee at the compliment to her taste.

I repositioned a pretty pink plate into the frame. 'You have some lovely pieces. They don't make tableware like this anymore.'

It turned out that the plates had been a wedding gift to Mrs Wheeler and her late husband, and the green glasses had been part of a set that her father had brought back from Italy after the war. It seemed that everything in the cottage told a story and Mrs Wheeler could remember the history of each item, fixture, and detail of the home she had lived in as a newlywed.

I asked her about the things I loved most – the honeysuckle growing around the door, the original glass in the windows, and the ornate tiles in the hearth of the tiny upstairs fireplace. She delighted in sharing the origins of it all and with every story she shared, I fell deeper in love with Puffin Cottage.

Mrs Wheeler's company was a great distraction, and I understood why my sister had enjoyed spending so much time with her. But within minutes of her leaving, I was back to stressing about Amy's phone. *Just follow the trail.*

The sugar rush had left Betsy in a chatty mood. I loved her but there was only so much eight-year-old conversation I could take, and I had to call for twenty minutes of quiet. She skulked back to her spot on the floor, her bottom lip in a pout. At least now I could focus.

'Auntie Izzy, what's your Instagram?' Betsy asked, her sulk seemingly forgotten.

'You're a bit young to be thinking about things like that.'

'Obviously, I'm not *on* Instagram.' She rolled her eyes. 'Like, I'm not allowed to post anything, but Mummy lets me look at hers.'

'Wait – what? Your mum was on Instagram?'

'She doesn't post anything, it's just so she can look up other people.' Betsy giggled. 'And she lets me look up people, too. I love Ariana Grande.'

I looked down at my phone, wondering if Amy had ever looked up my profile too. 'Do you know her password?'

'Yeah, of course. She keeps the same password for everything. Which you're not supposed to do, by the way.'

'Do you want to log into your mum's Instagram on my

phone?' I tried to keep the urgency out my voice.

Betsy enthusiastically grabbed the device from me, giving me just enough time to watch over her shoulder as she carefully punched in the password – 150694. The date Dad died.

I was itching to get into Amy's emails. I told Betsy she had ten minutes of Instagram time before she had to get back to work. Once she was safely distracted, I sat at the table and opened my laptop.

The password worked for Amy's email account. My pulse fluttered as I pulled up her inbox. There were dozens of new messages, and none of them had been read since the Friday she had died, which had to be a good sign – it suggested nobody had accessed her mailbox.

A quick scroll revealed nothing out of the ordinary. In fact, it seemed to be that with Amy, what you saw was what you got. Almost all of her emails related to the kids, their school stuff and activities, the community groups she was involved with, as well as the usual marketing promotions. There were a few messages that she'd exchanged with friends, longer catch-up emails, but nothing in them suggested she had any worries at home. I combed carefully through each email, making sure I wasn't missing something.

What else? I looked at my own phone for inspiration. Facebook!

The password worked. Amy's page was full of condolence messages that people had posted, and I couldn't see anything out of the ordinary. Then I noticed she had several unread messages.

Three of them were from Phil Turner – Rachel's husband.

A chill shivered through me. My hand shook as I opened the first message:

Dear Amy

I can't go on like this, my heart is broken. Every time I see you with him, I have to bury my feelings. I can't pretend any longer. I need to be with you. I want us to be together. Please, leave him and come to me. I can make you happier than you know.

What. The. Actual...? I tried to swallow, but my mouth had gone dry.

Are you there? Sorry I haven't seen you for a few days. I've missed you so much. I know you said you wanted to break things off, but I can't. I don't want to lose you. Please, let's find a way to make this work.

I felt sick. I opened the third:

I love you, Amy, I love you so much and I can't go on like this. I have to have you. We have to be together. Please, I am a desperate man.

My heart pounded.

I slowly closed the lid of the laptop. It took all my concentration to stand up and walk into the living room. The walls were squeezing in towards me and the ceiling was a crushing weight above my head. My stomach was a pit of caustic bile and I had to get to the bathroom before I threw up, but my legs were numb and everything was slowly spinning...

'Auntie Izzy, are you OK?'

Betsy's voice was faint. Where was she? She sounded so far away, but no, there she was, on the floor, getting up, moving towards me with her arms out as everything went blurry, then dark.

When I came around again, Auntie Sue was crouched over me, mopping my brow with a flannel. Betsy was sobbing, snuggled up on Mum's knee in the armchair.

'You fainted and hit your head,' Auntie Sue said, very matter-of-fact. 'Not too hard, it seems – thanks to Betsy, who managed to help you fall mostly onto the sofa. Her lightning-quick reflexes probably saved you from a concussion.'

I smiled at Betsy. Poor thing, I must have given her quite a scare.

'We'll take over here, and you're getting yourself off to bed.'

'Honestly, there's no need...' I started to say.

I would have to tell the police that there had been something going on between Amy and Phil Turner. It either gave another motive for Mike to want to hurt her – or gave them a new suspect.

And poor Rachel! When she had said she thought Amy wanted more, had she ever have imagined it was this? Her husband cheating with her best friend?

How could Amy have done this? The dizziness was back, my head spinning with what this potentially meant.

'Not another word, young lady. Get up those stairs and get into your pyjamas. I don't want a discussion.'

Auntie Sue always did have a way of speaking to me that made me do exactly as I was told.

I lay back in bed. The sheets were crisp and cool, and the weight of the blankets was reassuring. Even though I'd insisted I wasn't tired, Auntie Sue had taken my phone from me and tucked me in, promising to wake me up in forty-five minutes. I knew I wouldn't be able to sleep – I was picturing Amy and Phil together, and couldn't get the image out of my mind. How could she? And what consequences had it led to?

But the next thing I knew, Auntie Sue was sitting on the bed with a freshly-brewed tea.

'There, you've got your colour back. I told you a nap would

do you good. Now, are you going to tell me what's going on?'

I couldn't bear to tell her that Mike was having financial difficulties, or that Amy had been having an affair, so I just told her what I'd learned from Jake: that Amy was under the influence of some strong medication and there'd been some damage to the car before the crash.

'But it was an accident, wasn't it?' Her face was pale.

'It's suspicious. But the police look for motive first and foremost. That's what I'm trying to work out. Who, if anyone, would want to hurt her?'

Mike called in to collect Betsy on his way home. Did he look like a man who'd murdered his wife after finding out she was cheating on him? I wanted to push the thought away, but I couldn't unthink it. I tried to read him, but he just looked so weary. This whole situation with Betsy was spectacularly bad timing.

I wasn't going to give away what I knew. I'd been too quick to reveal that I'd found out about his financial troubles. If he knew Amy had been cheating on him, he didn't need to know that I'd found out. One way or the other, things would become clear sooner or later.

Was Mike capable of killing Amy? If he had known that his wife was having an affair with his friend, that was certainly a motive to hurt her. But why go after Amy and not Phil? Yes, there was the money to factor in, but setting up a car crash and making it look like a horrible accident seemed quite complicated for a crime of passion.

I logged on to Amy's Facebook from my phone and read the messages from Phil again. Had he wanted to hurt Amy, after she broke things off with him? I'd only met Phil a couple of times and he hadn't made any real impression on me. He was quite good-looking, in a rough-around-the-edges sort of way, and it was hard to say if he had a winning personality – whenever I'd seen him he had been on the verge of tears.

Come to think of it, he had been particularly upset by Amy's accident. I could picture him now, standing with us at the grave. He had been as upset as the rest of us. Was that because she was his wife's best friend and a mother of three whose death was an absolute tragedy, or because he'd had a hand in it?

I couldn't imagine Amy with him. But then again, how well had I really known my sister lately? If I'd learned anything in these past few weeks, it was that Amy and I had become complete strangers to each other.

Tormented, I knew that only a glass of wine would help. And mid-way through my second glass, I had a moment of clarity; I needed help to process this information, and there was only one person I could talk to.

Jake answered on the third ring and agreed to come over when I told him I'd stumbled onto valuable new evidence. He still hadn't arrived by the time I poured my third glass so I opened a second bottle.

It was raining when I opened the door. Jake's glasses misted up, and when he took them off I saw that he had droplets of water in his eyelashes. Up close, I could see a smattering of very light freckles on his nose that I hadn't noticed before. His hair was slick and black, wet from the rain. I vaguely thought of the roses I'd received with an anonymous note, and wondered again if he'd sent them.

The wine had left me way buzzier than I thought, and it

137

wasn't until I started to speak that I realised I was more than just a little tipsy.

Jake clocked the open bottle and the glass I'd poured myself. 'Are you feeling OK?' He asked.

'Long day. Make that a long week – or month.'

I poured him a glass and led him through to the living room. We sat at either end of the sofa, an awkward gap between us. I tried to find the words to start explaining what I'd discovered. When I'd invited Jake over it had felt quite urgent, but here I was losing focus again. And his eyes - at first, I'd thought they were brown but now they looked green. Or was it the firelight?

'You wanted to tell me something?'

'Erm, yes, right. Sorry, I'm just... it's a little hard for me to focus these days.'

Nice one, Izzy – use your sister's death as an excuse for your propensity for binge drinking. I cleared my throat and concentrated really hard on not sounding too pissed.

'I think Amy was having an affair,' I said, fixing my eyes on the carpet. 'I got into her messages, and there were several from a man that she seems to have recently broken up with. A man who just happens to be her best friend's husband.' I choked on the last few words.

'Are you sure?' Jake's eyes grew wide.

'Yes,' I said, feeling the tears start. 'She was cheating on Mike because she wasn't happy, because she wanted more from life. And I didn't know about it, and I wasn't there for her when she needed me...'

The grief hit me again: a surging swell of sorrow for having lost my sister – first to time and distance, and then to eternity. It swept over my head like a tidal wave, a tsunami I hadn't seen coming, and I was drowning before I realised what was going on.

'There, there,' Jake shuffled along the sofa and gently put one arm around my shoulder.

I flopped my head against his chest. The warmth of him was real and solid and comforting. He smelled like juniper and leather and rain.

'It's OK,' he said. His voice was a whisper, and he wrapped his other arm around me, folding me into him.

He leaned across and grabbed the box of tissues from the side table. I took one from him and sat back, trying to take deep, calming breaths. The air came in shallow gasps.

Jake sat there, contemplating me, waiting for me to finish – and probably unsure what to do next. This was not, I was quite certain, what he had imagined when I had invited him over.

What had he imagined?

The thought distracted me long enough to catch my breath. I came back to the surface. Treading water. Yes, this was better. And Jake was still sitting there, his face close to mine, gazing at me with those brown eyes that looked green by firelight. His lips were parted, just a tiny bit, but enough that I knew exactly what he was thinking.

I slowly leaned in towards him.

'No, Izzy...' He clamped my shoulders in both hands and my head was jerked back upright. 'This is not... I mean, that's not what... You don't want...'

'Oh, god.' I cringed, closing my eyes so I didn't have to see his embarrassment.

Perhaps the roses hadn't been from him after all. But how badly had I misread the situation?

'I'm sorry, I just...'

'Hey, don't worry about it. I'm flattered, but this is...' He patted my knee in a matey, not-here-to-take-advantage type way. 'This wouldn't be right.'

'Jake, I'm so sorry, I didn't mean...'

'No need to apologise,' he chuckled, maintaining a safe distance. 'Tell you what: let's agree to never mention it again.'

That sounded like a good deal. I smiled sheepishly.

'There you go!' He gave me a chummy pat on the arm as he smiled back at me. 'Listen, it's probably best that I go now. We can pick up again on this *discussion* tomorrow,' he said, putting way too much emphasis on 'discussion'.

'No, you don't have to leave!' I said. 'Stay! I want to talk about Amy.'

My words were slightly slurred, and I wondered if he noticed.

'I do, too, but I think you need to rest first.'

He was making me sound like a crazy lady and the worst part was, he was looking at me with pity.

Jake got up to leave. 'Goodnight, Izzy. I'll let myself out. Get some sleep and we can talk tomorrow.' He stepped out into the rain, pulling the door shut behind him.

My rage flared – at myself, for throwing myself at him, but also at Jake for knocking me back. He had been giving me all the signals, hadn't he? Maybe I'd got him completely wrong. But did he have to be such a *nice guy* about it? And the pity? That just made me feel even worse.

And Amy. I was mad at Amy. She had ripped up my life with her insane last wishes, dumping a whole load of her shit on my shoulders and expecting me to give up everything that mattered so that I could clear up her mess. It wasn't fair. Hot, angry tears rolled down my cheeks. I threw the empty wine glass against the closed door and watched it shatter.

Adam answered my FaceTime on the third ring. It was 3 a.m. in Hong Kong and he was out with Thierry and Mathilde and a group of friends, who all waved at me through the tiny screen. That's where I should have been – that was my life. Fun and glamour and money, working hard to play hard. Not this – pain and grief and responsibility, and confronting truth that only hurt more the deeper I went. Between sobs, I tried to tell Adam what had happened, but the music was loud – even from out in the street where he'd gone to hear me better – and I knew I was keeping him away from the party. We said goodbye and I went back to my self-pity.

I was bored with wine and needed something a little harder, so I poured myself a scotch. The fire was getting low, the embers glowing a livid red. I piled another log on and pulled the throw over my legs. I had find out what happened to Amy so I could get out of here, soon. Between my mum, the kids and the mess Amy had left, I was going certifiably mad.

Chapter Twelve

I rolled over and the room was suddenly full of light, shocking me awake. It took me a moment to realise I was still on the sofa. The cushion I'd been sleeping on bore the imprint of my face with two mascara-blurs for eyes and a little wet patch where the lips should be. My mouth was dry and everything was blurry, and I realised I'd slept in my contact lenses. *For god's sake, Izzy.* It was only mid-week.

I sat up and surveyed my surroundings. The fire had gone out at some point and I'd pulled a second throw onto the sofa rather than dragging myself upstairs to bed. The empty whisky glass sat on the side table like evidence. I'd refilled it several times before finally crashing out, and the rim was smudged with tell-tale lip marks. I padded into the kitchen to fill it with water. There were sparkles of broken glass all over the floor, and it took me a second to remember –

Oh god. Jake. The shame burned in my throat.

With the small dustpan and brush, I swept up the broken glass. It had been one of the pretty green glasses, and I felt awful that my drunken rage had got the better of me. Every movement hurt my head.

Maybe it would be better if I went to Amy's and watched Betsy there. The last thing I needed was a bored, angry eight-year-old cooped up in this tiny place with me. What time was it anyway? I glanced at my phone – it was already after ten. Why hadn't my alarm gone off?

I had three missed calls from Mike. I called him back, and he answered on the third ring.

'Izzy, are you OK?'

'Yeah, I'm fine,' I mumbled. 'Just a bit... under the weather. Where's Betsy?'

'She's over at your mum's. We were knocking for ages at your door, but there was no answer.'

His voice was so loud, every word made my head pound.

'Look, just take a day off if you're not well. There's no need for you to be watching her all the time. Let's share the work.'

Just a couple of weeks into my role as a co-guardian and I was too hungover to perform my duties. I really was not up to this. Amy had way overestimated me, and she would never have left me in charge if she knew what I was really like. I was just starting, and I was already failing.

Standing under the hot water felt good. I scrubbed my skin until I was pink all over. I was beginning to feel a little better, until I got out of the shower and saw that I had a missed call from Jake. I shuddered. I was starting to perk up, but there was no way I was ready to talk to him yet. I slouched back onto the sofa, exhausted from the effort of showering.

As I sat there, wondering what to do with myself, the phone pinged again. It was a message from Rachel:

I've got a day off. Are you at home with Betsy? Can I pop round? xxx

My heart sank, and I felt nauseous at the prospect of seeing her now that I knew what Amy had done. I sighed. This was

143

the universe punishing me. I had to face her sooner or later – might as well do it when I was already feeling rotten.

I'll come over to you, I texted back. *Remind me of your address? I'll bring the coffee xo*

I pulled on my jeans with Amy's big coat and a beanie and headed out. After last night's rain, the air was clean and the sky was bright, drained of clouds.

The coffee from Clarke's bakery wasn't anything special, but it was infinitely better than the jar of freeze-dried instant granules that Mum had given me. I decided I had to get one of those Nespresso machines for Puffin Cottage – maintaining my caffeine standards was non-negotiable. I bought two cups and two hot bacon rolls to go.

The main road cut through the centre of Seahouses and across Harbour Road, dividing the village into four quarters. Rachel and Phil lived on The Green, the small housing estate at the back of the village that had been built in the seventies as our part of the coast had grown in popularity among weekenders, inflating the prices of homes closer to the sea.

Dad used to complain about the people who snapped up the best properties to only use them a few days a month, pushing up house prices beyond the reach of everyone else. People on local salaries could just about afford to buy on The Green.

I walked along their street, looking out for number twenty. Rachel and Phil's place was a modest semi-detached, and one of the smarter houses on the street with its manicured garden and glossy white door.

'Those smell gorgeous,' Rachel said, taking a coffee from me and leading me inside.

The front half of the living room was dominated by a black leather sofa facing a widescreen TV, while the back was set up as a dining area. Rachel had been ironing her nurse's uniform and it hung from the top of the dresser like a ghost. A fake fire was roaring with golden flames, the mantelpiece above it crowded with framed photos jostling for position around a carriage clock that took centre stage. I ran my finger along the ledge. There was Rachel and Amy, Rachel with Amy's kids, Rachel and Phil... I picked up their wedding photo for a closer look.

'That's when Phil had more hair and I was still ginger,' Rachel said with a laugh.

I carefully put the picture back and joined her on the sofa. Rachel handed me my bacon roll on a plate and I took a sip from my steaming cup of coffee.

'We got married in 2006. I was only twenty-four. We thought we were so grown up.'

'Did you not want kids?' I said, before catching myself. 'God, sorry, I...'

Rachel shrugged and dismissed me with a wave. 'Don't worry about it. I think me and you are close enough by now to talk about things like that!' She gave me a brave smile. 'I mean, we tried for years, but it just never happened. We didn't have the money for more IVF, and in the end, we had to decide that we were enough for each other. By then I'd met your Amy and become an honorary aunt to her three.'

'How did you meet?' I was sure Amy had told me, but I couldn't remember, and now that I knew about Phil and Amy's affair, I had so many more questions about her friendship with Rachel.

'We moved to Seahouses right after we got married. Phil's grandma had a caravan up here and he used to spend weekends with her when he was a boy. He was taking over the garage and I was working in a care home near Newcastle, but I wanted a job closer to home. I thought that would be better once the baby arrived. I started working at the hospital and I met Amy in my first week. A few people confused us for sisters, which gave us a good laugh. We just clicked, I suppose...'

Her eyes were filling up. She turned from me, directing her attention out of the window at some faraway point. It was true, I thought: Rachel did look like Amy, with the same light brown hair – just like mine used to be, before I discovered highlights – and cut into a long bob, similar to how Amy wore hers. In fact, she bore more of a resemblance to my sister than I did, these days.

I changed the subject. 'God, this bacon butty was exactly what the doctor ordered. My head is throbbing.'

'Struggling a bit today?'

I mumbled something that sounded like agreement while biting into my sandwich.

Rachel reached out and took my hand. 'We're all devastated about Amy, but drinking doesn't heal the pain, it just delays it for another day. And drinking alone is never good.'

I didn't know if the delayed pain part was true – my head still hurt. Anyway, I hadn't been alone.

'Jake Ridley called in,' I said. 'The solicitor.'

Rachel's eyes grew wide.

'But it's not what you think!'

'I didn't say anything at all!' she chuckled, holding her hands up in surrender.

'He just came by to give me news on the investigation.'

Rachel stopped laughing. 'So they are investigating it? They really think it might have been more than just an accident?'

A young woman pushing a pram walked past outside, distracting me for a second. 'Some things just don't look right,' I said, keen to leave it at that.

I tried to change direction and asked how Phil was. I was hungry for any details she could give me, anything that might tell me why and how he and Amy had become involved.

Rachel just shrugged, but I pressed on. 'We should get out to the pub one night, drag Mike and Phil along. I owe him a beer to say thanks for the car.'

She pushed the remnants of her roll around her plate. 'That would be nice. We haven't been to the pub for a while. Not since before Amy...' Her eyes filled again and she looked away. Only the ticking of the carriage clock filled the silence.

'It would do Mike some good,' I said, watching her over the top of my cup. 'I know how close you all were.'

'Yup,' she said with a sniff. 'Me and Amy – well, we were best friends. And we dragged the boys along with us most of the time, so yeah – we were quite the foursome.' She sipped her tea, holding the mug with both hands.

'Phil must be upset about Amy too,' I said.

Rachel looked at me I had just said the dumbest thing in the world. 'He's devastated. He adored your sister.'

Her words hung in the air between us. There was no way she knew what was going on between them. The poor woman was completely oblivious to the betrayal right under her nose. What a mess.

I headed home, pulling my coat tight against the chill. Jake called me again, and I let it go to voicemail. The phone pinged with the arrival of a message from him:

I need to speak to you. Can you please call me back when you get this?

I cringed. What had got into me last night? Jake's 'no hard feelings' chat would have to wait until tomorrow, when I had the emotional strength to cope. Right now, I just wanted to eat crisps and wallow in my own self-pity from the safety of Puffin Cottage.

As I walked, though, I was hit by a sudden urge to see Phil. I wasn't sure how helpful it would be to just look at him, but it felt like the only constructive thing I could do right then. Or was this the action of a woman who was slowly going mad? Was this how an obsession started? I was almost at Sea Street. I pulled my beanie further down and carried on walking in the direction of the caravan park.

Phil's garage was busy. There were three or four cars parked out on the road and two inside that he was working on. From my vantage point across the street, I watched as he took a payment from a customer and handed back her keys with a smile.

So, this was the man that Amy had risked her marriage for. Had he been worth it?

He was chatting to his colleague now, a streak of grease on his cheek. He did have a nice smile, I supposed. Even from here, I could appreciate his rugged masculinity. Not that it was my thing at all, and I didn't think it had been Amy's thing either. But how well had I known my sister lately?

Phil had spent weekends here as a child, but I didn't remember him. Had he and Amy experienced a flash of recognition when they'd met again as adults? Or had he just been there, in the background, when she'd befriended his wife?

Where had they *had* their affair? Had he popped over to the house when Mike was away on business, or had Amy visited him at the garage? How often had they met; where had they had sex; how had they avoided being caught? Why had they ended things? Had Mike found out and wanted to hurt them? I had so many questions. I needed to know everything.

A memory hit me on the short walk back home. Me and Amy, standing in front of the school on a cold and dark evening. It had been after a rehearsal of *Much Ado About Nothing*, and we'd been waiting in the small carpark for Dad to collect us.

But Dad hadn't shown up. Mrs Wheeler had offered to take us home, telling us to stop making a fuss when we'd insisted that we were fine. These things happen all the time, she'd said.

The lights had been out when we got back. Mrs Wheeler had got out of the car with us to make sure everything was OK. I'd known it wasn't, but she wouldn't leave us alone. We hadn't had a key, so the three of us had walked around to the back of the house to retrieve the spare from under the flowerpot. When we'd got to the back garden, the lights were on in the living room and the curtains were open. Dad was asleep in the chair, inexplicably wearing a bobble hat, his head thrown back, roaring snores. A drink stood on the table in front of him.

Mum had been away for a couple of nights, probably at Auntie Sue's. Dad had been left in charge and had assured us he would be there to pick us up. But then he'd got home from a long day's work and had a glass of wine, or maybe something stronger. And this was the result.

I hadn't thought about that night in years but it came back now – the burning shame of having Mrs Wheeler understand exactly why Dad hadn't come to pick us up. She had made it ten times worse just by being there to witness it; I'd been so angry that she had seen him like that.

I remembered having been angry with her, but what about Dad? Had I been mad at him, or upset, or felt bitter resentment? I couldn't remember.

Because that's the thing, when someone dies. You forget all the bad things they did when they were alive.

It was impossible to be in Amy's kitchen and not feel her presence. Walking in there, it was as if she had been there just a moment ago and had only stepped outside to grab something.

While Mike supervised from behind his laptop at the table, Lucas had taken over the cooking. He was wearing an apron and had laid out his ingredients along the counter-top, ready to add to a huge saucepan. A pie crust sat cooling on one side. The windows of the kitchen had steamed up, and it smelled like home.

'I'm making baked bean pie.' Lucas smiled as he drained the sauce from a tin of beans.

He started describing how he had made the pastry from scratch, and the different types of pies he could make in the future, and I found myself zoning out.

I thought back to Amy's pastry phase – the day she'd discovered that it was nothing more than a combination of butter and flour, which had led to a period of experimentation of various pie, quiche, and tart fillings. Baked bean pie could feed two hungry girls for less than fifteen pence per meal, and had quickly become one of our favourites.

I was jolted from my memory by a scream from upstairs, followed by a thud and another scream. I jumped in alarm.

'Not again,' said Mike, holding his head in his hands.

Hannah burst into the room.

'Betsy hit me!' she wailed. 'You have to tell her, Dad!'

'What was it this time?' Mike's face was getting red. 'No, forget that, I don't even want to know. Betsy!'

Hannah sat beside me, rubbing the top of her arm and snivelling muffled little sobs. Betsy appeared in the doorway, arms crossed over her chest and lips pursed in defiance.

'Hannah was hogging the tablet, even though it was my turn!'

'I wasn't, I was just finishing my homework—'

'Enough!' Mike slammed his fist down, making the four of us jump. 'You all have to learn to share.' He pointed at the three of them, his eyes wide. 'And nobody hits anyone. Got that, Betsy?'

She started to bawl, and once more, I saw the little girl whose grief was spilling into an anger that she didn't know what to do with. Lucas went tentatively back to his cooking, silent now, and Hannah became absorbed in her phone. Even I felt like I was in trouble.

We ate dinner shrouded in the sulky silence of the children. I tried several times to get a conversation going, but failed at every attempt, and eventually gave up.

The kids sloped off after dinner, leaving me and Mike to clean up alone. He hadn't shaved again, and his grey stubble put years on him. The huge bags under his eyes told me he hadn't been sleeping well. He took a beer from the fridge and sat down at the table.

'You're not looking too hot there, Mike.'

He took a long, deep breath. 'Well my business isn't doing great, my kids hate me and each other, and my wife just died, so yeah – things are a bit shit right now.'

I helped myself to a beer, too. It would take the edge off my hangover and tune me up just a little bit. I needed some Dutch courage right now.

'Any more thoughts on who might have wanted to hurt Amy?'

Mike sighed. 'We've already discussed this. Amy didn't have enemies. What happened to her... however it looks, it was an accident.'

'You have to admit though, with the drugs and this mysterious damage to the front wheel...'

'I'm pretty sure there's an explanation for both of those things. Just leave it to the police to investigate. You're not helping here.'

Ouch.

'But you guys were happy, right? I mean, are you sure there wasn't anything going on that might have upset her...'

'Like what, Izzy? You think she was so distraught over the money I'd lost that she wanted to kill herself?'

His anger was starting to flare up again. I was prodding a sleeping dragon.

'Not that, I'm just thinking now about all the wild possibilities. We should explore every avenue, right? Like... Did you ever worry that Amy had a secret gambling problem? Or might have been unfaithful?'

He scoffed. 'You think my wife was cheating on me?'

I shook my head, but he carried on.

'Listen,' he said, his voice softening. 'Your sister was well-loved. She had no enemies or secrets. And I can promise you, Amy was not having an affair. We were happy. It was just a horrible accident.' He started to cry.

My phone buzzed on the table – Jake again. He was persistent, I had to give him that. I fired off a message to him:

Sorry, I'm tied up with family stuff. Can I call you back

tomorrow?

The reply came immediately:

It's urgent. The police want to talk to you.

I tried to keep a straight face as I texted back:

When? Why??

Now, he replied. *They're on their way to your place.*

Shit.

I started to write a reply, the phone trembling in my hand. I wanted Jake to come, but my pride wouldn't let me ask him. As my fingers hovered over the screen, searching for the words, another message popped up:

I'll be there.

Chapter Thirteen

I made my excuses to Mike and dashed home. What did the police want from me? And what was I going to say? At least Jake would be there with me.

Thankfully, the police had come in an unmarked black Mondeo – if any of the neighbours had seen a police car, the whole village would have known by the morning. By the time I arrived, I was sweating, and my hand trembled as I turned my key in the door to let them in. Jake greeted me with a shy smile and I was careful to keep our eye contact to socially acceptable standards, the heat already rising in my cheeks.

It was the same dinner lady and intern, and I invited them to sit down at the kitchen table. The cottage felt ridiculously small with this many people inside it. I could practically feel the intern breathing on me. I sat on my hands to stop myself fidgeting.

This time, I actually paid attention when they introduced themselves.

Dinner-lady-police-officer – or DCI Bell, as I was to call her – was leading proceedings while her work experience-police-boy colleague PC Knowles made notes in a tiny leather-bound book. She assured me that it wasn't a formal interview, and I wasn't under any kind of caution – they just wanted some background on the family. I glanced at Jake for reassurance and he gently nodded.

What was that thing about looking to one side when you lied? Not that I was planning to lie. I had nothing to hide, and I would answer anything they asked – but I was nervous that DCI Bell might think I was lying. Was it to the left or right? I decided I would try to keep eye contact with her as much as I could. Or was that weird, too?

I wasn't sure why DCI Bell made me so nervous. She was disarmingly ordinary, and if she hadn't been in police uniform, I wouldn't have given her a second thought. Amazing how a badge could transform someone.

DCI Bell asked me how close Amy and I were, and how frequently we had spoken in the weeks leading up to her death. I fought back tears as I explained that the time difference and my work schedule had meant we hadn't spoken that often. How often was not often, DCI Bell wanted to know? I struggled to remember the last time I'd had a proper conversation with my sister, sitting down to talk and giving one another our undivided attention. If DCI Bell judged me for that, she hid it well.

We talked about Amy's state of mind and what I'd learned from my family since coming home. I told them about Mike's outburst at the reading of the will, and how it had prompted me to search through their stuff. Was that a criminal offence? Surely Jake would stop me talking if I was inadvertently confessing to a crime? My heart was racing, and I could feel my cheeks burning up.

PC Knowles's voice was surprisingly deep, and it startled me when he started speaking. He referred to the Detective Chief Inspector and it took me a second to realise he meant the dinner-lady, and by then I had missed the question. Jake got up and poured me a glass of water. He touched my shoulder when he set it down and I flinched.

'Don't worry, I'll repeat the question: could you describe to me and DCI Bell how your brother-in-law reacted when confronted about the status of his financial affairs?'

I took a deep breath and focused on the glass of water in front of me, then remembered I was supposed to be maintaining eye contact.

'He was angry, I'd say.' I pictured Mike's face when I'd told him what I knew about his financial situation.

'And what did you understand to be the reason for his anger?' DCI Bell asked.

The three of them were watching me closely.

'He didn't think it was my business, clearly.' I took a shaky drink of water and a deep breath. 'He was hoping to have the insurance money to pay off his debts. He'd been planning to use some of it to pay back the people he owed.'

I looked up at DCI Bell, who glanced quickly at PC Knowles. 'Did he say that, Isabelle? Can you remember exactly what he said?'

I thought back to that night. I'd been drinking, but I could remember the conversation pretty clearly.

'He said that after the accident, he thought he could use the insurance money to get his business back on track.'

'That's great Isabelle, really helpful,' said DCI Bell. She smiled, but I noticed it didn't reach her eyes. There were smoker's lines around her mouth. 'We'll let you know if we need anything else.'

I shifted nervously in my seat. I'd told the truth, but how were they going to use it?

And I knew I had to tell them about the messages from Phil Turner. The words were right there, but saying them out loud would be an unforgiveable betrayal of Amy. DCI Bell and PC Knowles started to pack up.

'Wait!' I blurted out. 'There's something else.'

PC Knowles glanced at Jake, but DCI Bell didn't flinch. She kept her eyes on me, waiting for me to start.

I took a sip of water, my hand shaking as I set the glass down. 'Amy was having an affair. I logged on to her Facebook account and I saw messages from Phil Turner.'

DCI Bell's eyes stayed on me. 'And these messages, Isabelle, what did they say?'

I took a deep breath to steady myself.

'There were three messages. It was Phil pleading with Amy. Like they had ended things and he wished they hadn't broken up, that they could get back together. He said he was desperate.'

'Thank you, Isabelle. That's very interesting. We'll look into that right away, and I'll be in touch if we need anything further.'

I bit my lip. 'What do you think? Does it mean Mike had a motive?'

DCI Bell gave a polite smile that gave nothing away. 'Like I said, we'll be in touch.'

Jake got up and saw them out. I'd betrayed Amy, and it left a bitter taste in my mouth. I held my breath until I heard their car pull away.

'You did the right thing, Izzy. At least this way, they have the full picture.'

I tried not to look at Jake. I felt bad for throwing myself at him, but I was equally annoyed that he had pushed me off.

Now the police had left and my heartbeat was returning to normal, my embarrassment had started to creep back. I just wanted to get him out of there.

He, on the other hand, seemed to be stalling. I could tell he wanted to do the 'hey, listen, about last night' talk, but didn't know how to begin. Well, I wasn't going to make it easy for him.

I did a theatrical yawn. 'I think I'm going to make it an early night,' I said, getting up from the table.

He hesitated for a moment and then stood up too. 'Right, yes, I suppose it is getting late.'

I willed him to say something – to say it wasn't my fault, or that he regretted turning me down. Anything to make me feel better. Something to prove that I hadn't imagined our connection – that it wasn't just all in my head.

He looked down at his shoes. 'So, I guess it's just a waiting game, now. If you need anything else, you know where I am.'

I opened the door. 'Indeed. Well, goodnight then.'

He stepped past me, and for a moment, we were facing each other in the narrow space between the counter and doorframe. He paused there. Was he going to kiss me? There was something about his lips, the soft curve of his cupid's bow. I realised I was staring at his mouth, and quickly looked away.

'Goodnight,' he mumbled, bottling it.

He hadn't reached the yard gate before I'd slammed the front door shut.

I was angry with myself. I'd clearly misread Jake's intentions and I had to get over it. Anyway, why was I even thinking about men when my sister had quite possibly been murdered, and I'd just given the police reason to think that her husband had quite possibly been the one who had done it? I shuddered.

I hoped I'd done the right thing.

Could Mike have done it? It would have been easy for him to slip something into Amy's drink that evening, and he had access to her car. Would he have known how to loosen a wheel? Was that something you could learn on YouTube? And how could he have convinced her to drive afterwards?

I poured a vodka, telling myself I would stop at one. I called it a night after my third, climbing wearily into my cold bed, the lullaby of distant waves singing me to sleep.

The feeling of unease after my chat with the police lasted for days afterwards, a disquiet that I couldn't shake. I was still jumpy after I'd collected Betsy from school on Friday afternoon. The cottage landline rang, and the man's voice on the line startled me – I thought I'd only given the number to Mum. Why did it feel like I was in some kind of trouble? But it was just Richard, calling to check how Betsy was doing after her suspension.

There had been no major injuries, nothing and nobody broken, and only a few tears – on both our parts – so I considered it an overall success. Sure, she'd been bored, but for the most part she had been that calm and sweet girl that I loved. At that moment she was sprawled across my living room floor, in what had become her go-to position for doing her homework. Looking at her, I saw flickers of Amy. I could watch her all day.

Betsy's form teacher had recommended a child psychiatrist and Richard wanted to explain to me and Mike what we should expect from the sessions. He suggested stopping by on his way home from school to discuss it with me in more detail.

I glanced absentmindedly at the clock on the kitchen wall.

Mike had a work thing that evening, so Mum and Auntie Sue were having the kids for tea, giving me a night off. Meeting Betsy's headteacher to talk about her emotional well-being didn't sound like the most fun way to spend a Friday night, but it did feel like something a responsible co-guardian would do. Besides, I was still curious about how close Richard and Amy had really been.

As Betsy and I walked over to Mum's, I daydreamed about what I *should* be planning for my weekend: a Friday night after-work blow-out, followed by a Saturday morning of penance in the gym, perhaps coffee or lunch with a friend, then maybe a blow-dry or facial to sort me out before doing it all over again that night. If it was nice weather, we might even spend Sunday at the beach, or out on the water. Chiara knew a lot of guys with boats, and there was always someone willing to welcome us aboard.

I sighed. Hong Kong didn't just feel like the other side of the world, it felt a lifetime away.

Auntie Sue made a pot of tea and brought out fresh scones. She said Mum was upstairs, cleansing her chakras – I caught her eye and we shared a giggle. Lucas burst in, excitedly describing what he was planning on making for dinner. Auntie Sue nodded slowly, nervously biting her lip as he checked off a list of ingredients he would need. Hannah was quiet as usual, but there was something different about her.

'Are you OK, sweetie?' I asked her.

She nodded in response, but I knew something was wrong. Maybe it was my maternal instinct finally kicking in, but I could see she was carrying an even bigger burden than usual, and I had just the technique for getting her to open up.

I said my goodbyes and walked to the end of the street before taking out my phone:

Do you want to talk about something? I texted Hannah.

I need help, she replied.

What kind of trouble was she in? My heart raced. The icon on the screen told me she was still typing. I waited for the next message.

I think I've started my period and I don't know what to do.

I felt the familiar prick of tears and bit back a sob. This was not the time to feel grief. This was the time for sympathy, cuddles and a crash-course in sanitary products.

I walked quickly to the chemist and bought a selection of towels, tampons and liners. On a whim, I also got her a scented candle and a lip gloss. As I paid, I realised part of me was flattered – of all the adults in her life, Hannah had chosen me to confide in.

In my head, I started rehearsing the discussion we would have about what was happening to her body, although they'd probably done that at school. I remembered a cringe-worthy video they'd made us watch about how to insert a tampon, and shuddered at the memory. Maybe I should offer to take Hannah bra-shopping, too. I was going to nail this. This, I could handle. After all – I was the cool aunt.

I ran back over to Mum's: Auntie Izzy to the rescue. Hannah answered the door and pulled it half-closed, to give us some privacy. I handed her the bag.

'Do you want me to come upstairs with you, and show you what's in there?'

Hannah's face flushed red as she took the bag from me. 'It's OK, I know what to do. Thank you.'

To my horror, the speech I had composed completely escaped me – I could not remember one single piece of the motherly advice I'd rehearsed in my mind moments ago. Just to make matters worse, I could feel the blush rising in my cheeks too, and wondered who was finding this more awkward. 'Are you sure you're going to be OK?'

Hannah nodded weakly and went back inside, and my heart broke again.

It wasn't raining, and I decided to take the long way home to maximise my fresh air intake. I wandered aimlessly, telling myself that I had no clear destination or route in mind, until I found myself on the same street as Phil's garage. It was the fourth time that week I'd ended up there.

There was something pulling me here – a morbid curiosity? What was I hoping to find? Perhaps some answers to the growing list of questions I had about my sister, or a jolt of understanding. But when I caught a glimpse of Phil, I felt nothing but the empty expanse of the void that had grown between me and Amy.

Back at Puffin Cottage, I opened my laptop. My heart sank when I saw an email from my boss, Toby, with Annabelle Taylor copied in. The bank had approved my three-month unpaid leave of absence, and Toby was now suggesting that the two junior client managers who worked for me could continue to handle my clients under Annabelle's temporary supervision. I chewed a nail as I read the rest of his note. It all depended how long I planned to be away for, he said.

It was a good question – how long was I going to be away? Did I trust Toby to keep my job waiting for me until I got back? What would I be going back to?

The strange thing was that the longer I was away from work,

the less I missed it. Even the thought of Annabelle worming her way into my accounts didn't bother me so much these days. What did I actually enjoy about it? I had worked hard to get the high-value clients and the big corner office, but was it really bringing me any satisfaction? My career was like a hunger, a strange hunger where no matter how much I ate, I never felt full. And I had a voracious appetite. There was always another goal to chase, another target to hit and another bonus to push for, and never enough time to enjoy the achievement. But did it ever make me happy? Truly happy? Had I been missing something all along?

It was as if I'd been wearing a pair of Louboutin stilettoes for a long time, and only now that I had taken them off could I feel how much they squeezed and pinched my feet. Maybe an extended break would help me get some perspective.

Adam had emailed me – he'd found a friend of a friend who wanted to sublet my apartment. At first, the thought of someone else sleeping in my bed and using my stuff sat uneasily with me, but the more I thought about it, the more I realised it was just that: stuff. Meaningless objects. Puffin Cottage was starting to feel like home. Maybe I could stick around longer.

I'd promised myself I would wait until after Richard arrived before opening the wine, but it was Friday night of what had been a long week, and Toby's email had tipped me over the edge. What harm could one glass do? With a bit of luck, it would mellow me out enough to take Richard seriously. Child psychologist? There hadn't been anything like that when we'd lost Dad. Or adult psychologists, for that matter. Who knew how differently things might have worked out if there had been.

I went to freshen up, and couldn't resist assessing myself in the bathroom mirror. My expensive dye job was growing out at the roots, betraying my natural hair colour to the world. I could even see a few greys that I could swear hadn't been there before. And I desperately needed a facial. My once glowing complexion – the result of years of effort and investment in lasers, peels and injections – now looked dry and pale. Fine lines were becoming fully fledged wrinkles.

I rummaged through my washbag for the tiny bottle of rosehip oil that usually restored me to some semblance of glowing. It was almost empty. *Deep breaths, Izzy.* I used the last of my Touche Éclat to cover up the shadows under my eyes and brushed a coat of mascara over my lashes, then went back downstairs before my own reflection made my cry.

Something was niggling at me. Was it the embarrassment of misreading how much Hannah needed me, then forgetting my lines? Or was it the growing unease I had about Amy? Had I neglected my sister and allowed a gulf to grow between us, or had she been keeping secrets from everyone? I poured a second glass of wine and drank it in half the time it had taken me to finish the first.

I heard the yard gate and seconds later the doorbell rang. I quickly downed the rest of my wine and put the dirty glass back in the cupboard out of sight.

Richard was dressed in casual clothes – a zipped up chunky knit cardigan and jeans. He was wearing too much aftershave and holding a small bunch of flowers.

'An official house-warming,' he grinned, brandishing a bottle of wine in the other hand.

I was grateful, but wine and flowers were a strange way to start a parent-teacher meeting. I took the bottle from him.

'Tignanello – my favourite! How did you know...?'

'I have to confess, I checked out your Instagram to get the inside scoop.'

Who actually said things like 'inside scoop'? I quickly turned my back so he wouldn't see me smile and made a big deal of putting the flowers in water. Also, what was the point of Instagram-stalking if you told someone straight away? Richard was such a dork, it was actually quite sweet.

'Will you have a glass?'

I was keen to open the wine. There was nowhere locally that sold it, which meant Richard must have gone through quite an effort to procure it. Extra points that were definitely making up for the extra aftershave.

We sat in the living room, each with a glass of wine in hand, Richard looking awkwardly at his feet.

'You wanted to talk about Betsy?' I reminded him.

I took my first sip, not wanting to look over-eager, and wondered how long this might discussion might take.

'Yes,' he said, headteacher voice back now. 'We're obviously quite concerned about what she's been through, and how much there is for her to process and deal with. And while her support structure is going through a period of... *adjustment*' – he gestured towards me – 'we feel that a professional could help to guide her through some of those emotions.'

He was trying to cushion my feelings. Should I be offended by this? Was he saying that I wasn't doing a good job with Betsy?

'I'm...' I searched for the words. 'I'm really trying my best with her – with all of them.' The tears came from nowhere, catching me off-guard.

'I'm so sorry. I really didn't mean to upset you,' Richard

said, fumbling to put his wine down and retrieve a tissue from his pocket.

I was crying as much for me as I was for failing Betsy. I knew I wasn't good at the kids' stuff, and hearing other people confirming it wasn't especially hurtful, or even surprising. I thought of Hannah's reaction to me trying to help her and realised it was silly, really. Then I remembered that I did have things to cry about – the life I'd lost, and the job I had worked so hard for that might not be waiting for me by the time I got back, *if* I ever got back... And the fact that my sister might have been murdered. And I got more upset when I realised that the things that had set me off were my hair and skin and the fact that I hadn't tasted my favourite wine in weeks, which officially made me a superficial narcissist – and that made me bawl even more.

I heard myself weeping and but I couldn't stop myself, I couldn't rein it back in. I tried to take deep breaths and choked on them.

Richard carefully prised the glass from my hand and set it on the side table next to his. Kneeling on the floor in front of me, he placed one hand tenderly on my knee.

Suddenly it all seemed vaguely ridiculous. This whole situation – Betsy's headteacher, bringing me wine and flowers and telling me that she needed psychological help and me crying because my skin looked crappy – was hilarious. Richard's expression morphed from concern to bemusement as my crying turned into laughter. Now who was the crazy one?

'Sorry,' I said, wiping away a final tear. 'I don't know what that was, or where it came from, but I needed that.'

'Of course,' he nodded sagely, like I hadn't just had a meltdown in front of him. 'You're processing a lot right now.

166

You know, talking about it can really help. And I just want you to know, if you need anything at all, I'm here for you.'

I considered him. He wasn't bad-looking. In fact, he was quite attractive from a certain angle. If I just squinted my eyes a bit and pretended that he wasn't wearing a cardigan, he was actually quite handsome.

His hand was still on my knee, and with the lightest touch, he brushed his thumb against my thigh, watching me, waiting for my reaction. I didn't object. He pressed harder, and the pressure and heat from his fingertips was travelling through me, making me hunger for more. It felt so good to be touched, to be wanted. Maybe what I needed was right in front of me. To hell with Jake Ridley.

I leaned in towards him, ever so slowly, then stopped. Our faces were just inches apart. Did I want to do this? Did he want to? His eyes signalled a resounding yes. I parted my lips.

'You know, you remind me so much of her.'

I stopped. A chill ran through me. 'Excuse me?'

'I mean, you're so much like her. Like Amy.'

'That's...' I searched for the words. Richard's hand was still on my knee. I gently lifted it off. How did I even respond to that?

He shook his head. 'I'm so sorry – that was a stupid, insensitive thing to say. Please, don't hold it against me. I don't even know where that came from...'

'It's OK,' I lied. I suddenly felt very weird about Richard.

'Did you like the roses, at least?'

The roses. Of course. Hadn't it been obvious? I should have seen this coming.

I mustered the best smile I could manage. 'I think you'd better be going.'

'That was... Gosh, I am sorry.'

He followed me through to the kitchen, awkwardly shuffling around each other in the small space as I opened the door. Richard hesitated on the threshold.

'I'm sorry about that,' he said, eyes glistening. 'I'm sorry about everything.'

The goodbye was short and clumsy, and I gently closed the door as soon as he was at a safe distance. I leaned back against it and slowly exhaled.

My phone pinged, interrupting my thoughts. It was Hannah. *I'm sorry about before. I really do need you. Not to show me what to do or tell me about any period stuff. Just to be there.*

I didn't get this girl. She was like two completely different people – Hannah in person was not the same teenager who was so communicative through her phone. Or maybe that's how all girls her age were these days? She disappeared into her device for hours at a time. What little world had she made for herself in there?

Whatever it was, this was a window opening up to let me in. It might not have been a clear SOS, but it was a call for help from Hannah and a second chance for me to get this right. I had a great idea, and two-thirds of a bottle of good red wine to enjoy while I made it happen. Time to get to work.

I was envisioning a pamper day, Auntie Izzy-style. Lunch with champagne, nails, a facial, and a little shopping was just what I needed, and Hannah was giving me the perfect excuse. Getting your first period was a cause for celebration and she deserved a treat. It probably wasn't what Amy would have done, but she hadn't left a handbook on how to mother. I was going to have to do things my way.

Chapter Fourteen

T he car came to pick us up at nine for the hour-long journey to Newcastle. Hannah cooed at the black Mercedes that I'd managed to hire from an executive chauffeur company at the last minute, taking a photo with her phone. The driver held the doors open for us and she climbed in, shifting nervously around in the leather seat. The smell of a freshly valeted interior was a comforting reminder of my normal life.

Our driver, Henry, had clearly missed the day of chauffeur training when they were coached in the art of being silently attentive. He jumped straight in with questions, and when he got one-word shut-downs from me, moved on to Hannah.

She told him that we were celebrating a special occasion and looked across to give me a smile. Henry yapped on about how busy the 'town' would be, given the great weather. He spoke with a broad Geordie accent and his cologne was far too strong for such an enclosed space. I sipped on a small bottle of water from the armrest console and willed the journey by, gazing out of the window as the countryside rolled past.

Journeys to Newcastle had always signalled big events and special occasions – school trips, visits to the theatre or museums, Christmas shopping excursions. I remembered a

Saturday afternoon a lifetime ago when Amy and I had first been allowed to make the trip on our own. We'd taken the bus and spent four hours walking around, exploring in our own time, giddy with excitement and the possibility that a big city held. I'd decided then that even Newcastle was not enough – I wanted more, bigger. London, Paris, New York.

Growing up, I couldn't wait to get away from here. Amy had told me she was coming too and I'd taken it for granted that she felt the same. I could see now how she might have said that for my benefit. She'd have done anything for me, once upon a time. Perhaps Seahouses had been enough for her all along. And maybe there was something wrong with me – after all, it's normal to feel a desire for home. It had taken her dying wish to get me back here. And now there was a kernel of a thought, a seed of an idea deep inside me, that maybe I should have done it sooner.

Eventually, rural turned into suburbia as farmland gave way first to vast housing estates and then finally the towers and spires of the city itself. I hadn't been to Newcastle for several years, and I asked Henry to take us on a quick tour before our first appointment. So much had changed; new buildings had sprung up everywhere and a lot of streets were no longer recognisable to me. But as we traversed the river, the Tyne's familiar seven bridges slid into view, lined up one by one, framing the water below.

I had booked a salon the evening before, managing to get appointments for both me and Hannah to have our hair and nails done, followed by a facial. Hannah was wide-eyed as I explained this to her, even more so when I suggested she got some subtle face-framing highlights and layers cut into her hair. The salon staff spoiled her, bringing her endless treats while they glossed, buffed and trimmed her to perfection. As we were getting ready to leave, Hannah took out her phone to get a picture of her makeover and I realised that it was the longest I'd seen her go without it. She even took a selfie with me – surely the biggest compliment I was going to get.

We went to a brasserie on Grey Street for lunch – Google had suggested it was the most decent option. I ordered a martini to start and it didn't disappoint. Hannah was delightfully unselfconscious and took photos of everything we ordered, not even attempting to be discreet. I laughed as she posed for selfie after selfie.

'This day has been *epic,*' Hannah said, her eyes bright. 'You're totally spoiling me, though. Betsy's going to be so jealous.'

'Betsy had quite enough of me last week,' I laughed.

As I signalled to the waiter for the wine list, something outside caught Hannah's attention.

'Is that... Dad?' She looked over my shoulder, squinting.

I followed her gaze. A man who looked very much like Mike was standing on the opposite side of Grey Street, beside a row of parked cars. The street was wide but even at that distance I could see it was him. He was talking to a woman in a baseball cap.

'That's Dad. That's his car. What's he doing here?' She started to stand.

I put my hand on her arm. 'Just wait a second.'

'Who is he with?'

We watched and waited. The woman had her back to us but it was obvious that the pair were arguing. Mike was red-faced and jabbing his finger towards her.

'Do you know who he's talking to?' I asked her. My heart

was pounding.

'I don't know. I can't tell from here.' Hannah's voice was small. I silently willed her to stay in her seat.

'Isn't he supposed to be at some work thing today...?' My voice trailed off.

'I'm going over there,' Hannah said, squeezing out of the booth.

'Please, Hannah, just wait...'

I signalled to the waiter to get the bill, but Hannah was already walking out the door.

'Dad!' she shouted, waving.

'Hannah, wait for me!' I called, trying to keep the urgency out of my voice.

Two ladies at the table next to us were watching. I looked around for the waiter. What was taking so long?

Hannah was already outside the restaurant, about to cross the road. I didn't want to let her out of my sight. I could always come back to pay... I picked up my bag and followed her out the door.

'Hannah, wait!' I reached out a hand to her shoulder.

A red sightseeing bus rumbled past, hissing with the exertion of climbing the steep hill, blocking our view for a few seconds. When the road cleared, Mike and the woman had gone.

'He was right there, that was Dad,' Hannah said, frantically scanning the street, which was busy with Saturday shoppers.

We turned at the same time to see Mike's car turning left onto Mosely Street, disappearing from view.

'I'm calling him. That was him. He must have heard me.' She got out her phone and called, but there was no answer. She tried again. 'It's just going to voicemail. I don't understand.'

She looked at me for an answer I couldn't give.

We walked up Grey Street in silence, Hannah looking at her feet. Seagulls circled above us, bigger than the birds at the coast. The mood had soured, but I was determined to finish the day on a positive.

I took Hannah to Topshop and headed straight to the counter to collect the item I'd reserved online. The assistant disappeared and returned with a black leather jacket.

Hannah gasped, her eyes wide. 'Are you serious?'

I urged her to try it on, and we headed to the changing rooms. 'Every woman needs a black leather jacket. It goes with everything, and if you look after it, you'll still be wearing this when you're forty.'

She scoffed. Forty seemed ridiculously far away to her. So far in the future she couldn't see it.

'It's really expensive,' she said, stroking the butter-soft leather and admiring her reflection. 'I don't know...'

'I've already decided for you. Besides, every time you wear it, you'll think of your Auntie Izzy.'

I smiled at her in the mirror. She smiled back at me, but the sparkle had disappeared from her eyes.

Back in the car, even Henry was quiet.

We were heading to Mum and Auntie Sue's, as they had invited us all over for dinner, including Rachel. I had already decided that my coping strategy was going to be to not think about the Phil thing when I was with Rachel – which would be a challenge, especially because she liked to talk about Amy so much. I wished she didn't have to come, but I figured it was good for the kids to be around someone who was so close to their mum. I felt sick when I imagined what would happen if she ever found out what Amy and Phil had done. Or rather, *when* she found out. Secrets like that never stay buried for long.

Hannah sighed. 'Maybe he didn't hear us,' she said, gazing out the window. 'Or maybe it wasn't him?'

Maybe, maybe, maybe, I thought. Maybe Mike was hiding something after all.

'Listen,' I said softly. 'Don't say anything to your dad, about this afternoon. Not just yet.'

Hannah was about to speak, I could see the question forming on her face, but we were interrupted by my phone ringing.

'Izzy?' It was Rachel, and she sounded frantic. 'Where are you?'

'I'm in the car with Hannah, we're on our way back to Mum's. What's happened?'

'It's Phil,' Rachel said, the panic rising in her voice. 'The police came. They've arrested him.'

My hands trembled as I put the phone back in my bag.

'What's wrong?' Hannah asked. 'You're as white as a sheet.'

I didn't know where to start. My mouth had gone dry, and I was acutely aware of Henry listening in. My mouth moved but still no words came.

'What's wrong! Tell me!' Hannah was frantic now.

'Everyone's OK. That was Rachel. The police have taken Phil in for questioning.'

'Uncle Phil?' Hannah's face knotted into a question. 'Why?'

I couldn't see how to shelter her from this. I reached across the console and squeezed her hand.

'Mum's... accident. They're just making sure that it was an accident, and not... That someone might have wanted to deliberately hurt her.'

Hannah's hand flew up to her mouth.

'No!' She gasped and shook her head. 'No, no no...'

'I'm so sorry. But with anything like this, they need to investigate, just to make sure...'

'But Uncle Phil? Why? No. He wouldn't...' Hannah's eyes filled with tears and the words came out in gulps. 'He wouldn't. He wouldn't hurt Mum. Say it's not true?'

I caught Henry's eye in the mirror and he quickly turned his attention back to the road. Hannah rested her head against the car window and wept softly as the sea came into view.

Rachel was at Mum's by the time we arrived. Everyone had piled into the living room, with Auntie Sue comforting Rachel as she sobbed. Betsy and Lucas were tear-stained and dazed.

'Oh my god, Izzy I'm so sorry; I don't know what to do!'

Rachel crumpled into herself. I wrapped my arms around her as sobs wracked her body.

'It's OK, it's OK,' I tried to soothe her. 'We'll figure this out.' My head was thumping, the beat of blood loud in my ears. I looked over Rachel's shoulder at Auntie Sue. 'Where's Mum?' I mouthed. Auntie Sue gestured upwards, and gave me a look that warned me against asking more. Hannah sat down between Lucas and Betsy, pulling the pair of them into a cuddle. Betsy started to sob again.

'And where's Mike?' I asked, aloud this time.

'We can't get hold of him,' said Rachel, between choking, gut-wrenching sobs.

Auntie Sue sighed. 'He isn't picking up his phone. We've left messages.' The worry was etched onto her face.

I instinctively wanted to shelter Rachel, to comfort her, and

I pictured two girls holding hands across the gap between their beds, fortifying one another. Making each other whole. I held her firmly by the shoulders. 'I've got you. We'll figure this out.'

I willed her to be strong right then, at least for now, at least in front of the kids.

My mind was scrambled, but I frantically tried to think through my next steps. Where was Mike? I needed to speak to Jake. What had made the police suddenly switch their focus from Mike to Phil? Maybe they still had Amy's phone after all, and had uncovered damning proof. And where the hell was Mum?

First things first – the children. I crouched down on the floor in front of them. Betsy slid down from the sofa onto my lap and curled her warm little body into my side.

'Listen kids, this is horrible. There's no other word for it. But we have to stay strong.' I took Lucas's hand. 'We have to support each other.'

'Does it mean Mummy was murdered?' His lip trembled.

The word sent a shiver down my spine, and I was floored by fresh wave of nausea. I saw Hannah blink back new tears.

'No, darling, it doesn't mean that at all. We don't know anything yet. The police just need to be sure exactly what happened to Mummy. But we shouldn't think too much about those things.' I tried to speak slowly and deliberately, to give the kids some reassurance that this was all normal, that everything would be fine, even though I wasn't convinced myself.

Jake picked up on the third ring.

'Izzy, how are you? I was just about to call you—'

'Couldn't they have given us some advance warning?' I hissed angrily.

I'd come to the back garden to get some privacy. I didn't want any of the family to hear.

'It doesn't work like that. They can't tell you before they arrest someone, for obvious reasons.'

I put a hand on the wall to steady myself. 'What happens now?'

'They have twenty-four hours in which to question him - thirty-six hours at most. If they can't charge him in that time, they'll release him.'

Arrested. They had *arrested* someone for Amy's *murder*. The thought was like a hammer blow to my head. Even breathing became a struggle. I took shallow gulps of air and tried to focus. My head was spinning. *Now everyone will find out about the affair*, I thought.

'But what about Mike? Amy and Phil having an affair means Mike had a motive on top of the money from the insurance.'

'That's true, but it seems some additional information has come to light.'

'What was the new information? Can you find out?'

'Not officially, no.' A nervous edge had appeared in Jake's voice. 'But I heard a rumour. They had an anonymous tip-off.'

I heard him swallowing. Stalling. The sound of bad news stuck in his throat. I closed my eyes.

Jake sighed. 'The loose wheel. How it might have happened. Apparently, Amy took her car to Phil's garage for a service two days before... the incident.'

I slumped to the ground, my back against the wall and face to my knees, the phone still held up to my ear.

'Izzy?' Jake said quietly.

'Yep, I'm still here.'

'There's nothing you can do for now. Go and be with your family. Wait it out.'

'Rachel's here, too,' I said.

Silence from Jake.

'Does she know?' I said. 'Does she know about Amy and... what Amy and Phil did?'

Poor Rachel. How they had betrayed her. I felt sick again.

'Not yet, and you shouldn't say anything. The police will need to speak to her at some point, and it's important she hears it from them first.'

'You'll have to go with her,' I said firmly. 'We can't expect her to do that on her own.'

'Let's cross that bridge when we get to it.' Jake sounded tired.

We said our goodbyes and hung up. I wanted a drink, badly. A vodka. Or frankly, whatever I could get my hands on at this point. It was starting to get dark, the sky turning velvety, and the kitchen window cast an amber glow onto the lawn. I pulled myself up and headed back inside.

Mum was in bed. Auntie Sue had half-heartedly tried to talk me out of going to her, and I could see why. The smell of the room stirred deep memories within me.

The curtains were drawn, and I assumed they'd been that way all day. Despite the dark, I could make out the crescent of her body curled under the covers. She didn't move when I came in. I sat down beside her and reached out a hand to her shoulder.

'Amy?' She whimpered.

I sighed. 'No, Mum. It's me, Izzy.'

She rolled over towards me. Her wet eyes glinted in the dark. 'Sorry, love. I thought I was dreaming.'

I swivelled around, stretching my legs out alongside the length of her. I leaned over her pillow, cradling her head in the crook of my arm like a baby. Her hair smelled like apples. A sweet contrast to the sourness of the room. I breathed her in.

We hadn't been this close – this loving – since before she'd disappeared. Amy and I had spent weeks watching her like this before she'd woken up one day and decided to go. I prayed to the universe that she would recover, willing her back to us. And hopefully this time she wouldn't disappear completely first.

Auntie Sue was in the kitchen with the kids.

'Where's Rachel?' I asked.

'She's gone to bed.' She motioned upstairs. 'I've put her in the spare room. Mike called, he's on his way over. I got the impression she'd rather be on her own for now.'

She gestured to the kids with a barely perceptible nod, indicating there might have been more to the story than she could give right then.

'Poor Rachel,' I said, shaking my head.

We sat at the kitchen table, all of us at a loss for words. The silence hung over us like harbour mist. Auntie Sue looked drawn, and I could see the worry of the last few weeks etched on her face. The low light in the room cast shadows across her eyes, adding years. One hand covered her mouth, like she was suppressing a cry, or a scream, or something she might regret. She was well-practised in holding it together. But how much more could she take?

A car engine and the sound of a door slamming shut snapped

179

me back to attention.

'Daddy!' said Betsy, looking to us for confirmation.

Mike didn't make it past the doorway before Lucas and Betsy threw themselves at him. Hannah was slower to move, inching her way to her to father and folding her two younger siblings in her arms, making a knot of four.

I had almost forgotten about seeing Mike in Newcastle this afternoon. Not that it mattered so much now. I chided myself for being so suspicious of him. How could I have thought he would hurt Amy? His business dealings might be a bit dodgy, but that didn't mean he'd been out to kill his wife. And I'd been so quick to assume the worst about him, when all along it was Amy who hadn't been a saint. Amy who had been cheating with a man who turned out to be more dangerous than she could have imagined.

He was worn down. Threadbare. I recognised in him the same unease I was feeling, the same sense of emptiness, of being stretched to breaking point. And as hard as things had been until now, it was about to get even tougher. There were going to be some difficult questions asked very publicly about Amy and Mike's private life. Nothing would remain sacred.

Auntie Sue and I herded the kids up with coats, bags and shoes, and we hugged our goodbyes. I promised to call over in the morning.

'Cup of tea?' said Auntie Sue.

I was already looking in the fridge. 'Got anything stronger?'

'Good call.' She retrieved a bottle of sherry from the dresser in the corner.

I knocked back my first glass in one go. Auntie Sue looked at me with a raised eyebrow, then shrugged her shoulders and did the same. I poured us both a second.

We sat like that in an easy silence, each of us too dazed to talk and empty of words. A stillness had settled over the house, and only the clock on the mantelpiece sounded out the passing minutes. At last, Auntie Sue spoke.

'There's got to be some mistake. Why would Phil Turner want to hurt Amy? Why would anyone want to hurt her? It was an accident... I can't work out why they'd think someone did this deliberately.'

I shuddered, saying nothing.

Auntie Sue drew a deep breath and shook her head. 'I don't know if I can do this again.' She nodded upwards, upstairs, to where Mum was lying in the dark.

I finished my second glass of sherry and poured a third. My head was swimming and I needed to calm my thoughts so that I could focus. There was too much hurt, and I knew only one way to numb the pain.

'If it's any consolation to you, Izzy, I know what you're going through.' She pulled her lips inwards, wincing at the memory, and leaned forward in her chair. She smiled at me with sad blue eyes as she raised her sherry. 'So, let's toast the aunties.'

'To the sisters who pick up the pieces,' I said, chinking my glass against hers.

'Indeed,' she said, taking a big sip.

I looked at her, seeing her more clearly than I had in years. She wasn't just Auntie Sue. She was a whole person, a woman who had left her life to look after me and Amy. Twenty-five years later, here she still was. Still picking up the pieces.

It had never occurred to me how much she must have given up for us. One day she had just waltzed into our lives and started looking after us, filling the vacuum left by our parents, but giving us just enough space for us not to resent her. Caring for us just the right amount.

I had a sudden urge to know the answers to all the questions that the teenage Izzy had been either too self-centred or too preoccupied to ask.

'You know, I never really thanked you properly. For everything you did for us.'

Auntie Sue gave a little shrug, a barely perceptible tilt of her head, and filled our glasses again, higher this time. I took a sip. 'Except I never knew – I never thought to ask you...' I struggled for the right words. 'I guess I never thought about it before. How much you gave up.'

She sat back in her seat, the leather of the chair creaking, and settled in to her story.

'I would have done anything for my sister. I was always the practical, sensible one – even though your mum was six years older. We were close, growing up, despite the age gap. Your grandma worked full-time - still quite unusual, for that generation, so me and your mum were often left to fend for ourselves, albeit with the help of a full-time housekeeper. Nobody thought twice about things like that back then.

'Your mother, my god, she was dangerously dreamy. She would walk upstairs and forgot what she'd gone for. She was forever losing things, and I spent a good deal of my time looking for whatever she had misplaced. Once, she came home with only one shoe!'

She chuckled, and I could picture Mum in her bare-socked foot.

'I loved being outdoors. Even in bad weather I'd be outside, hiding in one of the dens I'd built in the grounds of our house. My most constant companion was the gardener, an old man called Tye. He taught me how to chop and store firewood, set mole traps, and forage for mushrooms in the woods. He knew different types of lichen by sight, and could tell you what the weather would do based on the colour of the moss. I would follow him around, hanging on his every word.

'Mum and Dad were determined that both of us would follow them into medicine, but Tye had inspired me to follow a different path. I graduated in Geology and horrified my parents by accepting a job in Scotland, working on rotation aboard an oil rig off the coast of Aberdeen. You should have seen your grandpa's face when I told them.

'Still, at least it was a career. Your mum never quite found her footing. She studied History of Art, which, I think, your grandma pushed her to do in the hope that it would help her find a husband. She came back to Northumberland with a degree but no prospect of a job or wedding. She moped and moped and moped.'

I tried to do the maths in my head. It would have been a few years after Mum graduated until she met Dad. That was a lot of moping.

Auntie Sue took a sip of sherry. 'So you can imagine how unapologetically thrilled everyone was when your mum got along well with one of the new junior doctors from the hospital. Dad – your grandpa, that is – invited Edward around for dinner one evening. They encouraged the courtship and were delighted when Edward eventually proposed.'

'That sideshow – the wedding, then you and Amy arriving – meant I could settle comfortably into my own life. Finally, I could live the way I wanted to, away from the scrutiny and expectations. It was only Aberdeen but it felt a world away from the village. I wasn't Susan anymore, I was Sue. I got my hair cut into a pixie crop and started wearing dangly earrings.

'I made just enough visits home to deter them all from coming up to Aberdeen. Don't get me wrong – I loved coming to see you girls, but I was always glad to get back again. I was young, carefree, and living life my way.'

'Until I got a phone call one day from a kind nurse, who told me that my brother-in-law was in Alnwick Hospital and my family was asking for me.'

I nodded, remembering that awful time.

Auntie Sue wiped a tear from her eye. 'I had to prop your mum up at the funeral, quite understandable, of course. I'd planned to stay for a week afterwards, helping her find her feet, helping you and Amy. When it became clear that she wasn't bouncing back, I took another week off work. Back in Aberdeen, I'd called her every day. She seemed to be improving, although some days were better than others.'

Those days – the darkest days of my life – came back to me now. Mum swinging between episodes of depression during which she lay in her bed in the dark, and hyperactive phases where she would describe her dreams in forensic, vivid detail. She would sit outside in the dark, looking for patterns in the stars, convinced that Dad was communicating to her through the universe. Amy and I had worried that if anyone saw her like that, she would be taken away. So we hid it from the world, including Auntie Sue.

'She stopped coming to the phone, so I would just speak to you and Amy. You girls used to tell me everything was fine, and I believed you. And you sounded OK, for the most part. There were days when I had an uneasy feeling. And of course, I longed to come and see you, but I was stuck on an oil rig 120 miles off the coast. There wasn't a lot I could do, besides worry.' She bit her lip.

'And then, one morning, Diana Wheeler called. I got a message from the office to call her back, and when I saw the name on the notice, my blood ran cold. I could barely dial the number, my hands were shaking so badly. She assured me there was no emergency, but she was worried that people hadn't seen your mum out for a while, and she thought it best if I could come home.'

'Well, I was out of there like a flash – they even scrambled an emergency helicopter to take me back to shore. I went back to my flat, threw some clothes a bag and drove straight to Seahouses. And of course, you girls admitted everything – or at least, everything that you knew.

'I was furious with our Anne – utterly livid. But I had to hide it from you. You'd been doing such a good job of taking care of each other, but you don't leave grieving teenage girls alone like that. I thought I'd never forgive your mum for what she did.'

A familiar wave of anger rose in me, too. I pushed it away, willing the swell to calm.

'It was clear that you were ready for help, though. You slept for almost two days, do you remember?'

I nodded.

'I didn't know how I'd cope, at first,' Auntie Sue said. 'But the three of us muddled through those first few weeks, and before long, I couldn't imagine life without you and Amy. In the end, there was no choice – I had to give up my old life. I thought I'd go back, eventually, picking up the pieces and carrying on from where I'd left off. But the weeks became months, and then years, and that life slowly faded into memories.'

My gut wrenched with a pang of familiar grief for the life that Auntie Sue had made and lost, and the pain of being asked to sacrifice everything for someone else. My job, my friends, my life in Hong Kong, the life I'd created for myself – it was still going on, just without me in it.

There was something else she wasn't telling me, a secret that flashed behind the sadness in her eyes, betraying its true depth. She had lost more than she was letting on. And suddenly it occurred to me. Auntie Sue had always been single. It was one of those things that had just been, that I hadn't questioned, and the circumstances of how she came into our lives meant that I'd never thought to ask.

'You were with someone, weren't you? In Aberdeen?'

'Yes. I was, yes.' Auntie Sue's eyes glistened.

I gulped hard. 'And you gave him up? For us?'

Auntie Sue took a sip of sherry and nodded. 'Her', she said. 'And her name was Emily.'

She wiped away a tear on the back of her hand and my heart broke again – a tightening in my chest that was harsher and deeper than any pain I'd ever known. The irony of my situation was suddenly too much to bear, a parallel line drawn across my family history and binding us in an unbreakable curse. I wept for everything we had all lost.

Chapter Fifteen

I stared at the ceiling from my makeshift bed on the sofa. It was early, too early to be awake, and the house was still. Even though Puffin Cottage was only a short walk away, I had stayed over at Mum and Auntie Sue's so that I could be there when Rachel woke up. My grief – all the many losses – had balled into one, a tangled knot of wool, so that I couldn't see where one ended and another began.

I ached for a chance to ask Amy what she had been thinking and how she had got herself in to such a messy situation. I wouldn't even have been mad with her. We had spent our whole lives easily forgiving each other's misdemeanours, and this could have been like all those other times when we would argue, sulk, and quickly fall back into the established rhythm of us. And while having an affair was worse than any fuck-ups either of us had made before, I just wanted to see her. It didn't matter what she had done, or the hurt she had caused, or the chain of events she had set in motion. I craved her face, her smell, the sound of her voice. I just wanted my sister.

After reminiscing with Auntie Sue the night before, I had more sympathy for Mike. Losing Dad had been hard for us, but it had almost killed Mum, and she had never properly recovered from it. As difficult as this was for me, my grief for

Amy was nothing next to the pain Mike had to deal with.

The dark clouds of a murder investigation and a trial were gathering on our horizon. There would be courtrooms, lawyers and judges, journalists. Amy's life would be ripped open and forensically examined, then held up for everyone to see. Nothing would be sacred, and there would be nowhere to shelter from the truth – or from the hurt. I could only imagine what it would do to Mike. I needed to be better for him, and for the kids. And Rachel, and Mum, and Auntie Sue... I needed to be better for all of them.

I wasn't going back to Hong Kong. I couldn't. Whatever I'd had before, wherever I had thought my life was going, that was over now. It would be easier for me to cope if I accepted it and moved on. A trial could take months. We would be battered and bruised by the process, from the scrutiny on us, and it would take years to recover – if we ever did.

I had to acknowledge what Amy had asked of me regarding the children, and I wondered if there was more to her wish than it first seemed. Had she known that Phil could do something like this, and made plans just in case? Was that what she meant by *running out of time*?

Auntie Sue had saved me and Amy, that much had always been clear to me. And now it was my turn. The circumstances weren't the same – at least Mike was still here. But a murder investigation would shake each of us to our core. It was my job to shelter the children from the storm that was heading our way and I knew then that I would do whatever it took to protect them, however long it took. It would be ten years until Betsy turned eighteen, and by that time, the life I knew today would be long gone.

With my mind made up, I could focus on what to do next.

The first priority was to resign from my job and sort out my apartment in Hong Kong, then find somewhere to live here and think about finding some kind of work. I wondered if Mrs Wheeler would agree to a long-term let on Puffin Cottage. Maybe I could move in with Mike and the kids? Their place was big enough... But that would be wrong. Perhaps Rachel and I could get a place and grow together into our new roles – the spinster aunt and the betrayed wife of the murderer. It was almost poetic.

Those were the big things, the long-term stuff. The most pressing concern was how to get Mum, the kids, and Mike – not to mention Rachel – through the next few days. There would be more questions from the police, and at some point, very soon, Phil would probably be charged with Amy's murder.

The thought knocked the wind out of me, and I shuddered, hugging my knees to my chest for comfort.

I heard soft footsteps coming down the stairs and the door slowly creaked open.

It was Rachel, fully dressed in yesterday's clothes. 'Want a cup of tea?' she whispered.

She knew her way around Mum's kitchen and didn't have to search for teabags, mugs or sugar. I closed the door so we didn't wake anyone.

'How did you sleep?' I asked.

Her complexion was ashy, and without make-up, the shadows under her eyes were purple. 'Not great.' She leaned back on the counter and wrapped her arms across her chest as we silently waited for the kettle to boil.

This woman had become such a good friend to me, had been there for me when I needed her, and now I didn't even know what to say to her. Could she guess the depth of Amy's betrayal? I wanted to know, but I didn't dare ask. How would she feel when she found out how much I knew, and had been keeping from her?

The silence was mercifully broken by the muffled sounds of someone moving upstairs. Without saying anything, Rachel took out an extra mug. Auntie Sue appeared at the door just as Rachel was pouring. In her dressing gown and with no make-up, Sue looked every one of her sixty years.

'Oh, love, come here.' Auntie Sue pulled Rachel into a hug and Rachel started sobbing on her shoulder. The two of them stood like that, bound together, while Rachel wept into the collar of her dressing gown. The three mugs of tea steamed on the counter beside them.

'I just... I just don't understand,' said Rachel as she pulled away from Auntie Sue and we sat down. 'Why would they think he was involved?

I tentatively placed my hand on hers, squeezing her fingers. Saying nothing.

We decided that Rachel should stay at Mum and Auntie Sue's for a few days, and I agreed to sleep over for a night, too. I longed for the little airy bedroom at Puffin Cottage and my bed with its sea view, but Rachel needed me. She had to go home and get some things, but she promised to be back in time for tea with her overnight bag. We hugged goodbye, and I told her to call me if she needed anything.

My first stop was to check on Mike and the kids. I wanted to be there in time for them waking up, and had decided to treat them to bacon butties. I let myself in and took the five paper bags of steaming bacon rolls from Clarke's through the kitchen.

Lucas's eyes grew wide when he saw my haul. Mike was already up and making coffee. I sat down at the table. I needed to speak to Mike without the kids around.

'Lucas, why don't you go and wake your sisters up?'

He rolled his eyes but got up, reluctantly leaving his bacon sandwich.

Mike poured me a cup of coffee. I held it with two hands, inhaling the steam.

'How could he have done this, Izzy?' Mike stared off into space. 'He's my mate, for god's sake.' He took a sip and corrected himself. '*Was* my mate...'

'Rachel's distraught,' I said. 'Absolutely beside herself. I don't know how she'll ever get over this.'

Mike stroked his knuckle slowly across his jawline, his two-day stubble bristling. 'I've been thinking about Rachel.' He shook his head. 'And all of this, now with Phil... I don't know. Clearly, they weren't the friends we thought they were. Maybe we should be keeping her at arm's length, you know? Until we know what's what?'

'Why? You don't seriously think for one second that she knew what was going on, do you?' I regretted the words as soon as I'd said them.

'What do you mean, "what was going on"?' Mike's face was white. 'What are you talking about?'

My mouth opened, but no words came to me. Panic rose in my chest.

I was saved by Betsy, who came bounding into the room, impossibly energetic for someone who had just woken up. I mouthed, 'Nothing,' at Mike, just as my youngest niece draped her arms around my neck and planted a kiss on my cheek.

Breakfast was painfully awkward. Mike was doing his best to

be normal, so much so that he was trying too hard and giving a very over-the-top performance of holding it all together. Hannah was withdrawn, and although she kept laughing at her dad's jokes, it was clearly an exhausting effort.

I grew weary just from watching them all trying so hard, and my appetite disappeared. The bacon that had smelled so good was now cold and greasy in my mouth, and the bread was like cotton wool. It took all my energy to chew and swallow, chew and swallow.

Mike was taking the kids to the beach for the morning and I'd agreed to spend the afternoon with them. I headed back to chill for a few hours.

Puffin Cottage smelled like home. The sweetness of the honeysuckle followed me inside, where it combined with the earthiness of yesterday's log fire. I slumped into my favourite chair. I had only been away for twenty-four hours, but it seemed like an eternity.

I noticed a piece of paper by the front door that I must have stepped on when I came in. I went over and picked it up, examining the handwriting before I unfolded it. My name had been written in a spidery, elaborate script.

Dear Isabelle

I trust you are well. I intend to call in to see you, and I am writing this note in the event that you are not at home when I do.

I'll endeavour to keep this short. I love Puffin Cottage – it was my home, and a piece of my heart will always remain there. I want to see it go to an owner who appreciates it for what it is, rather than someone who wants to conduct 'renovations' and install a 'breakfast bar'. I want someone who will treasure my possessions.

I suspect that despite your initial intentions, you might be staying in Seahouses for longer than you imagined, perhaps even permanently. If you would like to make Puffin Cottage your home, I would be willing to sell it to you for the price of £50,000, on the condition that you would be living in it and will promise to keep the property true to its original character. I'm confident that it is worth considerably more on today's market, and that this would represent quite a bargain.

I hope this proposal is agreeable to you, and I look forward to being invited to continue our discussion over tea and cake.

Yours sincerely,

Mrs D Wheeler

I put the letter down, steadying myself on the back of the chair. Fifty thousand pounds? The cottage had to be worth five times that amount, surely. Her daughter would go nuts. I giggled at the prospect of seeing Sandra Wheeler, face even redder than usual, lose her wits when she found out what her mother had done.

And what timing – it was almost too good to be true. Did Mrs Wheeler know I had decided to stay, or was she trying to tempt me back with an offer I couldn't refuse?

Could I accept this proposal? Was this an old lady who possibly didn't understand the ramifications of what she was doing, or a true friend being very generous? Mrs Wheeler had always been so kind to me, and to Amy. Would it be wrong to take advantage of her kindness once more?

If I could buy a place to live for that amount, I'd still have enough savings left to start again. Probably enough to start my own business, doing something for myself for a change. But what would I do?

I looked around Puffin Cottage, admiring Mrs Wheeler's quirky taste and eclectic collections as if I was seeing them for the first time. Maybe – just maybe – I could be happy here.

I pulled on my running stuff, along with Amy's fleece top. I needed to clear my head, and a bracing run along the beach would give me the headspace to think. Inhaling deeply, I stretched out my back, looking above to the clear blue sky. I pulled my phone out my pocket and sent a message to Amy.

I'll make you proud, Ames. Promise xo

I sniffed back the instinct to cry and set off at a steady jog. The seafront was getting busier and the carpark was slowly filling up with day-trippers who were keen to take advantage of good weather on a Sunday.

As I approached Richard Pringle's house, I tucked my chin into the top of my collar. I tried to keep my head down, but couldn't resist glancing up at the house with its big windows like eyes staring out at the sea. Upstairs, a lone shadow moved behind a curtain.

The beach spread out in front of me like a freshly made bed, smoothed over by the tide. A blank canvas. My feet hit the sand with a series of satisfying thuds. Only once I turned around and saw the line that I'd made in the sand did I realise how far I had come.

My phone pinged with a message from Jake as I got out of the shower.

Phil is denying everything. DCI Bell still working on him. Rachel has an appointment to come in this afternoon. J

Why was he denying it? The evidence against him was overwhelming – their affair, not to mention the sabotage of the car. My gut lurched, thinking of Rachel having to go in to the police station, of what she would find out. How would she ever get over the betrayal, once it was laid bare in front of her? I just hoped she had something to tell the police, that there was some information she could give – some piece of the puzzle – that might help them charge Phil. I dried myself slowly, my mind occupied by thoughts of court rooms and juries and judges in white wigs.

I needed a distraction. I had agreed with Mike that the kids and I would go through some of Amy's things from the loft. She hadn't liked to throw things away, and I knew that there were all sorts of things gathering dust in boxes. Although Mike was convinced it was all crap, I'd begged him to let us look through and see if there was anything that the kids wanted to keep. We would make a start that afternoon while he was out.

Hannah helped me to haul down the first box and slide it into the spare room, leaving a grey streak of dust across the landing. Lucas reached in first, and pulled out a CD in a clear plastic box.

'What's this?' he asked, holding it up, genuinely baffled. I took it from him.

'"Summer '01",' I read on the label. 'Your mum made this. It had all her favourite songs on. She made a new one every year. This was while we were at Edinburgh.'

I held the disk carefully by the edges and ran a finger over the handwriting, as familiar as my own. I could remember Amy as she had been then. Bodyshop lip gloss that smelled like apricot. A shell necklace that she'd worn for years. Her sweet smile – she was always smiling. Her rule about never leaving the house without wearing earrings.

It seemed a shame to miss the good weather, so we got more boxes down from the loft and each carried one out to the garden.

There was a Discman in one of the boxes that miraculously still worked once we'd located a fresh pair of batteries, and we spent the whole afternoon taking turns to listen to songs while looking through Amy's things, sorting out hidden treasures from trash.

Amy had kept most of the toys we'd had as kids, and I experienced flashes of recognition as the kids found a Barbie, an art class clay vase, and a pirate hat Amy had once worn for fancy dress.

Most of the objects had a story behind them, and the kids were keen to hear where everything came from. They were hungry for details of the life their mum had lived before them. I dug deep, trying to remember as much as possible, feeding them with memories.

'What's this?' Betsy pulled a yellow plastic folder from her box.

I took it from her, turning it over. No label, and it was conspicuous by its newness. Everything else in these boxes had been packed away for years, and had the dust to show for it. This folder looked to have been put away far more recently. The edges were sealed with Sellotape. I fingered it, trying to gauge the contents. Just a few sheets of paper.

'It looks like paperwork,' I said. 'I'll pop it in the office.'

I climbed the stairs to Mike's office, thumbing the folder. Just a few pages, hidden among Amy's things and too new to be anything old. I tried to prise a corner open, but couldn't get my thumbnail under the tape. I scanned the office for something sharper and found some scissors in the desk drawer. I was about to cut the folder open when the front door opened downstairs.

'Hello!' Mike called out. I froze.

'Out here!' one of the kids called from the garden.

I stood very still, until I heard Mike's footsteps passing down the hall and into the kitchen. I tiptoed back downstairs, carrying the folder under my arm, and went into the front room where I'd left my things. I buried it at the bottom of my bag, carefully draping my jacket over the top so that it wouldn't be seen.

The sound of footsteps came back up the hall and Mike stuck his head around the door.

'There you are. Everything all right?'

'Just wanted to check my messages.' I held up my phone.

He nodded in the direction of the back garden. 'Find anything interesting?'

I smiled and shrugged. 'I've introduced your kids to CD technology, blown their minds with Game Boy, and even taught them how to play dominoes.'

Mike laughed. 'She never could get rid of stuff. I don't suppose you could clear it all up again before dinner?'

With the house returned to normal and the kids' curiosity sated, I left them to a Sunday night of homework and Chinese takeaway. I walked back to Puffin Cottage at a brisk trot, the folder burning under my arm.

I sliced the tape with a knife and sat down at the kitchen table to examine the contents of the folder.

It was only six pages. Six pages of Mike's credit card statements.

I shuddered, a chill running down my spine. I hadn't noticed any pages were missing when I searched the paperwork in his office, but I hadn't been looking closely enough to spot a detail like that. The dates ranged over a period of a few months last year. I scanned the first couple of pages, looking for large amounts that would tell me more about Mike's financial problems. Nothing jumped out. What had Amy seen here that caused her so much concern?

The phone rang, pulling away my attention. It was Rachel. She didn't bother with hellos.

'They were having an affair!'

I gasped, the wind knocked out of me.

'My best friend and my husband.' She sobbed. 'How could she do that to me?' Her cries were of pure anguish.

'Rachel, I'm so sorry—'

'And that's why he killed her.'

The word was a blow, a stabbing pain, the piercing agony of toothache. I shuddered.

I wanted to run to Rachel, to scoop her up and soothe her. 'Where are you?'

'I'm at your mum's. Upstairs.'

'I'll be right there.' I hesitated. 'And please, don't say anything to them. Not just yet.'

She sniffed a wordless goodbye and I was already shrugging on my coat, ready to run to her side.

Mum was out of bed and seemed to be back to normal – as normal as she ever was, which was worrying in the circumstances. How long would it last once she found out about Amy and Phil? She was doing a cleansing ritual on Rachel, wafting the smoke from a smouldering bowl towards her with a small feather fan. The air was thick with the scent of sage and rosemary. Rachel sat in a chair in the middle of the room with her eyes closed as Mum moved around her, humming deep in her throat.

'A smudging ceremony,' murmured Auntie Sue. 'Rids the

mind and body of negative energy.' She raised one eyebrow at me and went back to Good Housekeeping.

Rachel was shell-shocked, a fragile baby bird of her former self, and the burning herbs didn't seem to be doing much for her. She anxiously gnawed at the inside of her bottom lip, her mouth pinched into a tight line. Dark shadows under her eyes betraying the enormity of the weight on her shoulders. As soon as Mum was done, I pulled Rachel into the privacy of the kitchen, her hand trembling in mine.

'Did you know?' she said, immediately.

Rachel glared at me, waiting for an answer, anger burning brightly behind her sadness.

Tears pricked my eyes. 'I found out a couple of days ago. I swear, I had no idea before that.'

'I just don't know how...' She steadied herself. 'I don't understand how she could have done that to me.'

Rachel's pain was physical. It was contagious. I felt it transferring from her, down my arms and into my chest, into my body, my head. We kept to whispers – I didn't want Mum and Auntie Sue to have to confront this ugly truth until I'd had a chance to prepare them.

'I'm so sorry,' I said, between sobs. It was all I had. Amy wasn't there to explain herself.

'I've lost my best friend, and now I've lost my husband. What did I do to deserve this?' Rachel fell forward onto me, resting her cheek on my shoulder.

'Hey, hey...' I made soothing sounds, stroking a hand on her back. 'Whatever she did, whatever terrible mistake Amy made, I know that she loved you.'

'I thought she and I were like family...' She blew her nose.

'You *are* family,' I squeezed her hand. 'You were like a sister to Amy and you're the auntie to her kids. You're like another daughter to my mum...' I wiped away a tear. 'None of that is changing. We'll get through this together, I promise.'

She folded me into a tight hug and we stood like that, holding each other, making one another solid.

Chapter Sixteen

I took the sofa again. Rachel had offered to share the queen-sized bed in the guest room, but I was afraid of disturbing her privacy – she really looked like she needed a good night's sleep. I lay awake for hours, tossing and turning, trying to quieten my mind. It was impossible to switch off, and the harder I tried not to think about everything, the louder the thoughts became.

I was woken early by the sound of a magpie chattering in the garden. Already, my head was swimming, making it impossible to fall back to sleep. Just when the magpie finally stopped, I heard footsteps on the stairs.

'Are you awake?' Mum peeked her head into the living room.

'Yeah, I suppose.'

I shuffled up on the sofa, making room for her to sit beside me. She rested her hand on my leg.

'I knew you were awake in here,' she said. 'I could feel you, from upstairs. All that worry and pain you're carrying.'

I rolled my eyes. My mum, the mystic.

'I know you don't believe me, but I can help you to heal.'

I scoffed. 'What, like you healed yourself after Dad died?'

She shuffled uneasily on the sofa. 'Well, yes... like I healed myself.' She hesitated. 'It took me a long time, admittedly...

It was a process...' Mum nodded to herself, agreeing with the words she had selected.

'A process that took a year and a half, and that you abandoned your kids for?' They were words I'd spat at her many times before, during the blazing rows that had erupted whenever we had tried to rebuild our relationship, but this time I was controlled. Calm.

'Izzy, I have apologised a thousand times, and I'll be sorry until my last breath for what it did to you—'

'What *you* did to us,' I corrected her.

'What I did.' She nodded. 'The hurt I caused. But I had to, love. I wouldn't be here today if I hadn't gone then.'

She leaned in closer and put her hand up to my face. Her palm was warm on my cheek. 'Let me heal you.'

I closed my eyes in consent, which seemed easier than having this discussion again with Mum. I was too tired, too sad, and no longer had the energy to fight her.

Mum placed her hands on my head and started to hum quietly. At first, it felt good just to be touched, to let her have this intimacy. The humming became louder and more rhythmic, and soon it evolved into a muffled chanting of words that I didn't recognise. Each sound reverberated through me. I could feel her voice in my chest, in my stomach, all the way down to my feet.

The strange thing was that it did make me feel better. I grew lighter, like a weight was lifted, but heavier at the same time – the mass of my body was pressing down into the sofa, and I could quite easily have closed my eyes and fallen asleep right then. The thoughts that had been swimming around in my head, causing me to lose hours of sleep, were suddenly quiet, and my mind was still.

Mum sat back and I opened my eyes.

'How did you do that?'

She looked down at her hands. 'It's a long story,' she said, her eyes sad.

'Well in that case, you'd better put the kettle on.'

We hadn't known where exactly Mum had gone, that terrifying morning when we woke up and realised she was missing. All I knew was that a hole opened up in our lives, like those sink holes that appear in the earth overnight, swallowing entire homes into the bottomless black.

At some point, it had dawned on us that she had left Seahouses. That was a terrifying realisation for two girls who had believed their mother was simply hiding out somewhere nearby. By the time Auntie Sue swooped in to our rescue, we had realised that she was no longer in the country. The line crackled on her infrequent phone calls home, which would come at odd times of the day.

The police confirmed this when Auntie Sue reported her as a missing person. Mum, who hadn't been able to leave her bedroom for several weeks, had pulled herself together enough to not only leave the house, but get on an aeroplane. When they gave us the news, we were open-mouthed, lost for words. She didn't want to be found, they said. She was safe and well and wanted her family to be reassured of that. Auntie Sue didn't push things – presumably, she was as scared as we were that we'd be taken away, too.

'It all started with a book,' Mum said. 'About coping with grief. I don't even remember who had given it to me. After Edward died, so many people had words of advice, or love, or encouragement, but the only thing that made sense to me at the time was what I read in that book.

'I had so many questions for the man who had written those words. I simply had to find him. The only problem was he was in India, according to the book. This was in the days before the internet, before Facebook, before you could just look someone up online. Maybe I wasn't thinking straight, but I made up my mind – I had to go there.

'I sent away for a visa and when it came, I simply packed a bag and went to the airport. It was easy enough to buy a plane ticket. As soon as I was above the clouds and on my way, the pressure started to melt – the pressure that had been there like hands around my neck since the day your father died.

'After a couple of days of travelling, I finally arrived in a town that I had never heard of before, surrounded by other towns that I'd never heard of either. The whole journey was a blur, and the last leg had been on the back of a rickshaw. Yet all these years later, I can still recall in vivid detail the moment the doors of the ashram opened. I was welcomed by a stranger in flowing robes with long hair that smelled like coconut, and I wept with relief.

'Our days began with sunrise meditations, breathing exercises, and chanting, practices that nourished the body and soul. I saw myself growing stronger again, growing more aware of my power and my connection to the world, and gaining an understanding of the universe that was deeper than I could have imagined knowledge could be – I just had to work out what it all meant.

'I had private audiences with the guru whenever I could. I would take along my copy of his book, with passages highlighted, and he did his best to answer all my questions. He used to constantly tell me, "just give it time". "Enlightenment is not a lightbulb moment," he would say, "it is like making a fire by rubbing two sticks together. If you try hard enough, and you are patient, one day you will get a spark."'

'But I didn't have forever. I needed to get better and get home. Eventually I left. There was lots of talk about a spiritual retreat in Bali, and a new guy that everyone was following. I wanted to meet him, to see what answers he could give me.'

I held up a hand to stop her. 'What, wait – you went to Bali? You never said.' I'd been there several times, but I had no idea that Mum had ever visited.

Mum sighed and shrugged. 'You never gave me the chance to tell you.'

I waved her on to continue the story.

'Spiritual detox, energy cleanses, fasting and live-food diets, sweat lodges, liver cleanses, acupuncture, reiki, tantric chanting, goddess circles – I tried it all. Somewhere out there was the secret I was searching for. But the answer still didn't come.

'One day, I got chatting to another guest, an American woman. She had travelled the world and was quite the expert. The best she had come across was an indigenous tribe in Peru. This tribe had set up a retreat on their lands that allowed outsiders to come in and experience their ancient rituals – not cheap, but worth every penny. And not for the faint-hearted, she warned me. Well, I needed no more convincing. I left the next morning.'

I heard a creak from upstairs, either a bedframe or a floor-board. Rachel and Auntie Sue would be up soon, and I wanted Mum to finish the story.

'Getting from Indonesia to Peru was not an easy journey back then, and the cheap ticket involved several connections.

By that time, I had been living in ashrams, retreats and yoga institutes for quite a while and was used to the rhythm of life in a commune. I was as committed as ever, and very confident that finally, there in Peru, I would find the answer to the meaning of everything.

'But the retreat was like nothing I'd ever seen before. It was buried deep in the rainforest, and the accommodation was beyond basic. During the orientation tour – if you could call it that –we were told that the lodgings were designed to help guests connect more easily with nature, but the reality was they provided little protection from the constant rain and bugs. Men with painted faces patrolled the camp. One of their jobs was to catch snakes before they got too close to the guests.'

I shook my head, struggling to picture Mum turning up at an indigenous camp in the middle of the rainforest. The idea was surreal.

'I booked in for the two-week package. I'd asked about a discount on longer stays, but the young lady who showed me to the dormitory said that nobody stayed longer than that. The highlight of the retreat was to be the traditional ayahuasca ceremony – it's a ritual that involves drinking an ancient medicinal tea brewed from the leaves of rare rainforest plants. It helps to cleanse and purify the body and mind and induces visions. They offered all kinds of add-ons, including one that used treefrog venom rubbed onto the skin to help you detox. Finally, the night of the ayahuasca ceremony had arrived and I was ready. I dressed for the occasion in my all-white yogis and drank my tea quickly, eager for the visions to start.'

'Wait, Mum,' I said. 'You took drugs? In Peru?'

'Not *drugs*, Izzy. It's medicine, traditional ceremonial medicine. The tribe has been drinking that tea for thousands and thousands of years.'

Mum shook her head and continued. 'At first, nothing happened. I was sitting on the ground, and a kind assistant helped me to a chair. The other guests were enjoying their hallucinations, dancing around the fire and singing and laughing, touching their bodies as if they were aware of their skin for the first time. One woman took all her clothes off and nobody minded, least of all me.

'It had all been for nothing. I just sat there, watching the rest of them. After minutes that could just as easily have been hours, someone reached out and took my hand. I hadn't even noticed him, but a man had come to sit in the seat next to me. He could obviously see how upset I was. But there was something familiar about the hand... I looked up and there, right next to me in the middle of the jungle, was Edward.

'I was speechless. He was as real as... well, real. Alive. Your father,' she said, nodding. 'And he looked exactly as he had before we set off for a walk that day after Sunday lunch – wearing the same jumper and everything. I reached out and touched his face, and he smiled back at me.'

Mum started to get emotional but I urged her on, fighting back my own temptation to tears.

'You know how I knew he was real?'

I shook my head, unsure of where this was going.

'He said, "Anne, get a bloody grip and pull yourself together." We sat there, in that rainforest all those thousands of miles away, after all that soul-searching, and he said something that only your father would say. It's how I knew it was him,' she said, smiling.

'Wait... what?' I stammered. 'That was the end of the search? That was the big revelation?'

'That was just it: there was no revelation. No big secret, anyway. It just made me realise what I should have known all along – your dad was always with me. I went looking for him, but he was already there. I'd been looking for answers to questions that didn't exist. That was the fire I made with my two sticks.'

She pulled me in for a cuddle, and I allowed myself the indulgence of snuggling under her arm – something I hadn't done in years.

'The people we love don't leave us, Izzy. They're part of us, and we keep them alive. It's like Amy. She is here with us, right now. I see her in the kids, in you. In Rachel, too. There's no big answer, no eternal truth beyond that.' She sighed. 'Of course, by the time I'd realised this, I had pushed you girls away. You were so angry with me.'

Mum shuddered at the memory and I winced.

'I know all the spirituality stuff irritates you, because it reminds you of why I left. But it's also why I was able to finally come home. It became part of my life, and I need it today as much as I did then – as much as you need to drink water.'

Perhaps I could be better at allowing Mum her hippy indulgencies. It certainly did seem to improve her state of mind.

'So if Amy's here, what would she say to us?' I asked.

Mum stroked my hair. 'I think she'd tell us we're doing well,' she said thoughtfully. 'She would tell us we're doing a good job with the kids, I'm sure.' Mum looked up at the ceiling. 'And she would tell us that she's with Dad now. She...'

I waited for her to continue, but she had stopped short. Like there was something had been going to say, but thought better of. Her gaze stayed on the ceiling, fixed to some spot only she could see.

'What else would Amy say, Mum?' I sat up and looked at her. Her lip was trembling.

'I don't know... I don't understand...' She mumbled.

'What is it, Mum?' I tried to hide the urgency in my voice. 'What do you know? What aren't you telling me?'

'I just feel like...'

A pause. She turned to me.

'I feel like Amy has been trying to tell me something. These past few days.'

My heart started to hammer at the mention of Amy's name, and when I spoke again, my voice was thin. 'What has she been trying to tell you?'

Mum shook her head. Her eyes were wide and her lips pressed together in a tight line. 'She says we're wrong, Izzy. We got it wrong.'

Chapter Seventeen

I couldn't stop turning Mum's words over in my mind. Had she really connected with Amy, or had she finally lost it? I had no doubt that she believed what she'd told me. The question was how much consideration I or any other sane person should give to what she had said. Maybe it was time to confront the very real concerns I had about my mother's mental health. Still, I couldn't shake my unease. I sent Amy a text.

Did we get it wrong? Did we make a mistake?

The phone rang in my hand, making me jump. I'd been on edge since last night when the police deadline for charging Phil came and went. It was Jake.

'It's complicated, but they're keeping him in for questioning for another twenty-four hours. This does happen sometimes with serious offences. It means they believe they have their man, but maybe don't have enough evidence to get it over the finishing line.'

'Thanks,' I said. I was so weary. 'Keep me posted.'

I couldn't see what further evidence they could they possibly need, beyond the proof of the affair and the fact that Phil had tinkered with her car.

Mum's words were playing on repeat in my mind. What

could we have got wrong? I needed to keep myself busy and distracted for another twenty-four hours.

Thankfully, my shipment was arriving from Hong Kong. It had been so long since I'd seen my possessions and I was eager to be reunited with my collection of shoes and bags. Thierry and Mathilde had coordinated the packing under Adam's direction after I'd decided I'd be staying for a few months, and I was curious to see what they considered as essential personal items. Now that I knew I'd be staying here indefinitely, I'd have to organize for the rest to be sent.

I had enlisted Rachel's help, figuring she could also benefit from the distraction, and Auntie Sue and Mum had promised to come along later to pitch in.

'You're going to need a bigger wardrobe,' Rachel said, pointing to the pile of clothes on the bed. The small closet was already jammed full.

Mathilde had also packed my jade Qing dynasty jewellery box and my prized pair of antique foo dogs – god knows what they had added to the air freight costs. I held one of the foo dogs, stroking the smooth edges of the ancient stone. It was a small piece of home, and I was beginning to imagine how Puffin Cottage might look with my personal touch.

We carried on unpacking, and each box revealed some new treasure. I squealed with delight as I came across my favourite Saint Laurent cowboy boots and a limited-edition silver Balenciaga cross-body bag.

Rachel unwrapped a vintage Louis Vuitton pochette. 'Is this real?' she raised an eyebrow at me.

I gulped. There were handbags in there that cost more than Rachel must earn in a month. More than her car was worth, most likely. Suddenly they seemed very out of place here, and not at all well-suited to my Seahouses lifestyle.

Auntie Sue arrived just before lunch, bringing sandwiches and scotch pies which she arranged on the kitchen table. Mum followed her in.

'These are beautiful,' Mum said, picking up one of the foo dogs from the windowsill. 'They're Buddhist guard-lions – they offer protection. But they don't belong here...'

She looked around the room carefully, considering several spots before placing the dogs on the floor either side of the living room door.

'There,' she said, looking pleased with herself. 'They're looking outward – it's excellent feng shui. The male goes on the right, and the female goes on the left. Can you feel that?'

The three of us exchanged puzzled glances.

'The energy!' Mum said, excitedly, 'the energy in the room just changed!' She looked expectantly for a response from us, and when she got nothing, shook her head disappointedly. 'Maybe it's just me...'

'No,' said Rachel, after a beat. 'I feel it too. The energy. It feels better now.'

'Me too,' I said. I said it because I didn't want Mum to feel bad, but something really had shifted in my mood – I suddenly felt lighter.

Her face lit up. 'Actually,' she said, with a new sparkle in her eyes, 'we can make it even better.'

Twenty minutes later, the four of us looked breathlessly around the room, admiring our work. Mum had convinced me to flip the layout around, repositioning the furniture and moving a mirror from the landing to the wall opposite the fireplace. The living room now looked bigger, and although I wasn't convinced by her insistence that the feng shui would balance the energy in my life and bring me good fortune, I had to admit that the space felt better somehow.

We moved upstairs and did some more rearranging in the bedroom and bathroom, with Mum giving me advice on colours and fabrics that would enhance and bring harmony to the rooms. I was visualising where I was going to position my Chinese antiques when they eventually arrived, and I could already imagine how the cottage interior would look with a new colour scheme. On a whim, I swapped the heavy green velvet curtains from the bedroom with the grey linen drapes that had been hanging in the living room, which reflected the tones of my sea view and made the window look instantly bigger. We repositioned the bed to face it, so that the sea would be the first thing I would see in the morning. I couldn't wait to wake up in it the next day.

'You've got a flair for this, you know,' Mum said with a smile. 'And the energy is spot-on.'

But as great as the feng shui was, I had another important opinion to canvass.

Diana Wheeler was punctual, giving me just enough time to arrange the cake I'd bought from Clarke's onto a blue glass cake stand. Her eyes were wide as she surveyed the room.

'Do you like it?' I crossed my fingers behind my back, praying for her approval.

'My dear,' she said, looping her hand onto my arm. 'It's utterly charming, and I insist on the full tour.' She glanced at the teapot. 'But take that tea out of there, for heaven's sake – it'll be stewed.'

After a full exploration of the cottage, complete with more

museum-length stories about her favourite items and the interesting tales of their provenance, we sat down for tea and cake. Mrs Wheeler asked me to pass her bag, which she reached into and retrieved a thin leather folder. She laid out its contents on the table.

'Now, onto our business for the day - the sale of Puffin Cottage. My offer still stands, if you are interested, and my terms are quite simple. All I ask is that you care for the property and maintain its original character, as much as that is possible. Besides,' she said with a wink, 'it's not like I'm going to be around forever to enforce it.'

I glanced down at the papers – it was the deeds to Puffin Cottage, and a transfer document with spaces for two signatures. She was absolutely serious.

'Mrs Wheeler, I am so grateful – I-I'm humbled, truly. You've always been so kind to me, and my sister, b-but shouldn't we discuss this first?' I was stuttering.

'My dear girl,' she said, in the same voice she'd used when I was fifteen years old. 'We are discussing it now. I have made my position abundantly clear, but if you have any questions or concerns, now is the time to raise them.'

'I guess I'm just worried...' How to put this? 'I am concerned... that your offer is too generous. And that it wouldn't be fair on your daughter.'

'Ha!' Mrs Wheeler laughed. 'You're worried she will come after you!' She leaned towards me, wagging a finger accusingly. 'You're afraid that she'll say you took advantage of an old lady who had lost her marbles.'

She sat back and took a sip of tea, a smirk dancing on her lips. 'My daughter will be well taken care of when I'm gone, don't worry about that. As for anyone who thinks I'm no longer of sound mind, I'm quite prepared to have that debate with them in person. After all, I'm not going anywhere just yet.' She cut herself another slice of cake.

I clasped my hands together, wondering what to do. It could all end up badly, but what did I have to lose? If Sandra Wheeler had any objections, she could take them up with her mother. And it was such a beautiful house. If losing Amy had taught me anything, it was that life is short. From now on, I was determined to be happy.

'OK,' I said, 'if you are absolutely sure. But I want to add one clause in the contract: if you change your mind at any point, I will sell it back to you at the same price. That seems fair to me.'

'It's a deal!' she laughed.

'And one final thing. We must get a lawyer to look at this.'

She rolled her eyes.

'Don't worry,' I said, 'I know just the man.'

That evening, I microwaved some of Auntie Sue's sausage casserole from the freezer and set the table for one, complete with a pretty tablecloth, fresh flowers, and candles. Rachel had declined my invitation, saying she needed some time on her own, which I understood. I just prayed she believed that I hadn't known about the affair. Even though we had only known each other for a short time, we had been through so much together. I was angry that our friendship was now at risk because of what Amy had done.

I'd had an online order of wine delivered, so I opened a bottle of Tignanello and poured myself a large glass. My plan was to run a hot bath and spend the rest of the evening winding down in the bubbles with my Kindle. I had offered to do dinner with the kids tomorrow while Mike had to work late, and I wanted to make the most of my free night.

I'd been thinking about what I would do, if I was to start my own business. The break from work had helped me realise that I wanted to do something creative. Something that I could be good at, that I was passionate about. Something that I could do from home, and still be there for the kids, and Mum and Auntie Sue. Planning the redecoration of Puffin Cottage had given me an idea – I'd always loved interior design, but had never considered it seriously as a career option. An idea began to form in my mind.

The phone rang, snapping me out of my daydream. It was DCI Bell. I braced myself.

'I'm calling to let you know that we've charged Philip Turner with your sister's murder. Again, I just want to say how sorry I am for your loss.'

I held my breath.

'Miss Morton? Are you there?'

'Yes,' I said, the word coming out as a high-pitched choking sound. 'I'll let the rest of the family know.'

'I've already spoken to your brother-in-law.' She sounded weary. 'It might be good for the two of you to tell Mrs Sanders' children sooner rather than later. Word spreads fast around here.'

I thought again of Mum's words. Of the message she'd claimed Amy had given her.

'Can I just ask... Are you sure he did it?'

'We don't take these matters lightly, as I'm sure you can imagine. Not only had Mrs Sanders and Mr Turner been in a relationship, but he had access to her car before the accident. And during a search of his business premises, officers recovered medication that fits with what was found in Mrs Sanders's blood samples. I don't often say this, Isabelle, but this is pretty watertight.'

We said our goodbyes and I slumped down to the kitchen floor.

Chapter Eighteen

This is what grief is: it's an elephant, sitting on your chest. The weight presses down, threatening to crush you. You can't breathe properly, it is impossible to take a full breath, and so you panic. It's having your limbs turn to lead. Just walking is exhausting, carrying the burden of all that extra weight. It is too much to stand, so you try to lie. The sheer weight of your own body, now strange to you, pushing down, pulling down.

It is back-breakingly tiring. You ache to sleep, every bone and sinew craving rest, your eyes stinging to close. But sleep does not come. It is growing ever wearier, ever more tired, and still being unable to sleep, until finally you crash, falling in to sweet, sweet slumber. It is wanting to sleep forever and ever, until you are cruelly crashed out of it with an electric shock, a bucket of ice water over the head, the full horror returning as you sit bolt upright in the dark, gasping for air and panting to catch your breath, drenched in cold sweat.

Grief is a black shadow in every corner of every room that never goes away, even when you shine a light on it. The shadow follows you outside, even on the happiest, sunniest days. You can almost forget it for a second, give it the slip, but it is right there again, still following you, always present, and you realise that you weren't even close to escaping it.

It is knowing you have nothing, of seeing all you have and knowing it is worthless, of being ready to give everything up anyway, disbelieving everything you thought you knew, questioning what it was all for, why are we here, what is the point? It is your loudest scream, but you don't make a sound. It is being hungry but having no appetite, eating without tasting, never satisfied and never satiated. It is being thirsty but being unable to swallow. It is hour by hour, day by day, watching the big hand on a clock inch painfully by, knowing it will never end.

Grief is survival, maintenance, keeping the wheels turning, doing the bare minimum. It is sorry for your loss, time is a great healer, stay strong, rest in peace, in sympathy, condolences, pity. It is people avoiding you lest the sadness be contagious, it is avoiding other people because you don't want to see that life goes on, because how can they not see that sometimes, it doesn't? It is moving on, working through it, getting past it, learning to live with it, and then having the pain come back suddenly in a searing shock that you never saw coming, and it is even worse than you could have imagined, let alone remembered. It is doing it all again, every hour just like the last, never getting easier.

It's losing the person you loved above all others without knowing it until too late, your lifeboat, your anchor, your lighthouse. It's learning what you had only after it's gone. It's the torment of being cast out onto a dark and unforgiving sea, tossed about on high waves, alone except for the searing agony of loss. The anguish of one Salt Sister who has lost her other.

We sat the kids down to explain what had happened and tried to give them some idea of what to expect. Mike had called and asked me to be there when he broke the news, saying he didn't feel strong enough to do it alone. We could probably shield them from most of the proceedings, especially when it came to the trial, but DCI Bell was right – this was a tight-knit community and murders rarely happened. It would be the talk of the entire county.

Mike had wanted to take the lead in explaining everything to the children, and I was glad to let him. I still could not quite put together the right words to make sense of the situation. Mum and Auntie Sue had also come over, so that we could put on a united front and remind the kids just how much of a support network they had.

I had suggested that Rachel came too, but Mike wasn't keen. It was unfair of him to cut her off because of what her husband had done, but with emotions running so high and the pain so fresh and raw, perhaps some breathing space wasn't such a bad idea.

The police had warned Rachel to expect media interest, so she packed a bag and went to stay at her mum's in Berwick for a few days. We'd promised to keep in touch and keep each other posted on developments. I hoped she and Mike could make up, in time.

Amy was right: Mike was a good dad. He had immediately cancelled all his work commitments so that he could be there for the children. He seemed to know exactly how to pitch this, striking just the right tone in his child-friendly assessment of what was likely to happen now. He was so reassuring that even I was convinced everything would work out.

Still, just knowing that there was now a charge sheet made

the murder feel very real. It was one thing to lose someone in an accident, but quite another to have them deliberately taken from you. I could feel an anger creeping in whenever I thought about how Amy had died, and I wanted to protect my memories of her, to insulate her life from her death. Most importantly, I wanted to shield the kids from that.

Betsy was clamped to my side as usual and sucking her thumb. I kissed the top of her head, which still smelled fresh from yesterday's bath, and admired the thick fringe of her eyelashes. She was listening intently to her dad.

Lucas was sandwiched between Mum and Auntie Sue, his eyebrows knitted together in a worried frown. He looked permanently anxious these days, only relaxing when he was cooking and could lose his thoughts in the dish in front of him. I made a mental note to get him working on some new recipes in the coming week.

I explored Hannah's face for any sign of emotion, anything to tell me that she was listening, but she was expressionless and unflinching. Her mouth was set into a tight line and she had locked her gaze onto a point on the floor. Only the quick rise and fall of her chest gave anything away. When Mike started to explain that Phil was denying the charge, and that meant the case would go to court, Hannah fled the kitchen. We all listened to the patter of her footsteps running up the stairs, then her bedroom door slamming behind her. Auntie Sue started to rise from her seat to follow her.

'Leave her,' said Mike, pinching the top of his nose between his thumb and forefinger. 'She just needs some space.'

We sat like that in silence, each of us digesting the news, giving each other time for it to sink in.

'Will Uncle Phil go to prison?' Lucas eventually asked.

'Yes,' said Mike. I went to interject, but he got there first. '*If* he did it.'

'And it's up to the *jury* to decide?' Betsy explored the sound of this new, foreign word.

'Yes,' said Mike. 'The jury is a group of normal people who listen to all of the evidence, all the facts from the police, and then they decide if someone is guilty or not.'

Betsy considered this for a moment. 'But why did he do it? Why did he want to hurt Mummy on purpose?'

I looked away, leaving Mike to answer.

'We don't know, love. We might never know.'

'What if the jury decide he didn't do it?' Lucas looked from me to Mike and back again. 'What if they think it was someone else?'

'Let's just take this one step at a time, eh pal?' Mike ruffled Lucas's hair. It was getting so long that he had to keep flicking it out of his face. I wondered when he'd last had it cut.

'Anyway, that's not for us to worry about just yet,' said Auntie Sue. 'Who fancies a walk down to the church yard?'

It seemed a fitting way to focus our attention back on Amy and get the kids out of the house. I was ready for a change of scene and some fresh air, and it was a beautiful evening for a stroll. Hannah didn't put up an argument when she was called down from her room, but stayed silent and stuck at the back of the group with Mum and Auntie Sue while the younger ones raced ahead.

Mike was quiet. It had been a tough few days, but he was holding it together so well. How had I got him so completely wrong? I resolved to be a better sister-in-law from now on.

The shock of Phil's arrest was already starting to subside, like a punch to the arm, leaving only a dull ache where there had once been searing hot pain. I could picture him in his blue overalls, working in the garage, the way he had been while I'd watched from across the street, and even the thought of him made my anger start to rise.

I took a deep breath and pushed the image away. I didn't want to think of him, to have him invade my thoughts and dreams of Amy. I wanted to keep my mind and my memories pure, leaving only my sister, untainted, preserved. My beautiful, kind, smart sister. The other half of me.

I felt her at that moment, as if she was walking with us. I even glanced around to check that she hadn't stopped back along the path. It was fleeting, as tangible as a wisp of cloud and little more than the whisper of a songbird, but her presence was unmistakable. I smiled up at the sky and sensed Amy smile back at me.

The next morning, I set off for Alnwick. I was already at the end of the street when I remembered that the Mini I was driving belonged to Phil. The thought of him caught me off-guard. I sat there with trembling hands, gripping the wheel as a new hatred rippled through my body. I tried to shake it off. Only when a car came up behind, beeping at me for blocking the narrow lane, was I able to slowly pull onto the main road.

Diana Wheeler was ready by the time I got to her house, even though I was five minutes early. I hadn't even knocked on the door when she appeared in a dress, boots and felt hat, looking like quite the country lady. I went to open the car door for her and she batted my hand away.

'No need for that, Isabelle, I'm quite capable.'

She rolled her eyes as she climbed in and I suppressed a giggle.

Jake's assistant welcomed us into his office. She had already prepared tea, the tray on the desk heavy with an old-fashioned silver set, china cups and biscuits. I'd called ahead, explaining the special proposition that Mrs Wheeler had made and fore-warning Jake about her unique approach to... well, everything. He had assured me that all walks of life passed through his office, and it would take a true eccentric to surpass the quirks he'd seen. He had also promised to give her the VIP treatment he usually reserved for judges on the county circuit.

He breezed into his office, dapper in a three-piece tweed suit. As he flashed me a broad smile, a familiar knot twisted in my stomach. I cast my gaze down and willed myself to stop blushing.

'You must be Mrs Wheeler. What a joy to finally meet you, I've heard so many wonderful things.' Jake smiled warmly as he shook her hand. Mrs Wheeler didn't even try to hide her pleasure.

Jake poured tea and his assistant brought in a plate of home-made shortbread. He seemed in no rush to get down to business.

'Now, I know you don't have all day, dear,' Mrs Wheeler addressed Jake. 'I already had my solicitor draw up a draft contract of sale, I have completed the particulars, and here are the deeds to the property which Miss Morton intends to purchase from me' – she smiled at me – '*if* that remains her intention. I think you'll find everything is covered, so perhaps you would be so kind as to give this a once-over and check it is legally sound?'

Jake took the paper from her and quickly read it, his lips moving silently to the words. 'Well, Mrs Wheeler, you seem to have done my work for me.' He looked at her over the tops of the glasses. 'I take it you have some background in the legal profession?'

'Heavens, that would be quite a stretch!' Mrs Wheeler beamed. 'Nothing beyond a passion for detective fiction.'

Jake's face lit up, and I had to interrupt before this turned into a day-long tea-party Agatha Christie convention.

'My main concern...' They both looked at me, clearly having forgotten I was still there. 'My main concern is that Mrs Wheeler has offered me the property at a very good price, well below the true value—'

Mrs Wheeler raised a hand to cut me off and turned to Jake.

'Isabelle wants to make sure that I am in my right mind.' She placed her hand over mine and gripped it with a surprising strength. 'I have always been incredibly fond of Isabelle and her sister, Amy. Besides, Isabelle loves Puffin Cottage and has promised to preserve it. Unlike my daughter Sandra, who wishes to install an *en suite*.' She shuddered. 'Or worse, knock it down and start again.'

Jake shrugged at me. 'I see no issue with this. I'm confident that Mrs Wheeler knows exactly what she is doing and is more than capable of making such a decision. If you could provide your solicitor's details, we can arrange the payment and get these transferred.' He waved the deeds to Puffin Cottage in his hand.

'Wonderful news!' Mrs Wheeler clapped her hands, beaming at me.

Jake's assistant brought in a fresh pot of tea.

'I feel like we should be drinking champagne!' I was giddy with excitement – this was really happening. I would be the new owner of the most beautiful cottage in Seahouses.

'Not until you've driven me home, young lady.' Mrs Wheeler

gave me a sideways glance as she sipped from her cup.

'So, Isabelle – any plans now that you're going to be staying in Seahouses for the foreseeable future?' Jake caught himself, his eyes widening. 'I mean, er, work-wise? I think you mentioned that you're in the financial industry?' His cheeks reddened and my stomach flipped.

'Actually, I have been thinking.' I gazed down at my tea cup. 'I'd really like to do something new, something different. I want to start my own business.' I took a deep breath, faking confidence with a tight smile. 'I'm going to try my hand at interior design.'

'That's a wonderful idea!' Mrs Wheeler clasped her hands together. 'Isabelle here has such a good eye for design, really, Mr Ridley, you *must* visit Puffin Cottage and see what she's done with the place.'

Jake caught my eye and we exchanged shy smiles.

'Yes, I must visit sometime.' The colour rose in his cheeks.

I didn't want to share too much with Jake and Mrs Wheeler just yet, but I had been thinking about how to make Izzy Morton Interiors a success. I knew from corporate life that a brand needed to have something unique if it was going to stand out, and I had just the idea – something that no other designer could offer.

I was also thinking of asking Rachel to go into business with me. I'd need all the help I could get if I was to get a fledging business off the ground, and it would be helpful to have someone I trusted in a back-office role.

Small towns have long memories, and I knew it would be hard for Rachel to go back to her life as it was – working at the hospital, where everyone had known Amy. It was a mercy mission, and I didn't know how much use she would be, but I felt determined to offer my sister's best friend a fresh start, if she wanted it.

Mrs Wheeler gasped, which made me jump. She grabbed my hand with a surprisingly firm grip.

'I have the perfect opportunity to get you started! My daughter, she might employ you!' She nodded to herself and picked up her tea. 'Yes, I'll organise an introduction as soon as possible. Strike while the iron is hot, Isabelle!'

'Your daughter?' I thumbed the rim of my teacup. 'Sandra?'

'No, not Sandra,' she said, as if I'd asked a stupid question. 'My *other* daughter. Jennifer.'

I wracked my brain. Jennifer... Nothing came to mind.

'Jennifer Wheeler?' said Jake. 'The owner of The Stables?'

'The one and same,' Mrs Wheeler said with a smug grin.

'The Stables is a boutique hotel,' Jake explained for my benefit. 'One of the most well-known hotels in the county – in fact, I believe it has won a number of awards?'

'Indeed it has! It is Alnwick's only luxury hotel, and Jennifer is planning a refurbishment this year. Your timing could not be better, dear.'

I gulped. It was one thing to enjoy decorating your own place and secretly dream of becoming an interior designer, but quite another to take on a hotel refurbishment. That sounded like the sort of project you worked your way up to, not something for novices. Why had I said anything at all? My mouth went dry as I tried to think of a way out.

'You could at least meet with her,' Mrs Wheeler said, as if reading my thoughts. 'Talk to her, see if there's some way for you to get involved.'

She spoke so softly and looked at me so kindly with those sparkling blue eyes, I couldn't say no.

When we arrived at Mrs Wheeler's, we had a back-and-forth as Mrs Wheeler attempted to give me Jennifer's number. She didn't know how to send a contact from her phone, and looking at her ancient handset, I wasn't sure I would know how to, either. In the end she went into her house and wrote Jennifer's number down for me. I promised to call Jennifer as soon as I could.

As soon as I felt brave enough, more like.

Once my mind was made up about leaving the bank, it made sense to make it official. Emailing my resignation letter felt like a weight had been lifted from my shoulders, and I found myself hoping that Annabelle would be happy in my big office. I sent a message to the woman who was subletting my apartment to let her know it was now available long-term. Tying up the loose ends of my old life was oddly satisfying.

That afternoon, I called a store in Newcastle that bought and resold designer handbags. I listed the bags I wanted to get rid of, and the girl on the phone sounded disbelieving that I had such a collection. Who knows, maybe they were used to calls from luxury-goods fantasists? She reminded me several times that they only dealt in genuine products and would thoroughly inspect all items for authenticity.

Despite her scepticism, she was interested, and told me that if the bags were judged to be of good quality, they could offer me as much as fifteen thousand pounds. I had already squirreled away a couple of my favourites, plus some to gift Rachel, and the girls, once they were old enough. As for the rest of the collection, I was happy to free up the closet space and boost my bank account. If I was going to even consider taking on a hotel refurbishment as the first project in my new venture, I'd need all the cash I could get my hands on.

My final call for the afternoon was to Jennifer Wheeler. I drank a glass of wine to settle my nerves, looking in the mirror and telling myself out loud that I could do this. It wasn't very convincing.

Jennifer sounded just like her mother, with that booming, no-nonsense voice. Thankfully, Mrs Wheeler had called ahead and briefed her, so Jennifer cut right to the chase. She was all for supporting local businesses, she said, and would much rather help a new firm get off the ground than spend her money with an established agency who blew half of it on overheads and outsourced all the work anyway.

So this was it – she was giving me a chance. She would email me a brief, with details of the rooms that were to be renovated, and I would be invited to pitch to her and the hotel manager. All I had to do was to prepare mood boards, propose new design concepts, and provide cost estimates. It sounded like a lot of work, but I hastily agreed, grateful to have this opportunity.

I poured another glass of wine and started flicking through Pinterest, jotting down notes as inspiration came to me. I lit a scented candle and dreamily thought back to some of the hotels I'd stayed in, wracking my brains for what had made them feel special. Once I started thinking about it, the ideas came quickly. A project of this size would take a lot of planning – I would have to assemble a team sooner rather than later.

I opened the cupboard next to the fireplace in search of another notepad. On the top of the pile was the yellow plastic folder of Mike's credit card statements that we'd found amongst Amy's things. I'd tossed it in here on Sunday when I got home and completely forgotten about it after Rachel's phone call.

Perhaps I'd missed something the first time around. I slid

the papers out and took a closer look. There was nothing on the first two pages but on the third page, one of the transactions was underlined in black pen. I flicked through the rest – there were a dozen lines, all highlighting transactions from 'The Highwayman Inn, Alnwick'. The print blurred as the pages began to tremble in my hands.

Chapter Nineteen

Was I reading this right? I checked the details again: Mike's credit card statements, or at least certain pages from them, with hotel transactions highlighted. All hidden away in a sealed file. I tried to think of a simple explanation, but nothing came to mind.

I noted several of the dates on my phone, pulled my shoes on and ran out of the door. It was raining lightly, but I didn't go back for my umbrella.

At Amy's, I let myself in. Mike called out from the kitchen.

'Izzy! We weren't expecting to see you. I hope you'll stay for dinner.' He wiped a hand on his apron, nodding towards the stove. 'There's certainly enough for one more.'

Lucas was cooking Amy's signature sausage casserole, which contained surprisingly few sausages and a whole lot of other ingredients, which he started to reel off to me with great enthusiasm.

'Sounds wonderful – can't wait to try it,' I interrupted him. 'Let me just go and see what the girls are up to.'

I made my way upstairs to Betsy's bedroom.

'Knock knock!' I called out, before sticking my head around the door.

Hannah was styling Betsy's hair in French plaits.

'Auntie Izzy – look at my hair!' Betsy cried in delight. 'This is how Mummy used to do it.'

Hannah grimaced, then looked up at me with a brave smile and a shrug of her shoulders.

'Looks awesome, guys. Mummy would be very proud of you both. Now, I've just got to check next week's activities on the calendar. See you downstairs in a second.'

I paused on the landing, listening to check that Mike was occupied with Lucas in the kitchen, before quietly slipping in to the office. I logged on to the computer, opening the calendar and pulling up the list of dates from the credit card statements on my phone. I scrolled back through several months until I arrived at the first date on my list.

The entries for that day showed that Betsy had football and Lucas had computer club. Mike was marked in grey – I clicked on his name. It said 'London – overnight'. My hands were shaking. I took a deep, slow breath.

I scrolled further back, looking for the next date from the statements. Mike was listed as being overnight in Dublin. I double-checked the date on my phone, just to make sure. I continued, checking through half a dozen dates, and each one listed Mike as having an overnight trip. None of them mentioned anything about Alnwick.

My breath was shallow. I was starting to pant as the panic was rising in my throat. A dark cloud was beginning to gather around the edges of my vision, and I felt the room slowly start to spin around my chair. I placed a palm on the desk to steady myself.

Had Amy figured out that Mike wasn't where he said he was? Had she gathered up proof and hidden it away for one of us to find, in case something happened to her?

'Are you all right?'

I gave an involuntary gasp, my fingers gripping the desk. I hadn't even heard Mike coming up the stairs. My pulse quickened.

'Just wanted to let you know that dinner's ready...' He trailed off. 'What are you doing?' He stared at me. 'Are you OK? You look like you've seen a ghost.'

All the calendar windows were still open on the screen in front of me, seven little boxes of proof that Mike had lied, and he was standing just on the other side of the monitor. I gave him a weak smile and slowly moved the mouse to start closing them. It made a loud click every time.

'What are you doing?' he asked again.

I wished I could look nonchalant and play it cool, but the heat was rising in my cheeks and the back of my neck burned.

'Just had to check something on the calendar,' I said, in as breezy a way as I could manage. Fake breezy. Trying-too-hard breezy. Mike eyed me suspiciously.

'Don't you have it all on your phone?' He took another step towards me, arms folded across his chest.

'I tried to add it, but I couldn't get it to sync. It's fine, I'm done here.'

I closed the last calendar window and rolled the mouse to bring the view back on to the current month.

'Let me see, maybe I can fix it.'

Mike reached out for my phone. The list of underlined dates from his credit card statements was still open and would be the first thing he would see.

I tried to grab it before he could get to it, my hand moving towards his, but I was too late – he picked it up and scrutinised the screen. My heart pounded in my chest.

Mike's face melted into a soft smile.

'Such a great photo,' he said, holding up the phone.

I'd changed my lock screen to an old picture of me and Amy.

He passed the phone back to me. 'Let's take a look after dinner,' he said.

I exhaled slowly. I hadn't even realised I'd been holding my breath.

Skylarks danced in the dusk sky above me. My legs were heavy, like they weren't properly connected to my body, and the walk home took twice as long as usual. I wished I could move faster. Back at Puffin Cottage, my key clattered in the lock like chattering teeth. I shivered as I bolted the door behind me, shutting out the world for the night.

As I poured myself a glass of wine, I kept running over the possibilities. Had Amy known that Mike was having an affair too? Had she run into Phil's arms when she'd found out that Mike was cheating on her? Maybe they'd had some kind of agreement – an open marriage?

Or perhaps Mike hadn't been unfaithful – maybe he had just needed a night away from home once in a while? I could understand the appeal of escaping from time to time.

But who had he been with in Newcastle last Saturday? It was definitely a woman, but I hadn't seen her face. I tried to remember the scene from the street that day, trying to recall the details, but the whole thing had happened in a matter of seconds. With everything that had happened since, I hadn't asked Mike, and Hannah hadn't brought it up again.

Still, there was no question that the folder of his credit card statements had been placed in that box in the attic quite deliberately, and I had to assume that it was Amy who'd put it there. It followed, then, that the lines marked the dates when she had been suspicious of Mike.

I ached for my sister in that moment. Not this Amy, who had been cheating on her husband, who had caught him out in a web of lies – Amy from before. From before I left, before Mike. The Amy from the time when all we'd had was each other. I focused on that girl, and the girl I'd been back then. I needed to find out the truth for her. For both of them. I sent Amy a message.

Did you find out about Mike? Did you know he was having an affair?

Adam had tried to call me. My finger hovered over the button to call him back – how badly I wanted to cry on his shoulder. But I needed to focus. I'd phone him once I was done.

The wine was making me fuzzy and I needed to be sharper. I took a bottle of vodka from the freezer and poured a small glass, downing it in one icy kick.

The Highwayman Inn in Alnwick didn't ring any bells, so I googled it.

There were some mentions on hotel review sites which initially sounded promising, and articles about historical sites of the same name, but none of them were local. Nothing showed up when I searched the online maps, at least not in Alnwick. I tried 'High-way', 'High Way', 'High Way Man'. Still nothing. The closest Highwayman Inn was in Durham, more than fifty miles away. In desperation, I called them, asking if they had another hotel in Alnwick – the receptionist was bemused by my question and politely told me that she couldn't help. Had Amy reached the same dead end?

I wished again that I had her phone – surely there would be some record, somewhere on it, of her having gone through this same search. Would she have shared her suspicions with someone? Who could she have confided in? She couldn't talk to her best friend, of course. Perhaps because she'd been involved with Phil, she'd felt like she couldn't speak to anyone about Mike. I kept circling back to my first question – had she strayed first, or had she turned to Phil for comfort when she discovered what Mike was doing? My heart ached for Amy – as mad as I was, I felt so sad that she hadn't had anyone to talk to. Not even me.

The timing was weird, too. The most recent page of the credit card statements was from October last year, just before Amy had changed her will. Nothing after that month. I went to look again at her letter. I had read it several times in my feeling-sorry-for-myself moments, usually looking for guidance on how she expected me to look after the kids, trying to read between the lines for parenting clues. There had been one part that had always stood out and hadn't made much sense. I scanned the page:

...I am running out of time.

When I'd first read it, I'd thought she was talking about never finding the time to speak to me. But could she have meant that there was some other pressure on her? Some deadline? What had made it crunch-time?

Perhaps she had been planning to leave Mike. But she had broken up with Phil – that suggested she wanted to work on her marriage. Had she been worried that Mike was going to leave her?

What had made her believe that things were coming to a head?

I stood up, looking around at the scattered mess of papers on the floor. There were also notes in my phone, screenshots, and some information I'd tried to commit to memory – I needed to file everything properly, make sure it was all written down in one place. There were gaps in this story, and I needed to see where they were. Grabbing a pen and paper, I started to put together a timeline of what I knew, and make notes about what I still had to find out.

When had Amy ended things with Phil? That seemed like a crucial piece of the puzzle. I poured myself another vodka and picked up the laptop to log back into Amy's Facebook account.

I hadn't looked at her page since I'd first found the messages from Phil, and it was full of new posts. Her friends had shared quotes, photos and memories of her. Some were paragraphs long and others just a line or two. As I scrolled down through her page, seeing them all knocked the wind out of me. I allowed myself to read a few, just for the sweet indulgence of seeing other people share my grief, validating my pain.

The newest posts were angry commentaries on Phil's arrest. I read these recent additions carefully, combing for clues, but nobody else seemed to know any of the details – yet. At least, nobody was sharing them here. Another nurse from the hospital had uploaded a photo of herself with Amy, and my sister's beautiful smile transfixed me for a moment before I scrolled on. People were sharing the donations that they had made to charities in Amy's name. There were tributes from university friends, work colleagues, people who she'd known from her various community groups. There must have been hundreds of messages.

I scrolled down, looking for names I recognised – there was Richard Pringle. He had posted a photo of Amy at a school bake sale, smiling down at kids as she handed out treats. He was standing behind her, and the angle of the photo had cast him in a shadow, gazing at Amy. He would be heartbroken when he learned that she wasn't as perfect as he thought.

Did people write such lovely tributes for everyone for who died, I wondered? What about unpopular people, or people who had done something bad – did they end up with everlasting digital monuments built in their name, too? Was that what it came down to, when we died – a legacy of likes and shares and emojis and words on a screen?

Had these people even known Amy that well? There was no way she'd had as many friends as this. These were strangers, intruding on our grief. What should be private was plastered here, permanently, for all to see. Had any of them really known Amy, known her like Rachel or I had? Would they feel differently when they found out what she had done?

I had allowed myself to get distracted – a quick scroll had turned into me falling head-first into a Facebook hole. Two minutes had become twenty. I clicked on the messages tab.

Some people had even sent her messages since her death – who did that? Apart from me, of course, but that was different. Amy was my sister, not theirs. My grief was in another league – bizarre behaviour from me was entirely permissible. I was tempted to read these other messages, but figured it could wait. I scrolled down, looking for the messages from Phil.

They weren't there.

At first, I thought it was a slip up, that the vodka had made me bleary and not focused enough. I blinked hard several times to make the screen clearer. I started again from the top, this time looking forensically, message by message. But they really had gone, vanished from the inbox, and I couldn't find any way of viewing deleted items. Had I imagined them? Hallucinated?

No, I was certain of what I'd seen. There had been three messages to Amy from Phil Turner, just a week ago – so what had happened to them?

Chapter Twenty

Amy was shouting to me. She was trying to tell me something, but the sound of the sea was too loud, overpowering, and I couldn't hear her above the crashing of the waves. I yelled at her – *Speak up!* She came closer and put her hands on my shoulders, shaking me. Her eyes were wide, her face contorted with the effort, but still she made no sound.

The dream started to slip away. I tried to hold on to it – to Amy's face, to her voice – but it was like trying to grab a handful of sea water.

My pulse was pounding at my temples. I pulled the duvet tighter around my head, keeping my eyes closed. There was no water by my bed and my mouth felt sandy, but the kitchen was miles away.

The pounding continued, and I realised that it wasn't my head – there was someone at the front door. I staggered to the bathroom, sticking my face under the cold tap, taking gulps of cool water and letting it splash over me. I dried my face on the sleeve of my dressing gown as I stepped carefully down the stairs.

I opened the door to Richard, a dark silhouette against sunlight that was unfeasibly bright. Definitely not the person

I wanted to see right now. I squinted, shielding my eyes from the glaring daylight.

'Sorry if I woke you.' He gave a nervous laugh.

What time was it, I wondered?

'I brought coffee?' he added. It sounded like a question.

I eyed the steaming cups in his hands.

'And I owe you an apology,' he continued. 'I was way out of line the other day, and I'm so sorry about... Well, you know.' He shuffled from foot to foot. 'Amy's death hit me harder than I'd realised, but that's no excuse...'

The sunlight was hurting my eyes and I willed Richard to stop talking. I did appreciate the apology, though. Besides, I wasn't exactly blameless – I had been about to kiss him, until he'd blurted out that I reminded him of my dead sister.

The coffee smelled so good. Wordlessly, I waved him inside.

We sat at the kitchen table – I didn't want a replay of our scene on the sofa.

'So, what's new?' he asked.

I prised the lid off my cup, inhaling the cloud of steam. Where to start? 'Something doesn't add up, about Phil. Hurting Amy. It... It just doesn't make sense.'

A long pause. Eventually, Richard shook his head. 'I can't work out what makes them think it was Phil Turner. He hardly seems the sort.'

A light rain started, the drops on the window blurring the world outside. I took a deep breath. 'Phil and Amy were having an affair.'

Richard's mouth fell open. Shame burned in my chest.

'Yup. Amy and Phil. Something was going on. Or something might have been going on... They had ended things a while back. Maybe. But now I'm not so sure...' The pressure started to build behind my eyes and I stopped talking, waiting for the threat of tears to pass. *Deep breaths.*

Richard considered it for a second, then shook his head. 'No way. That's not true. Don't you mean Mike was having an affair?'

His words floored me – did the whole village know?

Richard saw the look on my face. 'I don't mean he *was* having an affair, I just mean – I could believe it more from him. But not Amy. And Phil Turner!'

His expression was utter incredulity, his eyebrow twisting up into a question mark.

A lump rose in my throat. 'It's true. I logged into her Facebook and saw messages that Phil had sent her, and I told the police. I swear, they were right there' – I nodded at my phone – 'three messages, from Phil, and now they're gone.'

Richard's mouth was pressed into a hard line and his grip tightened on the cup in his hands. 'She wouldn't do that. Amy wasn't like that. She *would not* do that.' His knuckles turned white and his eyes were glassy with tears. 'You got it wrong. There's got to be some mistake – it can't be true. You have to tell the police – Amy wouldn't do that. She would *not* have an affair with Phil Turner.' He put down his cup and brought his hands up to his face, taking a long, deep breath.

I was frozen, unsure of how to handle his reaction. My pulse had quickened.

Richard went to say something, then stopped, as if he thought better of it. He stood up and shrugged on his jacket. His mouth twisted into something between a sneer and pity. 'Amy was your sister. Did you even know her at all?'

I didn't cry until he had closed the door behind him – I didn't want him to see how deeply his words had cut.

How come everyone around here seemed to know Amy better than I did? Richard's certainty was unnerving. But was he right? There was no other evidence Amy had been having an affair – if it was true, there would surely be some proof somewhere. A receipt, or an email, or a suspicious best friend.

Could I have imagined the messages from Phil? Perhaps part of me wanted to think the worst about Amy. Or had the messages been about something else - had I somehow got the wrong end of the stick? No, that was impossible. I knew what I had seen, and now they were gone. But would anyone believe me?

I missed Rachel terribly and really needed a confidante right now. I churned over the painful idea that I'd possibly ruined her marriage – ruined her life – for no reason. I owed her an explanation – when she eventually came home. If she ever came back.

Richard had made me feel horrible about Amy. My betrayal of my sister was etched across his face and his words rang in my ears. But the messages had been real. I had been meant to see them. Had someone deliberately set me up to frame Phil?

Mike was at home, alone. From the street, I could see him in his upstairs office, working at his computer. I stood outside, mustering as much bravery as possible before going in.

The hallway was lined with family pictures: baby photos and holiday snaps and school portraits. Smiling, happy faces. A happy family. Except I no longer knew what was real and what wasn't. Mike came into the kitchen.

'Were you having an affair?' I blurted the words out before I lost my nerve.

'What?' Mike's incredulity rang hollow to me. 'Where did

you get that from?'

'It doesn't matter how I know – what matters is whether it was true or not.' I balled my hands into tight fists. *Hold your nerve, Izzy, hold your nerve.*

'Don't be ridiculous.' Mike shook his head and sighed, as if my paranoid sister routine was wearing thin.

'OK, let me put this another way: I *know* you were having an affair. I've seen the proof for myself—'

'What proof?' he sneered.

'Enough proof to make it impossible to deny! And I know that Amy found out,' I spat, dealing my trump card. 'Does this have anything to do with her accident?'

He turned away from me, looking out of the kitchen window. There was a stack of unwashed dishes in the sink. Even with his back turned, I could see his breathing had become ragged.

'It's not what you think.' He turned to face me, holding up his hands in a plea before realising they were shaking. He folded his arms to hide them.

'So tell me what it is, Mike. Explain it to me.'

'It was a mistake!' He pressed his knuckle to his lips. 'A stupid, stupid mistake. Yes, Amy knew about it, and we'd moved on.'

'Was that who we saw you with in Newcastle?'

His eyes brimmed with tears. He nodded. 'It ended ages ago. But she got back in touch. I met her in Newcastle last weekend, to tell her we could never see each other again. I swear, this has nothing to do with what happened to Amy...'

'Who was it, Mike?' I clenched my jaw.

'Does it matter?'

'Did Amy know who it was?'

'No.' A beat. 'No, she didn't. But we had made our peace...'

244

'Hannah saw the two of you, Mike. You ran away from your own daughter.'

'I'm sorry!' He crumpled, legs first, falling to kneel on the floor in front of me. 'I'm so sorry! Just don't say anything, please...'

'What's her name?'

'It's not important. Please, Izzy. Don't do this.'

He was begging. I had to hold my ground.

'Tell me who it was.' My voice was low and level, unnaturally calm.

'Julie!' he blurted out.

The name was familiar. Where had I heard it? I wracked my brain. I had seen it last night. What had I been doing? I closed my eyes, pressing my fingertips to my temples. *Julie, Julie.* I turned the name over in my mind. There was a Julie who had written a tribute on Amy's Facebook page. It was one of the poems that I'd taken the time to read, and the name had stayed with me because it had been familiar.

'Julie Knox?'

'What?' Mike looked up at me from the floor, incredulous and enraged. 'Who...? How...?' His jaw dropped, then he caught himself. Pulled it together.

'Yes,' he said, staring at the floor.

My vision clouded with thick, acrid anger. I wanted to kick, rain blows, smash something over his head.

'Please though, Izzy, you can't tell anyone about this. Swear to me that you won't tell!'

'Why shouldn't I? Why should I keep your dirty little secret?'

Mike sobbed on the floor before me.

'Because I don't want my kids to hate me. I'm the only parent they've got left.'

The car grumbled to a halt outside the police station and I realised that I'd arrived in Alnwick without knowing how I'd got there. I looked over my shoulder, as if the answer was on the street behind me, unable to recall any details of the journey. My head was swimming.

DCI Bell was waiting at the front desk and silently led me into a meeting room. She flicked a switch and the grey walls were cast in the sickly glow of a fluorescent light. The plastic chairs scraped against the floor as we sat down.

She listened to my explanation – or lack of – of how the messages from Phil Turner had just vanished. Her face stayed neutral, and I knew that this was not news to her. I wondered how many hours of police time had been spent ascertaining that I'd given them a false lead.

'But I swear, I know what I saw,' I said. 'And I think I was set up.'

DCI Bell held my gaze, offering only a curt nod tin response. Did she think I was a fantasist, a liar, or just a heartbroken sister?

She listened wordlessly as I told her about the plastic folder that had been hidden away in the attic. I handed it to her and she spread out the credit card statements across the table, looking over the lines that had been highlighted. Only when I told her about seeing Mike in Newcastle last Saturday did her expression finally change.

'This clearly gives us more to consider. I'll hold on to these' – she waved the statements – 'and I'll be in touch if we need anything else.'

I stood to leave. I wanted to tell her about Amy's missing phone, and how I was sure that was important to the case – but so far, my attempts at detective work had caused more problems that they had solved.

'And do please keep this to yourself, Isabelle. We'll take it from here.'

I walked back out of the police station with my hands clasped in front of me to hide the shaking. Had I done the right thing?

I needed to take my mind off things. My meeting with Jennifer was in two days and I had a lot to prepare. It was time to get my secret weapon on-board. I called in to see Mum.

The concept for Izzy Morton Interiors was simple: a bijou agency that married a modern approach to design with the ancient Chinese art of feng shui, establishing the perfect balance between style and function, harmony and sophistication.

A broad smile spread across Mum's face as I explained my idea.

'That sounds wonderful.'

'I'm glad you think so,' I said, 'because I'll need your help.'

Auntie Sue stopped stirring the tea and looked at me. Mum fidgeted with the Tibetan prayer beads around her neck.

'In fact, I was hoping you would agree to be my business partner.'

Mum couldn't hide her delight. 'Sue! Did you hear that? Izzy wants me to be her business partner!' She clapped her hands in glee.

'That sounds like a lovely idea, Anne,' Auntie Sue said, smiling at me.

'Silent business partner,' I quickly clarified, before Mum got too carried away.

I explained how it would work – I would do the styling, choosing the colours, furnishings and fabrics, and Mum would lead on the positioning of the space. We would accessorise together, and I would source stuff from Hong Kong whenever Adam's husband Thierry could get me a good deal. I couldn't wait to tell Adam my plan. I really should call him back, I realised. He had tried to call me again last night and I'd let it ring out.

The business wouldn't make me rich or famous, but it would allow me to indulge my creativity and hopefully earn enough to get by. Most importantly, it would mean I could be there for the kids, and give me and Mum a chance to make up for some of the years we had lost.

I showed Mum my sketches for The Stables and watched her become completely absorbed by the work, drawing diagrams to show me the ideal positioning for a bed, a mirror or a plant, and suggesting accessories that might enhance the energy of a space. Soon, we were sitting in the middle of her living room floor surrounded by pages of our drawings, and for the first time since I'd got home, I saw a weight lifted from Mum's shoulders and a sparkle in her eyes.

In that moment, like so many others, I wished Amy was there – a deep longing, a yearning, to see her again and share that kernel of joy. To show her that maybe, just maybe, we would all be OK. Out of habit, I took out my phone and sent her a message.

Wish you were here. You would be so proud of Mum. Miss you every day xo

As I watched, the little icon beside the text turned green – delivered.

I checked back over the messages I'd sent Amy – they had all been delivered. When had that happened? The phone had been switched off when I'd tried calling it, and I remembered that my first message had stayed grey. When had I last checked?

Amy's phone had been switched on. But who had it?

Mike had to have taken it. Maybe there had been something incriminating on it – something he hadn't wanted the rest of the family to see. Some evidence of his affair with Julie Knox, something that proved Amy had found out who he had been seeing – perhaps something that had given him a reason to want her dead. A chill ran through me, making me shiver. But where could he have hidden it? I'd already searched the house. Could I have missed something? I could tip off the police, but then I pictured them turning Amy's home upside-down, going through her stuff, the kids' stuff. I chewed the ragged edge of a fingernail.

I needed Jake.

We arranged to meet on the seafront at Amble. I pulled into the small, sand-swept car park, and he climbed into my passenger seat. It was easier to talk to Jake like that – sitting side-by-side and looking out to sea rather than face-to-face. At least I couldn't get distracted by him, and I had to admit to myself – I was finding Jake increasingly distracting. But this was most definitely not the time to fall for someone. My sister needed me.

I showed him the messages I'd sent to Amy that were now mysteriously delivered to a phone that had apparently been lost. We had to work out who might be hiding it. I allowed myself a peek at Jake as he took my phone from me, chewing pensively on his bottom lip.

Jake explained that the box of Amy's possessions had been given to Mike two days after the accident. None of it was considered evidence, so the family were free to take it. I filled in the next piece of the puzzle for him – Mike claimed that he had given the unopened box to Mum, who had taken it home with her. By the time I had collected it, the phone was gone.

'So did Mike take the phone before he gave the box to Mum, and lie that he hadn't gone through it? Or did he go back for the phone *after* he gave it to her, when he realised what we might find...'

Jake twisted in his seat to face me.

'Why are we here?'

I started to stutter, struggling to articulate a sound reason. It was a good question. I looked down at our hands, side by side on the armrest. Our fingers almost touching.

'I know you want to find Amy's phone, but I don't see how I can help you with that.'

I fixed my gaze ahead towards the horizon. Saying nothing.

'This is a difficult time for you, I understand—'

'Don't, OK?' I cut him off. 'It's fine, you don't need to explain yourself.'

The words were bitter on my tongue.

'No, but I do. I do owe you an explanation.'

I turned ever so slightly towards him. Just enough to be able to see him from the corner of my eye.

'I like you, Izzy – I really like you,' he said in a quiet voice. 'In fact, I haven't *liked* anyone – felt this way about anyone – in quite a long time. But you just lost your sister, you're grieving – and I'm a partner at the legal firm that's handling her estate. Not to mention how much I've become involved in the investigation. Do you understand?'

I shook my head. I knew that if I tried to speak, words would fail me.

'I wish we had met under different circumstances,' Jake said, running a hand through his hair, 'and that I could just ask you out for dinner, or to the cinema, or the pub.'

'But we didn't,' I croaked. Tears pricked at my eyes.

Jake brushed a fingertip against the side of my hand. His touch was barely perceptible and electrifying all at the same time. It had been so long since I'd felt this way about someone – it was like being a teenager again. Like those first flushes of adolescent pining, when Amy and I had whispered secrets to each other about the latest objects of our infatuation.

Amy.

Jake was right – we couldn't get involved. Not now. I was falling for him, but he was out of reach. His finger was still touching mine. I looked back out to sea.

Jake's let-down had been gentle, but I was deflated – it felt like yet another thing that Amy's death had taken from me. Still, he had left me with some hope – that perhaps one day, when all of this was over, our friendship could become something else. If this was ever over. My determination hardened to find out what had happened to Amy.

I sat Mum and Auntie Sue down and told them to cast their minds back to the first few days after the accident, focusing on the box of Amy's possessions. We needed to work out who might have had access to it.

Those initial days after I'd got home had been a blur, and I struggled to put them in order now. The memory of that raw grief washed over me as I thought back, and I winced under the weight of it. Auntie Sue flinched too, hit by a similar force. Only Mum was still, sitting with her eyes closed and a serene expression on her face.

'Self-hypnosis,' said Auntie Sue, with a look that told me this wasn't the first time she'd seen it. 'It might take a while.

I'll put the kettle on.'

Auntie Sue's recollection of the days after the accident was slightly better than mine. She had helpfully kept a list of who had sent cards and who had phoned, knowing that she wouldn't remember who to thank later. She'd also kept note of people who had taken flowers to the site of the accident. I had no intention of visiting the scene of the crash and had been deliberately avoiding that road out of the village. I pictured a tree on a sharp bend of a country lane, black skid marks pointing towards a makeshift shrine of wilted blooms in plastic wrappers, and shuddered.

Almost all of the visitors after Amy's death had been at her house. That had been the family base for most of that time, where we had huddled in shock and congregated in our misery. There had been a couple of days when Mum had taken to her bed, and Auntie Sue had stayed home to watch her. Sue couldn't remember who had called at their house during those days, but she didn't think Mike had been.

'There,' said Mum, brandishing a sheet of paper.

She had scrawled a dozen names with notes beside them. I quickly scanned her list. Mum was not only claiming to remember who had been to her house, but when they had been there and how long they'd stayed for.

'How can you even remember all of this? You were in bed.'

'Just because I was in bed doesn't mean I wasn't present,' she said with a shrug, 'I was very much here, and focusing very hard on... not drifting away. I was practicing hyper-mindfulness.'

Auntie Sue looked at Mum's list and nodded.

'This does seem about right,' she said, taking a sip of tea.

Mike had not been to the house, not according to Mum's

252

list at least. Rachel had been of course, several times – but I already knew that. I was only listed as visiting once. I swallowed, a lump rising in my throat.

Diana Wheeler had visited. The only other name I recognised was Richard Pringle. According to Mum, he had been over three times.

'What's the deal with Richard Pringle?' I asked them. It was a question I'd been mulling over for a while.

Mum and Auntie Sue exchanged glances. Mum bit her lip. 'His heart is in the right place…' She hesitated. 'And he was very fond of Amy.'

Auntie Sue frowned. 'He's a good person. I know what people say about him, but Amy always had time for him. And she knew him well – better than most.'

'What do people say about him?' I asked, trying to keep the concern from my voice.

'Oh, nothing,' Auntie Sue said, with a dismissing wave of her hand. 'Nothing important. You know how people here like to gossip, no matter what truth there was to any of it…'

'What are you talking about?'

Mum and Auntie Sue looked at each other.

'Go ahead,' Mum said. 'You might as well tell her now.'

Auntie Sue took a deep breath, shook her head like she was thinking better of it, and then began to tell me before she changed her mind.

'Richard's not from Seahouses, so even though he's lived here for years, clearly that still means he's an outsider.' She pursed her lips. 'He's also not married, which would make him an eligible bachelor in most places, but oh no, not here. Here, that's a cause for suspicion. And he has the audacity to live alone in a large house. You get the picture - people are jealous. They don't know his life history, he didn't share it, so they've filled in the blanks themselves.'

She sighed. 'There have been various rumours about him over the years, but the one that has persisted is that he left his last school after becoming involved with a former pupil. Can you imagine?' Auntie Sue said, exasperated. 'Absolutely no truth to it whatsoever!'

She shook her head and continued. 'The man can't do right for doing wrong. People decided that he's a bit creepy, and any time something happens, the finger of blame gets pointed at him.'

'Like what?' I asked.

Auntie Sue rolled her eyes. 'Underwear stolen from a washing line. A mysterious dark figure spotted in the back lane one night. An anonymous love letter posted through someone's letterbox. Richard Pringle gets the blame for everything. It's a wonder he still lives here.'

'He was very keen on our Amy, though,' Mum said, raising an eyebrow.

'Anne! Don't you start!'

Mum pursed her lips into a sulk. 'I'm just saying... That man has a strange energy. And he moped after Amy. Even she got exasperated with him at times.'

The idea was needling at me, like a tiny stone in my shoe. I pictured Richard in my house, about to kiss me, then telling me that I looked just like my sister. I thought of the roses he had sent with an anonymous note, and the feeling that he was watching from the window whenever I went past his place. And he had been here, to this house, three times in the week after the accident.

Then I remembered: Richard had mentioned Amy having

money worries without me having said anything. And he'd seemed to know about Mike's affair when apparently, nobody else did. My blood ran cold.

I hadn't questioned how he knew those things. But had he been reading it all in the messages I'd sent to my sister?

DCI Bell answered on the third ring. 'Isabelle. To what do I owe the pleasure?'

I swallowed, a tennis ball of guilt in my throat, and told her about the missing phone. She was silent as I explained my suspicion that Richard Pringle had possibly taken it from my mother's house, coupled with his fondness for Amy and his behaviour towards me. I tried my best to stick to the facts and cringed when I told her about the almost-kiss. She thanked me and abruptly hung up, and I could almost hear her disdain in the buzz of the dead line. I poured a small vodka and took a sip to steady my nerves. Then I called Jake.

Jake sat up with a start when he heard my voice – I heard the familiar creak of his big office chair – and I wished I was calling with better news.

'Well if the phone has been switched back on, it should be straightforward to find – they can locate it by the signal. They should know right away if he has it.'

'He's got it, I'm convinced. So you think they will act quickly?'

I pictured Phil, languishing in a cell somewhere. Falsely accused, thanks to me stumbling across those messages and assuming the worst about Amy without questioning it. And meanwhile I'd failed to see what was right in front of me. My head pounded.

'I'll give my contact a call this evening and see what I can find out. Try not to think about it in the meantime.'

I hung up, thinking about the fact that I'd told the police about Mike's affair. Had I laid out my sister's dirty laundry for everyone to gawk over, for nothing? I topped up my vodka, hoping to get some clarity.

Mike had been having an affair, that much was certain. But the messages to Amy – someone had set me up to frame Phil. And Richard had Amy's phone the whole time. I just hoped that Rachel and Phil would forgive me one day.

I was late for dinner at Amy's. Mike was helping Lucas to cook again, and something had gone wrong – the smell of acrid smoke was all that remained of a failed experiment. He was scrubbing at the burned pan and gave me a sheepish tilt of his chin as a greeting. I glared back at him, just daring him to say something. Even the sight of him was more than I could bear.

I helped Lucas to dish out and served Mike last, roughly spooning a dollop of fish pie onto his plate. Auntie Sue raised an eyebrow but said nothing.

My head was swimming, and I found it hard to concentrate for more than a moment before another ugly thought appeared. Betsy was trying to tell me some long and convoluted story, with the enthusiasm and level of unnecessary detail that only an eight-year-old can muster, and I struggled to follow. The buzz from my vodka was wearing off and I had to steal away to the bathroom midway through the meal to refresh myself.

I cleared up after dinner, dismissing the others' offers to help. I plunged my hands into the basin of too-hot water, watching them disappear beneath the layer of suds until the pain was too much and pulling them out again, angry and raw.

Mike came back into the kitchen and stood at a safe distance across the galley. 'I said I'm sorry, Izzy...'

I didn't turn around. 'It's not me you should be apologising to. Besides, sorry isn't going to change anything.'

He sighed. 'No, it's not. All I can say is how much I regret it, and I'll regret it every day for the rest of my life... But please. We were doing well here. We were OK at this, me and you.'

I thought again of Amy's will, and her letter to me. She'd wanted me and Mike to work together, to be parent and guardian, even after she'd known that he had been unfaithful.

Or had she wanted that? Maybe the reason she had asked me to come back was because she didn't trust Mike anymore. I put my hands back into the hot water.

There was a knock at the door.

'I'll get it,' called Hannah.

The front door swung open with a gasp, and a draft of cool evening air blew down the hall and into the kitchen. Mike and I turned at the same time.

DCI Bell and PC Knowles were standing on the doorstep.

Hannah turned and looked down the hallway towards the kitchen, to me and Mike, her eyes pleading for one of the grown-ups to come and deal with this.

Mike walked down the hallway, rolling down his shirt sleeves back towards his wrists like a schoolboy who had been disciplined for sloppy uniform. He put a hand on Hannah's shoulder, still doing up the button on his shirt cuff. I edged up the hall behind him, my eyes fixed on the officers' boots. Auntie Sue appeared at the living room door, her mouth dropping to a surprised 'oh'. The birdsong of Betsy's laughter rang out from inside.

DCI Bell had her hat under her arm.

'Mr Sanders, Miss Morton – could we speak in private for

just a moment?'

'Come on, Hannah.' I put my hands on her shoulders, steering her gently away from the door.

Auntie Sue beckoned her over and pulled her into the living room. Betsy had gone quiet. The only sound was the blaring of the television. I followed Mike outside and pulled the door closed behind us. My heart was hammering.

'We've released Phil Turner without charge.' DCI Bell said, her voice hushed. 'The evidence against him was not as it initially appeared. I'm now of the opinion that it could have been fabricated.' Her eyes locked with mine.

'Even the medication in his garage?' I said.

'He insists he's never seen it before. In light of other recent developments, we believe it could have been planted there.'

I shivered and wrapped my arms tightly around myself.

She carried on. 'And we've taken Richard Pringle in for questioning. Mr Pringle has come in voluntarily to discuss Amy's accident and will be interviewed under caution. He had Amy's phone in his possession, and he has admitted to accessing her messages.'

The thick night air started to close in on me and my throat seized up.

Mike shuffled from foot to foot. 'When will you arrest him?'

PC Knowles was quick to answer. 'There's no evidence at this stage that would prompt an arrest. We're just talking to him. What would be helpful from the family is any idea why he might have had Amy's phone. Something you might have seen or heard, or something Amy said. Anything you can tell us, no matter how insignificant it might seem.'

A chill breeze swirled along the street, picking up leaves and tossing them in the air before carelessly letting them fall back to the ground.

My mind was racing. 'Could Richard have planted the medication at the garage? If he was trying to frame Phil?'

'That's for us to look in to.' DCI Bell's mouth was pressed into a pinch. 'And we'd like you to come in tomorrow as well, Mr Sanders – nothing official, just a few details to go back over.'

I looked down at my feet.

Mike cleared his throat. 'I see. Do I need a lawyer?' He chuckled nervously.

'Nothing like that,' said DCI Bell. 'It's just formalities, really. Please pop in for a chat when you can. I'm free at eleven.'

It was a command, though, rather than a suggestion. I wondered if Mike had heard it, too. I kept my eyes fixed firmly on DCI Bell's boots as she turned and made her way down the path back to the car, with PC Knowles following her.

A silhouette appeared at a window across the street. How long would it take for the whole village to find out about Richard?

We retreated to the warm hallway, shutting the door against the evening. I leaned back against the wall. The living room was quiet, and I pictured the kids, Mum and Auntie Sue anxiously waiting behind the door to hear the news.

'I knew that creepy bastard was up to something,' Mike hissed.

You have no idea, I thought, as I pictured him in Puffin Cottage.

'Wonder why they need to speak to me again. You don't know anything about that, do you?' His eyebrows were raised in a question.

I shrugged, trying to keep my face neutral. 'Probably just a formality, like she said.'

There was no point delaying the inevitable. Mike went into the living room, took a deep breath and told the kids that Phil had been released, and the police had taken Richard Pringle in to answer some questions about their Mum's death. His gentleness belied the rage I knew was brewing inside him.

Mum began to cry and Hannah was the first to comfort her – showing a kindness that made me feel Amy was right there in the room with us.

Mike took the lead, coaxing the children to talk about what had happened and trying to get a discussion going. But we had so little to share, and we had agreed not to tell them that Richard had Amy's phone.

Only Lucas had questions, and they were purely logistical. Was Mr Pringle sleeping in a cell? Were there bars on the door? Was it locked?

Mike mentioned in passing that he would being going in tomorrow to help the police, and nobody responded, but Hannah glanced at me. She would have questions later that she didn't want to ask in front of the little ones.

The news about Richard hit Auntie Sue the hardest. I found her a little later in the kitchen, standing alone at the sink and staring out the window into the dark of the garden. She kept her back to me.

'Just because he's an outsider doesn't mean he's evil. He's just different – it doesn't make him bad.'

'He had Amy's phone! He stole it from us!'

'I know, I know,' she said, holding up a hand to stop me. 'But... maybe there's some explanation. It doesn't mean he murdered her. I just hope the man's life hasn't been ruined for nothing.'

She dried her hands and went wordlessly to join the others. I stepped up to the window to see what she had been staring at, but all I could see was my reflection.

My phone buzzed in my pocket. I took it out to find a message from Adam:

Why aren't you answering? Call me back.

There was also one from Jake:

Heard the news. How are you all holding up? It's late already, they'll keep Richard overnight at a minimum. I'll let you know if I hear anything else.

I chewed on a fingernail. So that was it. Phil was out and on his way home, and Richard was in custody.

I had built Phil up in my mind to be such a monster that it had been difficult to even consider he might be innocent after all, even after I'd realised his messages to Amy had probably been faked. At first, I had even been trying to imagine scenarios where Mike and Phil might both be guilty, although that made no sense. How wrong I'd been about it all. In my grief and desperation, I'd seen things that weren't there.

We had all been too quick to believe Phil had killed Amy, even his wife. What that meant for him and Rachel, it was too soon to know. And now I'd told the police about Mike's affair for nothing. A knot hardened in my stomach.

My instinct on Richard had been way off, and I shuddered as I pictured him sitting on my sofa. Had he come on to Amy as well? She would have spurned his advances. Was that what had pushed him to breaking point?

He must have planned all along to frame someone else for her death. His reaction to the suggestion that she had been having an affair with Phil was bizarre, considering he had sent the messages – but presumably that was all part of his attempt to cover his tracks. It was an elaborate scheme, though, and for just a second it struck me that it was implausible. But Richard had stolen Amy's phone and could have accessed her Facebook, which meant he could have framed Phil. It had to have been him. But why?

And if it wasn't him, then who?

'Care for a nightcap?'

I jumped. I'd been so deep in thought that I hadn't heard Mike come up behind me.

Chapter Twenty-One

None of the kids wanted to go to bed – at least, nobody wanted to sleep alone in their own bedrooms. Lucas insisted that he would have nightmares, and Betsy refused to even go to the toilet on her own. Auntie Sue agreed that it would be good for us to stick together and proposed a sleepover. She popped home to get a couple of sleeping bags for her and Mum, while we set up in the living room, pushing the furniture back to make room for us all to sleep in the middle of the floor, lined up like sardines.

I excused Mike from the slumber party and watched him climb the stairs, taking the bottle of scotch with him. He had been holding himself together remarkably well, but his expression changed whenever he thought nobody was watching. He was ready to crack, and as much as I was still furious with him, the idea that I had betrayed him was gnawing at me.

Betsy was sandwiched between Mum and Auntie Sue, where she promptly fell asleep, her jaw slackening on her wet thumb as her breathing slowed into soft snores. Lucas was reading with a small pocket light clipped onto the top of his book, casting him in a halo of yellow light. He fell asleep slack-mouthed, the book fanned open on his chest. Auntie Sue gently teased it free from his grip and pulled the sleeping bag up to his chin.

Hannah propped her head up on her arm, her face just below my shoulder.

'Do they think Mr Pringle killed Mum?' She was barely audible.

Instinctively, I shook my head.

'No, darling, I'm sure—'

'Don't *lie*,' she hissed. 'They let Phil go – they wouldn't do that if he was guilty. And why does Dad have to go in again? There's obviously something going on!'

She rolled onto her back, flopping her head back against her pillow, staring up at the ceiling.

'I wish Mum was here,' she said, whispering to the dark.

I slept in fits and starts, lying awake for what felt like hours at a time. Eventually, the daylight beyond the window became too bright to ignore. I scanned the row of sleeping bags – everyone was still asleep, except Auntie Sue.

'Fancy a coffee?' she mimed drinking from a cup.

We gingerly climbed out of our sleeping bags, trying our hardest not to make any noise. In the kitchen I stretched, my back making a series of loud cracks. Auntie Sue put the kettle on. I checked my messages. There were three from Rachel:

OMG Izzy. I heard what's happened! This is awful! They don't really think Richard could have done it, do they? How are the kids? xxx

They've released Phil. He's going to stay at his mum's for a few days. I don't know what's going on. I don't know what to do!

I miss you guys, all of you. Can't get through this without you. Coming home tomorrow xxx

And another from Adam:

IZ: CALL ME. IT IS IMPORTANT.

What was so urgent? I doubted it was more pressing than my sister's stalker being questioned about her death. I looked at the clock – it would be just after lunch in Hong Kong. I'd give him a call after my coffee.

Breakfast was a sombre affair, the kids silently spooning mouthfuls of sugary cereal, except for Hannah, who just stirred hers. Poor girl – only thirteen and already she had bags under her eyes. Lucas was yawning too, and I realised I wasn't the only one who'd only managed a few hours of sleep.

Mike appeared, clean-shaven for the first time in days. He joked and bantered with the kids, trying too hard, a false lightness to him that everyone saw right through. I studiously avoided eye contact, busying myself with clearing away the breakfast things. Despite my resentment over what he'd done to Amy, my disloyalty sat souring like a saucer of milk left out in the sunshine.

Clearly, nobody was going to school. I couldn't bring the kids' mum back, and I couldn't hide the fact that the local headteacher was about to be arrested for her murder, but I could protect them from the stares, the whispers, and the gossip of the world outside.

I remembered what it had been like to be the hot topic of the village. In a frighteningly short space of time, Amy and I had gone from getting condolences for losing Dad to worried queries about how well Mum was coping, and then thinly disguised attempts to mine for gossip.

Mum hadn't been seen out in weeks by that point, and everywhere we'd gone, people had turned and whispered, or spoken to one another from behind raised hands, their eyes on us. The rumour was that Mum lost her mind and retreated to the attic like Mrs Rochester – or something like that. Little did they know that she had retreated to the other side of the world. They speculated, conjectured, hypothesised and guessed, made up stories to fill the void, created a narrative to make their boring little lives more interesting. They thought that I wouldn't see, or I wouldn't realise that they were talking about us, or maybe they just didn't care. Only Mrs Wheeler had shown any true kindness.

No wonder I hadn't been able to wait to get as far away as possible from this place.

I wanted to keep the kids in a bubble, at least for now. As soon as we knew what was happening with Richard, then we could make a plan. If he was guilty, we were going – never mind Amy's last wishes. I would not, could not let them stay here. I would pack up the entire family and we would start a new life somewhere else, far away from Seahouses, where nobody knew what had happened. Far from here, where murderers and memories lurked around every corner. For now, I just had to keep them occupied and as sane as possible.

Mum was not herself, at least not the lively, happy woman she'd been just the day before. She hadn't dressed yet and was silently nursing a cup of tea that must have gone cold. I'd barely heard her talk all morning, and the puffiness around her eyes made me want to cry. She stared straight ahead at an invisible point on the table, drowning in her thoughts. I could see that she was withdrawing into herself by the minute, and I was afraid to lose her again, just as she was starting to make progress. Even Auntie Sue was giving me one-word answers.

They needed a distraction – we all did. Thankfully, I had a pitch to finish.

It was a crazy idea, but I put everyone to work. Before long,

Betsy was helping Auntie Sue to glue scraps of fabric and colour swatches onto my mood board while Lucas edited a 360-degree model of a hotel bedroom on the family laptop.

I asked Hannah to look at my PowerPoint, expecting some feedback on the design, and when she screwed her nose up at it, I told her to make me a better one. She was now putting together a short conceptual video to present Izzy Morton Interiors, scouring the internet for abstract footage and images that represented the brand vision. For once, I was lost for words.

Slowly but surely, Mum started to come around. Lucas nudged her gently with questions about the positioning of furniture in the 3D model, and as she described the flows of energy in a room, the light began to return to her eyes.

Lucas suggested that energy flows could be built into the model, an additional layer of graphics to give a visual representation of the chi so that everyone could see it as she did. Under her direction, he animated swirling patterns that looked like streams of molten gold and shimmering diamonds, pouring in through the windows and doors and bouncing around the room, reverberating and echoing off the energy points she had strategically placed, and Mum's smile finally returned.

We were disturbed by the sound of the front door opening. Auntie Sue gave me a questioning look as she got up to see who it was.

'Rachel!' Auntie Sue said. 'My dear girl.'

She pulled her into an embrace, and Rachel gave me a feeble smile over her shoulder. She was pale, with sunken hollows beneath her eyes, and I wondered how much sleep she had managed to get. The last few days had added years to her. I wanted to feed her, provide hugs and cups of sugary tea.

At least working on the pitch was providing a great distraction for everyone. I had been so absorbed by the work and by making sure that everyone had something to do, I had barely thought about drinking.

We proudly showed Rachel our progress, and I could see how much the kids had missed her. They asked about Phil, and she was honest – she didn't know what he had done or where he was. Her voice faltered as she spoke.

'But no matter what, I'm still your Auntie Rachel. I love you all so much. And I'm not going anywhere.'

I pulled her into the privacy of the kitchen the moment the kids got back to work. 'What's going on? Where's Phil?'

Rachel shook her head, tears pooling in her eyes. 'I've got no idea. He's not answering my calls. The police told me he went to his mum's, but she says he's not there.'

I reflexively wrapped her in a hug. 'Don't worry, love. He's probably just cooling off, getting over the shock of it all. He'll be home soon.'

She nodded, wiping her tears on her sleeve.

'And he's innocent, that's the main thing.' I hesitated for a second, wanting to press without adding to the pressure on her. 'So they must be convinced that it was Richard. I wonder what else they have on him, besides the phone. Are you sure Amy never said anything about him? Anything about being afraid of him?'

'I don't know, Izzy, I don't know what to believe any more. I don't know what's real...' Her lip trembled and she stopped short. I folded her back into me.

By midday, there was still no news. Rachel started making lunch, while the rest of us reviewed the results of a morning's hard work. What we had managed to produce in just a few hours had surpassed even my grandest expectations. Izzy Morton Interiors was suddenly beginning to feel very real. Maybe, just maybe, I could pull this off.

We sat down to eat. Rachel's hand trembled as she ladled soup into our bowls, so I gently took it from her and finished serving. Perhaps, when this was all over, I thought, we could take a break together – just to get away from Seahouses. A girls' trip would do her so much good.

The chatter started to slow down as the family ate, and in those growing moments of silence, I could see worry flashing across the kids' faces. Hannah kept looking at the clock and was constantly checking her phone – although that was nothing new. She was a bright kid, and she knew what she had seen that day in Newcastle. I wondered how much she had worked out for herself and how her loyalty to her father would be tested if she found out what he'd done. Mum began to hum, and Betsy started sucking her thumb as soon as she had finished eating. We needed to get back to work.

I stood at the front of the living room, my presentation on the TV screen and my mood board serving as a backdrop. Looking at my 'audience' I suddenly felt nervous – I needed to not let them down. They had as much invested in this as I had. I took a deep breath and started my pitch.

We hadn't got far when the doorbell rang. Auntie Sue answered it and led Jake into the living room.

'Just calling by to see how you're all doing.' He flashed me a heart-melting grin.

Auntie Sue raised an eyebrow at me as Jake wedged himself between the kids on the sofa. I tried to avoid the gaze of my newest audience member and concentrate on my script, but I felt the blush rising in my cheeks. Why did this man give me butterflies every time I saw him?

I stuttered my opening lines but soon found my stride, and actually started to enjoy it. I knew the idea was good and I was confident we were proposing a great concept. If Jennifer Wheeler would give me this chance, I wouldn't let her down.

My rhythm was broken by Jake's phone ringing. His face fell when he saw the caller ID and he excused himself to take it outside. I tried to carry on, but my concentration was shattered.

'OK everyone, quick break time!' I said, hurrying out of the room after him.

Jake was in the back garden, and I watched him from the kitchen window as he paced across the patio. His shoulders sank, and I knew from the curve of his neck and the way he held his head that we were back to square one.

He put the phone back in his pocket and I went outside to join him. His face said it all.

'Richard had an alibi.' He sighed. 'A solid one. He was nowhere near Seahouses the night that Amy died.'

Something like fury bubbled up inside me. 'That doesn't mean he didn't do it! Why did he have her phone?'

The ground started to spin, and my balance faltered. Jake was suddenly at my side.

'Easy, there.' He gently took my elbow. 'Let's just sit down here for a second.' He put an arm around my shoulder and eased me onto the doorstep.

'I don't understand,' I said. 'He had her phone. He framed Phil.'

'He took the phone – he's admitted that, and they'll charge him with theft, but there's nothing to suggest he sent those messages from Phil Turner. There's no evidence linking him to the accident.' Jake shook his head. 'Apparently, he says he loved her. He was planning to return the phone. He only took it to get photos of Amy.'

'That's stalking!'

Jake held up his hands.

'It's creepy all right, and it's illegal, but it doesn't mean he had anything to do with her death. Richard was at a conference in Edinburgh when Amy died. Hundreds of people saw him. Apart from the phone, there's absolutely nothing connecting him to any of it.'

I folded myself forward and buried my head in my hands. I'd let Amy down again. And Auntie Sue was right – Richard wouldn't recover from this. The people here, they'd never let him forget it. The story would grow and bend and twist and mutate into something hideous and unrecognisable from any version of the truth.

Perhaps that's what he deserved. He had stolen her phone, after all. Or maybe he'd seen Amy for who she really was and couldn't help but love her, and had been reckless in his desperation to cling on to any morsel of her memory. Maybe it was nothing more than that. Maybe he had loved her like we all had. Maybe Amy, if she were here, would forgive him for that.

We stepped back into the kitchen. Auntie Sue was waiting by the open door. She shook her head and for the first time in my life, I saw her disappointment in me and remembered afresh that there is no greater pain than letting down the people who love you.

I braced myself, but before she could say anything, the front door burst open, clattering so hard into the wall that the whole house shook. The noise was splintering, and I was running to throw myself in front of the kids before I even had to think about it.

Mike thundered into the hallway, his face a storm of fury and red with rage, lips carved into a snarl, fists balled at his side. He saw me first.

'Get. Out. Of. My. House.'

He ground out each word through gritted teeth, his jaw clenched.

'Mike, look – I mean, you can't think any of this is my fault...' I tripped over the words, inching backwards as he moved towards me.

'Get out my house and get away from my kids.'

Auntie Sue came running down the hallway, her face shattered with panicked incredulity. 'What on *earth* has happened?'

Mike peered around the living room, doing a double-take when he noticed Rachel sitting in Amy's chair. She stared at her feet with heavy eyes.

'It's her!' He bellowed, pointing at me. 'She's trying to set me up!'

'Mike,' I said, trying to stay calm. 'Let's talk about this, please. I had to tell them...'

Auntie Sue shook her head and looked away.

'Get out,' Mike said, now eerily calm. Staring me down. He glanced at Rachel. 'You too. Get out of my house and stay away from my kids.'

'Come on, Mike.' The words cracked on my tongue. 'You can't keep me away...'

'I can, and I will.' His voice was as still and deep as the sea, ready to whip into a storm at any moment.

I planted my feet firmly in the carpet and tried to summon the bravery to fight him, but it was no use. He was right. Then a hand at my elbow – and there was Jake, with his kind eyes. He ushered me and Rachel out of the room.

The kids were crying again, all three of them now. I gave a watery smile and mouthed to Hannah, 'It's OK…' as Jake steered me through the doorway, the first tears rolling silently down my cheeks. Auntie Sue was holding Mum, still avoiding my eyes. From the hallway, I could hear the kids sobbing, Betsy properly wailing now, just on the other side of this wall. What had I done?

Only Hannah had the presence of mind to scoop up the things I needed for my pitch and pass them to me as we filed outside the front door, a motley crew straggling along the garden path, shell-shocked and shoeless.

'Mike, come on, please don't do this,' I tried one last time.

He glared at me and slammed the door closed.

I pounded my balled fists against it, pleading. 'Please, Mike. Please!'

But I knew it was futile.

I collapsed downwards, folding in on myself like a concertina until I landed in a crouch on the doorstep, sobbing into my knees, my arms wrapped around my legs. The village rumour mill would be sent into overdrive, but I didn't care who saw or who heard any more; they could talk about us all they wanted. I had thought before that I'd lost everything – now I realised how losing everything really felt.

Jake crouched down beside me, folding me into his strong arms. I fell against his chest and he whispered into my hair, words that I couldn't hear over my sobs. My face was a gluey mess of tears and snot and something inside me – something that had been stretched and twisted and borne more weight than it was designed to hold – finally broke.

I tried to stand, but couldn't feel my legs. I didn't want to move, anyway – maybe Mike wouldn't let me in, but I could sit here on the doorstep all day. Stay close to the children, be ready when they needed me.

How long would he keep me away from them? Did I have any legal rights to see them? The panic was rising in me, a flutter beating in my chest.

Maybe if I closed my eyes and wished very hard, I could transport myself away from here – to another time, another place. Another life. It had been a favourite game of Amy's. We would crawl under the bedsheet with our torches, our heads making a tent peak, close our eyes, and focus on the place we wanted to go to.

I wished myself away from there, away from the shouting and Mike's fury, away from Seahouses, away from the people and places where everything reminded me of Amy. Away from Phil and Richard and the mistakes I'd made. From my failure to make everything better. From all the pain I had caused.

Jake was still at my side and he was trying to talk to me – I could hear him, but his words didn't make sense. None of it made sense. Everything was spinning.

And then another voice.

'Dear god, Izzy. Could you not have just answered your bloody phone?'

And there, at the garden gate with an overnight bag at his feet, was Adam.

Chapter Twenty-Two

'**I**'m not calling this an intervention, but I need some time alone with Izzy.'

Adam sent Rachel home and told Jake to go back to the office before whisking me off to the pub and installing me at our usual corner table. Only by the second glass of Sauvignon Blanc did my teeth finally stop chattering.

'What are you doing here? You're not due to visit until the end of the month.'

'I got so worried when you stopped taking my calls that I had to change my flights. Looks like I got here just in time,' he said, looking me up and down.

I took stock of my appearance. My hair badly needed some maintenance. I had gained at least three kilos and tiny threads of wrinkles were now creeping from the sides of my eyes and across my forehead – a combination of the emotional strain of the last two months and being long overdue for my regular Botox appointment. I had bitten my nails into short, frayed stubs that would have horrified the old me. My make-up routine had dwindled to the most basic – a lick of mascara and a swipe of lip balm.

Two months ago, I would have been embarrassed for Adam to see me looking like this – for anyone to see me like this, for that matter. Now, I couldn't care less.

'So apart from your family imploding on itself, what else have you been up to?'

Where to start?

I quickly filled him in on everything – going to the police with the evidence I'd discovered of Amy and Phil's affair, who arrested him – only to release him when I realised that he and Amy hadn't been involved after all, and that it was Richard who had Amy's phone all along and had been reading her messages, and then seeing the police release him too – and my underlying suspicion that Mike was hiding more than an affair. And now Phil was nowhere to be found and Richard's life was probably ruined.

'OK,' said Adam, taking a deep breath. 'Tell me – have you found any time at all for quiet, reflective grief? Quality time with your family, with the children?'

I ignored him.

'The worst part is I know Mike is covering something up – I'm not saying for sure that he killed Amy, but he had the biggest motivation and Phil was framed. Who did that, if not Mike? I need to find the woman he was having an affair with. There's more to that than he's letting on.'

I chewed on a fingernail. Finding Julie Knox – that was my next step.

'Would you listen to yourself, Agatha Chr-Izzy! Why don't you leave the detective work up to the professionals? You have enough on your plate, and this' – he motioned towards me – '*this* is not healthy. You're drinking far too much, and you've become obsessed with Amy's accident. Your family are worried about you.'

I scoffed. 'No, they're not.'

'Auntie Sue is. She said you're constantly drinking and the accident is all you talk about, that you're convinced Amy was murdered and it's eating you up.'

'Auntie Sue? When did she say that?'

'Oh, all the time.' He waved a hand dismissively. 'We've been speaking every couple of days.'

Adam registered my surprise.

'Well, it's not as if you've been calling me back!'

I winced under his blow. It was true that I had neglected our friendship, but it had been too hard to hear about my old life carrying on without me. And maybe Auntie Sue was right. Maybe my obsession with finding out what happened to Amy was becoming unhealthy.

Gina arrived with more drinks. Suddenly the wine seemed less appealing.

'So, what else is new?'

I started again from the beginning, telling Adam how hard it had been with the kids at first, but that we were finally finding our feet, and that things were starting to heal with Mum. I even used that word – *heal* – which just showed how much influence she was having on me.

I smiled as I described my friendship with Jake and was wholly unconvincing when I insisted there was no potential for romance. The blush started to rise in my cheeks and I quickly changed the subject.

Adam listened as I explained how Izzy Morton Interiors had quickly gone from pie-in-the-sky idea to harsh reality, and how I'd roped everyone in to help on the pitch for Jennifer Wheeler.

'Shit!' I looked at my watch. 'The pitch! It's tomorrow!'

There was still work left to do on the proposal, and I wasn't remotely ready for the meeting.

'Well, let's leave these for now.' Adam pushed our drinks away. 'Session postponed until we have something to cele-brate. Sounds like we have work to do.'

We went back to Puffin Cottage and worked late into the night. By the time Adam had finished weaving his magic, the pitch had been transformed from a solid home-made effort to something that looked and felt polished and professional.

Adam even helped me to pick an outfit to wear the next day. It had been a while since I'd worn anything except my casual clothes and at first, it felt like I was playing dress-up. I was relieved to find that my black wool trousers still fitted, and Adam paired them with a white silk blouse and cashmere wrap.

We surveyed the result of his makeover. It wasn't my old look – in fact, Hong Kong Izzy would have been seriously worried for this girl. But it was smart and somewhat chic, without trying too hard. It felt good to be wearing heels again. I was holding my chin higher and my shoulders were down. This was me, doing something for me. Something came back to me in that moment – something I hadn't realised I'd lost.

Adam yawned and I offered him my bed, insisting I would be comfortable on the sofa.

'Don't be daft – you need to get a good night's sleep.' He shrugged on his coat and kissed my cheek.

I opened the door for him. The wind had changed direction and a cool salty breeze wafted into the kitchen.

'You've got this, Izzy,' he said, as he closed the yard gate. 'Break a leg!'

My nerves got the better of me, pushing away the sweet

softness of sleep and jolting me back to consciousness with a gasp. A glance at my watch on the bedside table told me it was only 5.15 a.m. I knew I wouldn't get back to sleep again.

I made a coffee and took it to bed, pulling back the curtains to the dark and opening the window a slice, just enough to allow in a cool trickle of sea air. The blackness began to part across the middle, the sea now distinguishable from the sky that slowly came into focus. A sliver of gold light appeared along the edge of the water, growing, casting a glow on everything it touched.

I pulled on some warm clothes and headed down to the beach, streetlights guiding the way to the start of the dune path until the thin morning light took over. Despite my layers, the cold air bit at me. I tucked my chin deeper into Amy's fleece jacket and pulled the collar as high as it would reach.

Adam's words rang in my ears. Auntie Sue was right – finding out what had happened to Amy had become an obsession. Drinking had numbed the ache of my loss but blinded me to the pain I was causing. I had neglected the people I cared about and too many people had been hurt because of me. I could see that now.

Without thinking, I took my trainers off, tucking my socks inside them. The cold sand slapped against the soles of my feet as I ran towards the shoreline, where I stood, gasping at the shock of the water's icy caress, washing over me, cleansing me.

I bargained with the sea: *let me have this. Just for today, for one day only, let me focus on this and forget all the other stuff – forget Richard, forget Phil, forget Mike. Forget Amy, too, if I can. Just for a few hours. I need it.*

Jennifer Wheeler had her mother's sparkling blue eyes. She shook my hand firmly, smiling at me with a warmth that immediately put me at ease. I had been so nervous on the drive to Alnwick that I'd had to pull over at one point and wait for the trembling to stop.

She led me through to a function room. The Stables was all dark wood panelling with a deep red carpet and period decorations. I could see immediately how lightening the walls and wood and restyling the window dressings would refresh the room, making it brighter and improving the flow of chi.

Mum had given me some positive affirmations as a technique to control my nerves, and I repeated them in head as I set up for my presentation: *I am creative, I am professional and I am capable. I can do this.*

My voice quivered slightly as I delivered the opening that Adam had helped me to craft, and my hand trembled as I talked Jennifer through the styling elements on the mood board. But I quickly found my stride. I loved the proposal we had put together and tingled with pride at Jennifer's positive reaction. As I explained how the positioning of elements in the room would balance the energy of the hotel and improve the experience for guests at The Stables, I felt a genuine excitement.

By the end of my pitch, I was standing an inch taller than when I had walked in, and I couldn't shrug the smile from my face.

Jennifer was beaming back at me. 'Wow, Izzy, what can I say? I love it. I love all of it.'

'Fantastic!' My heart skipped a beat and I started to get dizzy with the potential.

'How soon can you start?'

Adam had advised me to reassure Jennifer that we could be up and running right away, and not to bother her with the hurdles I still had to climb – the administration of setting up a new business, securing a bank loan and negotiating contracts with suppliers. Auntie Sue had agreed to help me with all of that and was primed to start as soon as I gave the green light. As long as she was still speaking to me.

I couldn't wait to tell them all, and I just hoped that Mike would let the children join the celebration. Surely he understood the position I had been put in? Maybe I could invite Jake to join us, too. Strictly as a friend.

Jennifer offered me a tour of the rest of the hotel and I enthusiastically agreed. I had only seen a couple of the rooms that we were renovating, and I was keen to explore the rest of it.

The Stables was a rambling warren of crooked passageways leading to low-ceilinged rooms, with discreet signs everywhere warning visitors to mind their heads. I struggled to concentrate on Jennifer's explanation of the building's history because I was so distracted by the beautiful exposed wooden beams and stone floors that had been worn smooth by thousands of feet passing over them.

A twisted passageway opened onto the main restaurant and my eyes were drawn upwards to the double-height vaulted ceiling, propped up by centuries-old timber arches. The staff were setting up for the midday seating – the quiet murmur of pre-lunch rush chatter echoed from the kitchen.

'And this section leads on to the stable itself – the inspiration for the rebrand.'

Jennifer smoothed an invisible crease from one of the starched linen tablecloths and held up a gleaming wine glass for a closer inspection. 'You should have seen the state of this place before we took it over. Ghastly. It took a lot more than a lick of paint and a new name – we practically had to gut the place.'

'So it wasn't always called The Stables?' My heart started beating faster. A rebranded hotel, in Alnwick. Was it possible? Could this be the place I'd been searching for?

'What was it called before? Is it still known by another name?'

'It's had a few names over the years – perfectly normal, for a historic pub. You probably knew it as the Black Swan when you were growing up.'

I tried to keep the impatience out my voice. 'This might be a silly question, but if I stayed here, what would my credit card statement say?'

Jennifer rolled her eyes.

'Don't get me started on that. I've tried for years to resolve it with the bank, I don't know what else to do. I've gone round and round in circles with them, and the bureaucracy – you wouldn't believe...'

I interrupted her. 'And what name would it show?'

But I knew the answer before she said it.

'The Highwayman Inn,' Jennifer said.

Blood thundered in my ears and the cavernous room started to close in on me.

Chapter Twenty-Three

The drive home was one of those journeys where, after arriving, you don't remember how you got there. Before I knew it, I had pulled up outside Puffin Cottage. I sat in the car, parked in the back lane, staring down the road.

I hadn't imagined it – I hadn't been seeing shadows where there were none. Mike had been having an affair right under Amy's nose – no wonder she had found out. And he had lied when he'd told me that he and Amy had made their peace. They hadn't moved on at all - that's why she had hidden the evidence away for me to find.

I tried to pull myself back to the moment, walk myself through the next steps, but all I could think of was Amy. Had her suspicion built over time, or had it come as a shock? How much had she known? Had she ever confronted Mike, or had she been collecting evidence against him? Had he killed her when he'd thought she'd been coming too close to discovering his secret? My mind raced with the injustice of it all, too many thoughts jostling to be heard.

A loud knocking at the car window startling me, snapping me out of my reverie. Adam and Rachel. I wound the window down.

'And? How did it go?' Adam asked, their faces full of expectation.

For a second, I struggled to work out what he was talking about.

'The pitch? The pitch! It went great, really well, thanks,' I mumbled. 'We got it. We got the job.'

'Seriously?' Adam started bouncing up and down, grinning, and Rachel smiled proudly. 'You got the contract?' he said.

'Yes...' I forced a smile. 'I'm now officially in business.'

Adam opened the car door. 'Well, what are you waiting in there for? Champagne all round!'

I shuffled into the cottage in a daze, wishing I could enjoy the moment as much as I knew I should. Mum and Auntie Sue were already in the kitchen and there was a bottle of champagne on ice waiting for me, the bucket sweating onto the table next to a bouquet of white lilies.

Adam popped the cork and poured us each a glass.

'To Izzy Morton Interiors, and the start of something very special.' He held his champagne high. 'Cheers!'

We chinked our glasses together. Auntie Sue gave me a smile that told me I was forgiven – by her, at least.

The bubbles were mesmerising, and I could see a whole universe in my glass – galaxies suspended in gold, a sky of stars winking at me. Had Mike drunk champagne on his little jaunts to The Stables with Julie Knox? I felt sick at the thought.

'Izzy... Earth to Izzy... Is everything all right?' Rachel rubbed my shoulder.

They were all staring at me. Auntie Sue and Adam exchanged a worried glance.

'She's fine,' said Mum. 'I know my girl. Perhaps a little too much excitement for one day?'

I nodded in agreement, grateful for any excuse to sit down. My head was spinning again. The champagne had left a bitter aftertaste.

'Mike rang this morning,' said Auntie Sue, her voice ringing with a false lightness. She spoke as if she was addressing the whole room, but I knew this was just for my benefit. 'He's very sorry about what happened yesterday, and of course he isn't serious about keeping anyone away from the kids.'

The temperature dropped at the mention of his name. From the corner of my eye, I saw Mum pull her cardigan closed. I bristled at the thought of him, seething inside. How dare he threaten to keep me from the children? After what he had done. He had no right.

'I think he's ready to say sorry, if everyone else is...'

She was talking as if he had threatened everyone, but his anger yesterday had been directed squarely at me. He'd made me look like the bad one, like the crazy person. And now I had to apologise to him?

'Izzy?' Auntie Sue raised an eyebrow at me. 'Will you say sorry to Mike so we can all move on?'

I reluctantly agreed. Anything to see the kids.

Mum and Auntie Sue left, leaving me alone with Adam and Rachel. With my champagne almost untouched, I explained how I'd put two and two together at the hotel.

'That's scandalous!' said Adam, gobsmacked. 'The audacity of that man. No wonder you're out of sorts.'

Rachel had gone pale.

'Just think – all that time he was doing it right under her nose,' she said, shaking her head sadly. 'What are you going to do? Are you going to tell the police?'

'No, she is not,' said Adam, looking at me with a stern

expression. 'Izzy has done quite enough amateur detective work and she's learned the hard way that it doesn't do any good.'

'Well...' I said, considering it.

'You cannot be serious! Izzy – tell me you're not actually thinking of telling the police that you've worked out which hotel your brother-in-law was taking his mistress to?' He started to laugh nervously. 'What good would *that* do!? What does this even change, anyway?'

Adam hopped out of the armchair and onto the sofa beside me. 'I know you're angry,' he said, winding an arm around my shoulders. 'I know you're looking for someone to blame, and I know you think Mike did something wrong – well yes, he did... But not *that*. You can't decide that he murdered her just because he was cheating on her!'

The corners of my eyes started to blur with salty tears.

'You've got to give this up, Izzy.' Adam's voice was softer now.

Rachel crouched in front of me, offering me a tissue. 'Your sister would be so proud of you, you know.' She put her hand over mine. 'But Adam is right, you have to let this go. Let go of the anger. We all miss her. But this... It doesn't mean Mike is to blame. Perhaps it was just an accident after all.'

The tears started to flow, and I couldn't stop them.

Adam and Rachel went out for a walk while I took a nap, waking from an exhausted sleep when a wisp of cool air blew in from the window and tickled my cheek. The wind changed direction when the tide turned. Most people didn't notice it, but for coast folk, the ebb and flow of the sea was like a sixth sense. The more time I spent in Seahouses, the more I felt myself growing back in tune with the water. I no longer had to look out of the window to tell if it was high or low tide – the sound of the waves and the smell of the air gave it away.

We'd planned to go over to Amy's together that evening – safety in numbers, as Adam had murmured. I was desperate to see the kids. Just to make sure they were okay. And even though it had only been a day, I missed them.

Rachel was right – Amy would be proud of me. I'd done what she'd wanted me to do, made the sacrifice she had asked me of me.

At the beginning, I'd thought I'd be a burden on Mike, that I had so much to learn and that I would only get in his way. That between him, Auntie Sue and Mum, the children didn't need me. I was starting to realise that I'd been wrong – they did need me, just as much as I needed them.

I had started to worry about how much they were eating and if they were getting the right nutrition for their growing bodies. Reflexively, I checked them every morning for signs that they were getting enough sleep. Whenever I wasn't with them, I worried that they were safe and that they weren't upset. For the second time in my life, I knew what it was like to have someone who was more important to me than myself. The first had been Amy.

When Mike had told me to stay away from the children, it had cut like a knife. Just thinking of him made my rage start to simmer, and I didn't know why. Nothing had changed since yesterday – except that now I knew where he had gone with Julie. Now I had a location for his cheating, but did that make it any worse? It wasn't as if Mike had lied to me – I hadn't asked him where he had gone. And when I had confronted him with Julie's name, he'd come clean right away.

Perhaps Adam and Rachel were right – maybe I just needed to get over this. I had already got it wrong twice, and at what cost? Having an affair did not mean that Mike had murdered Amy, and I had to stop looking for proof of something that clearly didn't exist. The past was in the past, and we needed to forgive each other and move forward. Let the tide wash it all out to sea and start over.

Something else was niggling at me, too. I had replayed my discussion with Mike over and over in my head, and something didn't add up. It was like a jigsaw, with a final piece that almost fit, but not quite. From afar it looked fine, but if you ran your fingers over it, you would feel a bump where the pieces didn't quite belong. Was it my imagination, or had he admitted everything a little too easily?

Julie Knox. Julie Knox...

Why was the name familiar? Was she local? I'd read the tribute she'd written for Amy on Facebook, but I also had a vague memory of meeting someone called Julie Knox. Had she been at Amy's funeral? No. It was long ago, a lifetime ago. I couldn't put a face to the name. But there was an easy way to remind myself.

I opened Facebook on my phone, scrolling though Mike's friends until I found her: Julie Knox. Her profile picture was a flower. I was holding my breath as I clicked the thumbnail and her life unfurled across my screen.

My pulse thudded in my ears and my jaw dropped. I scrolled through her pictures, my eyes growing wider. Who was this? My head spun as I tried to make sense of what I was seeing.

Julie was in her seventies, a proud grandmother of five from Scotland. Not even one of those glamorous seventy-somethings but a proper old lady, with a silver perm set, shin-length skirts, and silk scarves knotted above her cardigans. Her Facebook profile was like a family photo album, including pictures with her husband. There was Julie at the WI, Julie at the church bake sale, Julie surrounded by her grandchildren.

No way was this woman having an affair with Mike.

I re-read the name to check I had the right person, and went back to the list of Mike's friends to make sure I wasn't missing something. How did this woman even know Mike and Amy? The text and photos started to swim on the screen in front of me. I clicked back to the top of her page and combed through her friends.

I opened the profile of her husband, Douglas Knox, and scrolled through his photos – and there was Mike. The two of them were standing with a third man on a golf course, smiling at the camera, squinting in the sunshine. The photo was several years old.

It didn't make any sense.

More scrolling, back through the years, then I saw it – a photograph of the Knoxes at Mike and Amy's wedding. And then I remembered – a vague, dusty memory, stashed away in the far corner of my mind, of being introduced to them. Douglas was a friend of Mike's father, a business partner or something like that, and Mike's dad had invited them to the wedding. He had already been a widower by then and had insisted on inviting some of his friends – Amy hadn't been happy about it but had been persuaded by Mike.

I had, of course, been completely disinterested in meeting them at the wedding. I'd been merrily drunk, smiling politely and saying just enough to be charming, wondering how quickly I could get back to my champagne and my date and the dancing. I hadn't thought of them since. Mum and Auntie Sue might remember more.

Not that it was important – this was clearly not the woman that we had seen with Mike in Newcastle. So why had he blurted out her name when I'd confronted him?

Or had he? Had Mike simply said the first name that popped into his head and I'd filled in the rest?

But he had admitted it was her.

Why had he lied?

And if it wasn't Julie Knox he'd been having an affair with, then who was it?

Chapter Twenty-Four

I needed to stay calm. Adam had suggested meeting at the pub before we went to Amy's and it seemed like a great idea. I was jittery, chewing on the inside of my lip now that there was nothing left of my fingernails.

My heart started to race whenever I thought of Richard. He would never be able to come back here, not after what he had done. Not after everyone found out. I had to keep telling myself that he had taken Amy's phone, and he had been accessing her messages – he would have brought police attention on himself sooner or later. But I kept picturing Auntie Sue's face and her look of disappointment in me when we realised that he'd been arrested for nothing.

At least Rachel was on my side. If she was holding Phil's arrest against me at all, she hid it well.

Phil must have known that it was because of me that he'd got arrested – and if he didn't already know, he would soon. Nothing stayed secret in Seahouses. I hoped he would come home soon, and that he and Rachel could work things out. I would get on my knees and beg his forgiveness – do whatever it might take – to help them save their marriage. Rachel had lost so much already.

He'd clearly expected a little more from his wife – at least a public show of support. She hadn't exactly leapt to his defence when he'd been accused, but we had all been so shocked, and in fairness to Rachel, she was also grieving for her best friend. Our entire worlds had been tipped upside-down and it was hard to exercise good judgement when you were so emotional. I had been quick to take the evidence at face-value, too. A wave of nausea washed over me as I remembered how easily I had believed that Amy had been unfaithful too.

But someone had wanted me to think that. Someone had planted those messages to frame Phil and gone back later to delete them – making it look like I had faked the whole thing. Someone wanted me to look paranoid, delusional. And that same someone had planted the medication at the garage for the police to find. I had no doubt that Mike was behind it. I just needed to prove it.

I went to the pub early and got myself a glass of wine. It was funny, I thought, how I was habitually late for almost every meeting or appointment except those that involved alcohol. The strength of my craving was frightening, enough to scare me into not touching my wine. I needed to get a grip – on my drinking and on my nerves.

Everything was becoming clearer. Mike had killed my sister, then set me up to frame someone else for it, and I was being forced to play happy families with him until the police figured this out. My legs trembled under the table.

By the time Adam and Rachel got to The Ship, I had bitten the inside of my lip so hard that it was bleeding and the shaking in my legs was almost uncontrollable. Adam clocked the full glass on the table but said nothing.

My mind was spinning – one thought had not finished before another began. Everything came to me in a jumble, my thoughts jumping from Mike to Amy, to Phil and back to Mike, from the funeral to the reading of the will and Amy's car in the garage and that small grey room in the police station, everything blurring and blending into one.

There should have been an outcry, we should be protesting, banging on the door of the police station and demanding that they do more, dig deeper. Yet here we were, in the pub making chit-chat, while my sister's murderer was free.

Adam asked how the kids were doing and Rachel answered before I could open my mouth – I suppose she still felt like she knew them better than I did. She was probably right. Besides, that wasn't the most important thing right now.

I tuned out their conversation and let the thoughts come to me, trying my hardest to focus.

Mike was lying – he had been lying all along. He had lied so much, it was difficult to know where his lies ended and the truth began, like a tangled ball of string. Lies stacked on top of lies – all in an attempt to cover up what he had done to Amy. But this – Julie Knox – this was the first time I had caught him out and could prove it. This was a cold, hard, fact – a bare-faced lie that I could prove was untrue. This was my starting point – the end of my string. From here, this was where it would all unravel.

The Stables. Jennifer – she would be able to help me.

An idea hit me, and I gasped. Adam and Rachel stopped talking and stared at me.

'Are you OK?' said Adam. He didn't wait for an answer, glancing anxiously at his watch. 'That's probably enough for now. I'll settle up so we can get going.'

As soon as he was out of earshot, I grabbed Rachel's arm. 'It was Mike,' I said, breathless. 'Mike did it, I know he did.'

She sank in her seat, shaking her head. 'You've got to let this go...'

'No, listen – I know Mike is hiding something and I can prove it. But I need your help.'

I looked over Rachel's shoulder to the bar, where Adam had been sidetracked into a conversation with Gina and a man in fishing overalls. Rachel twisted around to check that he wasn't listening, and leaned in towards me.

'What's happened now? I thought you said you would leave it up to the police?'

'Yes, yes. I know. But Mike lied about cheating on Amy, and then he lied about who he was cheating with, and I've thought of a way to find out who it was! And if we know that, then we can start to piece the rest together.'

She looked over her shoulder again, and I saw the desperate hope in her eyes for Adam to come back and talk some sense into me. 'I just think...' she began.

'Rachel!' I hissed. 'You have *got* to help me. If I get this wrong again, he'll cut me off from the kids for good. I just need to do this one thing and then I'll hand everything to the police, I swear. Just cover for me while I make a phone call. Tell Adam I'm talking to Jake or something.'

She bit her lip and gave a resigned sigh. 'All right. But keep it quick. I'm rubbish at lying.'

I slid out of the booth and slipped out of the pub's side door into the street. It was a warm spring evening by Northumberland standards, but my teeth were chattering. I paced from foot to foot and wrapped my arms around myself as I dialled Jennifer Wheeler's number.

She was surprised to hear from me, but she listened patiently as I explained the stalled investigation into Amy's death. It didn't take much to convince her how important it was to find out who Mike had stayed at the hotel with. She promised to head over to the hotel right away and call me as soon as she had checked the records.

We walked along the road in the direction of Amy's. Adam kept checking his watch, and I realised he had probably coordinated with Auntie Sue to make sure that everyone arrived at the same time. For him this was a peace-keeping mission, and we were envoys heading into hostile territory.

I understood why everyone wanted me and Mike to smooth things over – but they didn't know what he had done. They would be devastated when they found out, and this was one time that I wouldn't enjoy saying 'I told you so'. An image came to me, of Mike standing at Amy's funeral, his arms around the kids, a solitary tear rolling down his cheek.

That bastard.

The fury was bubbling and rising inside me like a vat of boiling oil. I took a deep breath and visualised a giant pot on a stove. I turned down the heat, the flames flickering smaller and smaller, and I carefully put a lid on. I instantly felt better.

I was so busy concentrating on my visualisation that I hadn't noticed a figure waiting on Amy's doorstep.

'Jake! Fancy seeing you here!' Adam exclaimed, giving Rachel a theatrical nudge and wink.

They fell about giggling and Jake blushed, looking bashfully at his shoes before glancing up at me. I gave him a weak smile and wondered if he knew he had been invited to make sure I behaved myself.

'Uncle Adam!' Lucas squealed as he answered the door, wrapping his arms around Adam's waist.

Uncle? I glanced at Rachel, who shrugged her shoulders.

Adam hadn't even made it into the hall before Betsy hurled herself on him too, and even Hannah was uncharacteristically affectionate, greeting him with a tender hug. He revelled in his hero's welcome, inching his way towards the kitchen with all three children draped from him and jostling for attention. The three of us followed, trudging down the hallway after them.

'You're popular...' I said to Adam, muttering as we shuffled into the kitchen.

He turned and raised an eyebrow.

'Just because Auntie Izzy won't take my calls doesn't mean I'm not regularly checking in on my tribe.'

Everyone crowded around the table. Mike started busying himself with drinks for the newcomers, looking thankful to have something useful to do. He fidgeted with cutlery and napkins, making only fleeting eye contact with me and Rachel as he handed us our glasses. I forced myself to smile at him. It left a bitter taste on my lips.

Mum was resplendent in a matching kaftan and turban, and I wondered who she had dressed to impress – Adam or Jake? Auntie Sue was cooking at the stove with Lucas by her side, and I could tell from the angle of her head that she was keeping one eye on dinner and one ear on the room. She had spoken to Mike and smoothed things over – I just hoped he didn't think it was necessary to talk everything out. It wasn't that I didn't want to say sorry, it was that I would sound so wholly unconvincing he would suss me out right away.

Nor did I want to hear his apologies – he could keep all of that, for all I cared. I would keep my cards close to my chest until I had an answer from Jennifer and could work out my next step.

Jake fit in seamlessly, and I watched as he chatted comfortably with Mum and Auntie Sue. I wondered if Amy would have approved of his boyfriend potential. Not that anything was going to happen. Not until all of this was over, at least.

'What's on the menu tonight, Jamie Oliver?' Adam leaned over Lucas's shoulder to see what he was stirring.

'Ham and mushroom risotto,' said Lucas with a wide smile.

'Well that sounds straightforward enough...' Rachel mumbled to me and Jake.

'Only, instead of rice, we're using porridge oats.'

The three of us gave a collective wince and Auntie Sue offered an apologetic shrug.

Adam, on the other hand, loved the idea. 'You're a genius, my boy, a genius! Is that one going in the book?'

Lucas nodded excitedly.

'What book is this?' I said, taking a sip of water, trying to sound casual.

Lucas shook his head and looked down, hiding a shy smile.

'Lucas is writing a recipe book,' said Adam. '*Amazing Amy's Adventures in Alimentation*. Working title, anyway. It's going to be a tribute to his mum, with all of her inspired inventions and her twists on the classics.'

He winked at Lucas, who was beaming.

'That's such a lovely idea, I...' I choked back a sob that came out of nowhere, the emotion cutting my vocal cords. My eyes met Rachel's, then Auntie Sue's – we were all filling up.

'I've been working on it since Mum died,' said Lucas. 'Every time I'm cooking. I try to remember how Mum made something, and when I get it right, I write everything down. Adam says I could be a chef when I grow up!'

How had I not known he was working on this? I kicked

myself – I should have been encouraging him, helping him. That's what a good aunt would do. Adam had only known Lucas for a matter of weeks and he'd given him more guidance and spiritual direction than I had managed to in his whole life time.

'A chef, eh?' Mike ruffled his son's hair. 'Your mother would be proud.'

Mike's mention of Amy sent a shudder through me, but nobody noticed. Adam was too busy enjoying the surprise on our faces.

'Maybe if you ask her nicely, MySelfHan can promote your book on her IG.' Adam winked at Lucas.

'What's IG? And who's MySelfHan? Am I missing something?' Auntie Sue was bemused.

'Instagram, Auntie Sue!' Adam laughed. 'Hannah here has gained quite the following. Who knows, we might make a social media influencer of her yet.'

'What?' I looked at Rachel and Mike, but the shock on their faces told me they knew no more than I did. 'You're posting *what* on Instagram? To who?'

Alarm bells were ringing – this was a serious oversight on my part. I was still mastering the basics of childcare and hadn't even thought about how to keep them safe online. Hannah could have been exposed to all kinds of dangers, and I had been too preoccupied to notice.

'Calm down, dear,' said Adam as he pulled out his phone. 'It's all very age-appropriate – no parental guidance necessary.'

'You didn't think to tell me about this?'

Adam rolled his eyes and pushed the phone in front of me. There was Hannah, but not as I knew her – she had a real talent for self-portraits. The pictures of her were mixed with random images – a shell on the sand, a wildflower, a close-up of the leaves on the tree in the garden. Her captions were little notes of positive affirmations, tips for self-confidence and dealing with bereavement. And Adam was right – she had more than eight thousand followers. My jaw dropped in disbelief.

Was this how Hannah was spending her time when she was glued to her phone?

'It started right after Mum died and we were off school,' Hannah said in a quiet voice. 'I wanted to talk about how I was feeling and then it just became this thing, where I was helping other people in the same situation handle their feelings.' Her tone was almost apologetic. 'I've been doing mindfulness exercises and meditation with Betsy, trying stuff out together.'

Betsy beamed at her sister.

'You know what, Han – I think it sounds fantastic.' Mike squeezed her hand. 'And your mum...' He gulped. 'Your mum would be so incredibly proud of you for helping other people. That was what she did, she was always thinking about others before herself. You're cut from the same cloth.'

A silence fell over the room and I felt the tension harden in the air, solidifying in the spaces between us. I wanted to scream at Mike, to smack him with something. Strong, violent, angry thoughts clouded my vision like a storm blowing in off the sea.

It was such a simple comment, and the obvious thing to say to a grieving child, but it felt like he was taking Amy's name in vain. How dare he invoke her memory? How did he have the audacity to proclaim himself as the expert on Amy's feelings, after everything he had done?

Mum shuddered. 'Did you feel that? The chi is abysmal

tonight. We'll have to do an aura cleansing before we eat, or we'll all get sick.'

Adam discreetly placed the palm of his hand on my shoulder and gave me a little squeeze. I glanced at him and saw the warning in his eyes, pleading with me to calm down. I forced myself to smile back.

Mum had us all sit down around the table and join hands. Before all this had happened, I wouldn't have even stayed in the room, let alone participated, and I would have been mortified to have Jake see the weird stuff she was in to. But I could see how much better it was making Mum, and that it was rubbing off on Hannah – not to mention Betsy – and I was beginning to appreciate it. She seemed to be on to something with feng shui, and after her meditation session the other day I did feel lighter and more relaxed. Mum would say that it meant I'd been spiritually cleansed – I preferred to think of it as a chill-out session.

Mum pulled a pale pink crystal from her bag and placed it in the middle of the table. I checked the group – everyone had their eyes closed and looked like they were taking it very seriously. Even Betsy had adopted a serene expression that made her look like a much older girl.

Mum started speaking, her voice dipping up and down in a strange sing-song pattern.

'Remember everyone, focus on the intention – bad energy out, good energy in. Take deep cleansing breaths and be mindful to let out any negative thoughts, any regrets, any darkness as you exhale...'

My phone vibrated in the pocket of my jeans. I opened one eye just to peek – everyone else still had theirs closed. Jake was holding my hand on one side and I had Rachel on the other.

'And now think of the energy in the room. I want you to visualise any toxic energy and harmful feelings and watch them blowing out of the door, blowing out of the window... And as they leave, they create space for light, warmth, and good energy. Imagine water flowing over you, cleansing you, leaving you feeling lighter, happier and free from earthly worries.'

The phone burned in my pocket and I willed Mum to finish so that I could check my messages.

'There,' she finally said, smiling around the room, still speaking in her up-and-down voice. 'You can now open your eyes and take a moment to express gratitude to one another.'

Jake looked like he had just woken up from a nap. 'That was marvellous, Anne,' he said, stifling a yawn.

'I know, right?' Adam beamed at Mum. 'I've missed my spiritual guru!'

Mum blushed and shrugged him off.

'Will you excuse me for a second?' I muttered as I climbed out from the bench.

Rachel caught my eye and I silently pleaded with her to keep quiet. I darted out the kitchen and ran upstairs to the bathroom, locking the door behind me.

There was one new message, from Jennifer.

I've been through the guest log – your brother-in-law was indeed a regular visitor. I also have an ID of the woman who checked in with him. I don't know how to tell you this. Can you please call me when you get a chance to talk?

I splashed my face with cold water.

The woman staring back at me in the mirror was almost un-recognisable. Pain was etched onto my tired face and my skin was pale and dull, but there was still a steely determination in my eyes.

'I'm getting closer, Amy,' I muttered under my breath, as I dried my hands on the towel.

Adam was waiting for me on the landing. I hadn't heard him follow me upstairs.

'You startled me!' The adrenaline was pulsing at my temples.

'Seriously, are you all right?' he asked. 'You're acting really strange tonight.'

It would be impossible to make a private phone call in this house. There were too many people and nowhere was out of earshot.

'I'm fine – better than fine. I have to pop out for a while though, I just have to ring someone...'

'What? Why? Who do you need to call so urgently?' Frustration fizzed in his voice. I cupped his shoulders in my hands and looked him in the eye, pleading for him to understand.

'I told you, I'm getting closer to the truth. I'm nearly there...'

'Please – you need to stop this. Please.'

'I'll only be gone for a few minutes – I'll tell everyone I forgot something at home.'

'We're about to eat dinner! Jake is here! You're supposed to be making up with Mike!' Adam's hands were balled into fists by his sides and I knew that I was wearing his patience down to breaking point.

'This is important, OK? Just don't say anything. I'll be back before you know it.'

Auntie Sue was helping Lucas to serve dinner, passing out steaming bowls of porridge risotto.

'I have to run home,' I blurted out. 'I think I've left a candle burning.'

I carefully avoided Adam's glare and focused on Jake, giving him a forced smile. Rachel shrugged reluctantly, shaking her head. It reminded me of the shrug that Amy used to give whenever someone disappointed her. Only, I wouldn't let Amy down this time.

From the corner of my eye, I could see the others exchanging raised eyebrows. But I didn't care what anyone thought – we would all know the truth before too long.

'I'll come straight back – fifteen minutes, tops.'

'Do you want me to come with you?' Jake asked.

'No, no – please stay. Enjoy dinner. I'll eat mine later,' I said as I pulled on my jacket. 'Sorry, everyone – be right back.'

I trotted down the hall and pulled the door closed before anyone had a chance to try and stop me.

Chapter Twenty-Five

It was a quiet evening, and the hollow crash of waves sang the familiar song of the tide on its way out. A solitary gull circled high above the harbour, tracking a returning fishing boat. The sun hung low, slowly dipping towards the hills. I walked as fast as I could.

I checked my watch – 7.25 p.m. I could get home, call Jennifer and be back at Amy's by 7.40 p.m. My hands were shaking, and I stuffed them deeper into my pockets. I wouldn't confront Mike with his lies tonight – I wouldn't confront him at all, but I would do my best to make sure I was there when he got arrested. I wanted to see the look on his face.

I hurried down Cedar Road and turned onto Swallow Street. From an open window on the back lane came the noises of dinner time – the scrape of a knife on a plate and the low murmur of table conversation. A ginger cat was lying on my neighbour's wall, basking in the dying light of the day.

The familiar scent of firewood greeted me as I opened the door to Puffin Cottage – my sanctuary. I locked the door behind me and didn't even take off my jacket before dialling Jennifer's number. My finger hovered over the call button, trembling. My heart was fluttering – I needed the sea to help me stay calm. I walked up the stairs, gripping the banister tightly, not trusting my legs to get me there. I sat down on my bed and fixed my gaze on the horizon just as Jennifer answered.

'Thanks for calling me back. I thought it was better to speak on the phone than tell you this by text.'

The sky was streaked with shades of gold and pink. I focused on the horizon, steadying myself. Deep breaths. The line crackled.

'Hello, Izzy? Are you there?'

Bad energy out, good energy in.

'Yes, I'm here.'

'It's just – this is really bizarre, but the guest who stayed here with Mike Sanders was his wife. It was Amy Sanders.'

I had been holding my breath and I choked on it now, coughing and spluttering.

'*What?* How? That can't be...'

Amy had been there with Mike? But why had she highlighted the dates on his credit card statements and hidden them away? Why had he admitted to having an affair? And there was the woman in Newcastle...

This wasn't making any sense.

'There's some mistake – it must have been someone pre-tending to be Amy.'

'I did consider that.' Jennifer was chewing on something – a pen perhaps.

It couldn't be right. Mike must have done something to cover his tracks. But how?

Jennifer sighed. 'I even pulled up the CCTV footage of them checking in together and showed it to Mum. She *thinks* it's Amy...'

'What does that mean, *thinks* it's Amy? She isn't certain?'

'The picture is grainy, and Mum's eyesight isn't the best.'

'But she couldn't say for certain? It could have been some-one else?' There was a frantic edge to my voice.

'Well if it isn't Amy, it's someone who looks a lot like her.'

I froze.

'Someone who looks like Amy...' I mumbled.

Someone who looked so much like Amy they could almost be sisters.

When I spoke again, my voice was nothing more than a croak.

'Could you email me the picture, please? Just so I can see it for myself?'

My pulse was pounding in my ears. I hung up on Jennifer and stared out to the sea, watching the rolling waves growing darker in the dying light.

A ping told me that her email had arrived. I clicked on the attachment and the picture started to download. It was agonisingly slow and I had to remind myself to breathe.

And there it was – grainy, but unmistakable. Mike, at the reception desk of the hotel I knew as The Stables. An overnight bag slung over his shoulder, a credit card in one hand and his other arm around... Rachel.

I zoomed in, squinting at the image, trying to see beyond the blur. Someone who didn't know Rachel as well as I did could look at this picture and see Amy. After all, plenty of people remarked on how alike they were.

It had been Rachel all along. Rachel was Mike's other woman.

Realising this brought me nothing. There was no release and there was no relief – just a sad emptiness.

Then I heard a thud from downstairs.

Had I imagined it? The noise must have come from outside. I had locked the door behind me when I came in.

I slipped my phone into my pocket. The last of the day's light was fading and the harbour lights were blinking to life. I tiptoed down the stairs and stood at the bottom in the darkness, pressed against the wall, listening outside the open living room door. There was a faint scuffling sound, so soft that it could be a mouse.

But I knew it wasn't.

My heart was pounding against my ribcage and I dared myself to look again. There was a light, a golden flickering that cast dancing shadows across the floor. I took a deep breath and stepped into the room.

Someone had lit a candle.

And then a voice from behind me.

'You couldn't help yourself, could you?'

I spun around on my heels, fists in front of me, ready for fight-or-flight.

Rachel laughed as she stepped past me and slowly folded herself into the armchair by the fire, tucking her legs up to one side as if this was one of our cosy nights in. I froze in disbelief.

'You just couldn't stop. Why? You had to keep pushing. And now here we are.' She laughed again, smiling at me with a snarl.

I took my phone from my pocket to call Adam. Rachel leapt up and snatched the phone away from me, slapping me hard across the face. The shock was more painful that the sting on my cheek. I touched a finger to my face, stunned into silence. I'd never been hit before.

'Seriously? You think I'm going to go through all of this and come this far, just to have you fuck everything up for me now?'

She spat the words at me with venom as she coiled herself back into the chair.

The shock subsided and I was pulled back to the surface, buoyed by adrenaline. I could feel my feet again.

I had to get out.

I was closer to the door than she was. Rachel must have let herself in with her key, but had she locked the door again behind her? It was worth a shot, and I decided to make a run for it – if I could make it as far as the lane, I could scream for help.

I ran through the kitchen towards the door, moving faster than I had in a long time. My weight slammed against the timber as I grabbed the knob and tried to twist – it didn't budge. She'd locked it from the inside. Where was the key? My pulse pounded in my ears.

Rachel hadn't even moved from the chair. 'That's your problem – you think I'm stupid.' That laugh again. The leather groaned as she stood up from the chair and started walking towards me. 'You know, Amy thought I was stupid too. And just look where that got her.'

She was laughing at me, at Amy. The panic was rising in me, and I struggled to think clearly. I needed something to defend myself. *A weapon!* I yanked the cutlery drawer open, ready to grab a knife. It was empty.

Rachel was suddenly at my shoulder, one arm around my neck and the other wrapped around my waist, pinning my arms to my sides. Her breath was warm on my ear.

'We could have been happy, me and you. We could have been sisters, played happy families. Shared the kids. Me and Mike could have got together. You might not have liked it at first, but you'd have wanted us both to be happy...'

CHAPTER TWENTY-FIVE

Her lips brushed my neck. She smelled of freesias – Amy's perfume.

'You'll never be my sister,' I said. 'You're nothing like Amy.'

How long had I been gone now? Adam or Jake would come looking for me soon. I just had to keep Rachel talking for long enough.

'Don't think that any of them are coming for you,' she said, reading my thoughts. 'They all think you're a basket case. They sent me to help you.' Her laugh was like glass shattering. 'After all,' she purred, 'I am like a *sister* to you.'

She was gripping me painfully hard and slammed me against the door. I tried to remember the moves I'd learned at the self-defence class Adam and I had taken in Hong Kong. I had probably missed any opportunity I'd had to fight Rachel off, and she was freakishly strong. I knew she would overpower me.

'Why did you do it? Why did you have to kill her?'

'Have to? *Have* to? I didn't *have* to kill Amy. I *wanted* to.'

Fresh anger burned like acid in my chest.

Rachel carried on, satisfied with her captive audience. 'Mike was going to leave her for me. He'd been saying it for ages, and somehow never got around to it.'

I pictured her and Mike together and felt repulsed.

'I had to bring things to a head. Make him decide, once and for all. So I told him I was pregnant, and you know what that bastard did? He told me to get rid of it!' She screamed, a frustrated, angry bark, and threw me against the door again with a new strength. 'He asked me how I knew it was his. After everything we'd been through, he told me to get a fucking *abortion*. Can you imagine? And then he wanted to end things, I know he did. He didn't have to say anything. I could see it in his eyes, the moment I told him. He was going to break up with me.'

Sadness curled at the corners of her words and her grip relaxed a little.

'It was a test, and he failed. Big time. So I had to find another way to solve the problem. Because, can't you see? *Amy* was the problem. That spoilt little bitch.'

She pushed me harder against the door.

'Little Miss Fucking Perfect Life. You were the perfect wife, had the perfect house, the perfect kids, the perfect husband... You even had the perfect best friend.'

Was she talking to me or to Amy? With her arm around my neck, it was hard to breathe. I desperately fought for tiny gulps of air.

'And what?' I gasped. 'You wanted what she had, so you *killed* her for it? Or you wanted to get back at Mike?'

Rachel hesitated for a second, as if remembering where she was. Who she was with. 'Nah...' Her bared teeth brushed against my earlobe. 'I killed her because I knew I could,' she hissed.

'Amy', I stuttered. 'Amy knew about you two. She found out. That's why she changed her will.'

'She found out about Mike. Never had concrete proof, but knew he was up to something. She was starting to keep tabs on him, going through his bank statements and stuff. She confided in me, at first. I was her shoulder to cry on. And then one day, there was just something different about her. The way she looked at me... And I could see it had occurred to her that maybe, just maybe, it was me. So I decided it was time. It was just a case of waiting until the right moment.'

'I came over that night – I knew Mike was at the pub, so I

called in on Amy for a nice cosy chat and spiked her drink. I made my excuses – told her I wasn't feeling well. She was off with me anyway. I saw myself out, then ducked beside her car and loosened the lug nuts on her front wheel - even took one all the way out. Turns out all those evenings I spent helping Phil at the garage weren't a complete waste of time after all.

'The car was parked right outside the house – can you believe it? She'd have seen me if she'd looked out the window.

'I gave it just enough time for the meds to kick in before I rang her, saying there was an emergency over at Howton Farm and I wasn't up to going. That would always get Amy out, even if she had drunk a glass of wine. Always on district duty, that one. The timing had to be perfect – she had to leave while she still felt OK to drive. The car was a ticking bomb by then. It was just a matter of time.'

Rachel's grip tightened on me. If she pinned me any harder, I would choke.

'And guess what? I pulled it off! It all went to plan – until you showed up.'

'And Phil? You framed your own husband?'

'He was the two-for-one! It was easy enough to send messages from his Facebook to Amy, he didn't even know I'd done it. You thought you were going mad after I deleted them. And I left the sedatives in his garage for the police to find – they were all ears when I tipped them off. Amy was dead and he was going down for it. He's a dead weight anyway.'

Rachel laughed, then laughed again, catching her own joke.

'He's actually a *dead weight* in every sense, these days. He's out at Southend Rock, in front of the caravan park. I knocked him out and rolled him over the edge. The water's deep over there, by the cliff. It'll take them ages to find him and when they do, they'll assume it was suicide.'

My insides turned to ice. I had to get out of here – she had killed Amy and Phil, and I was next.

'And you were too easy,' Rachel laughed. 'I couldn't believe how quickly you believed Amy was cheating on Mike. You wanted to believe she wasn't happy and you were so ready to think the worst of her. You really didn't know your sister at all, did you?'

My anger flared, reigniting my instinct to fight. But how? Everything in the self-defence class had been about kicking or hitting your attacker in the groin, but that wasn't going to work here. I couldn't move any part of my body except my left leg, and if I moved that, I'd lose my balance. But maybe that was just what I needed.

I threw myself back against Rachel, leaning my weight onto her. She was startled by the sudden movement and momentarily lost her balance, stumbling a little. I swung my free leg up in front and kicked hard against the door, sending us both tumbling backwards.

We landed together on the floor with me on top, the impact knocking the wind out of me. Rachel's head hit the ground with a sickening thud and her arm flopped to the side. I jumped to my feet, my breath a ragged panting, ready to kick or punch.

She was out cold. I carefully nudged her with my foot. Nothing.

Where was the key? I tiptoed into the living room, panic thundering in my chest. Where could she have tossed it? I rummaged through her bag and jacket pockets with shaking hands. She must have hidden it somewhere.

I glanced back over my shoulder – Rachel was still lying there on the kitchen floor, still out for the count. My heart hammered. I wiped my face with the back of my hand – sweat mixed with snot and tears. I prayed to Amy that I would get out of this in one piece.

The phone. I would ring Adam for help, then barricade myself upstairs until the police arrived. Rachel had tossed my mobile to the ground when she'd snatched it off me. There it was, under the TV table. I picked it up, found Adam's contact details, and pressed 'call'.

Come on, come on... I silently pleaded with it.

Then there was a thud, and everything went dark.

Rachel was sitting over me when I woke. I was on my back on the living room floor, my wrists and ankles bound tight with plastic cable ties, a dull ache in my head. I tried to speak, but she had put duct tape over my mouth.

'Wakey, wakey...' Her face twisted into a grimaced smile.

I retched. How long had I been knocked out for? It was properly dark outside now.

'You sent a text to Adam telling him that you want some space, and to pass the message on to everyone that you just want to be left alone.' Rachel held the phone out to me to read. I looked away. 'It worked, because he has just replied to let you know that you're selfish and he's had enough of you. So don't expect anyone to be running to your rescue, just in case that's what you were thinking.' She was pleased with herself. 'And later, after you've downed the rest of your vodka, and swallowed these' – she shook a jar of pills – 'you'll send him another message to say goodbye.'

I squirmed and the ties cut into my wrists. Rachel bent down to examine the angry red lines they had made, holding my wrists up for closer inspection.

'Hmmm... I might have to slit your wrists too, just to cover this mess.' She stood up and stretched, her neck giving a violent crack. She gazed out of the window, considering, her face twisted into a snarl. 'I think that's quite *you*, don't you? Very *Izzy*. You would be thorough. And look – these are the same pills that I used for your sister. How poetic is that?'

Rachel squatted down in front of me and hauled me over her shoulder in a fireman's lift. I screamed and squirmed, and she punched me hard in the ribs.

'I would keep still if I were you. A drunken fall down the stairs is still an option.'

She carried me upstairs and dropped me into the bath. My wrist hit the edge of the avocado tub with a sickening crunch.

'Don't move.' She pushed me back and turned on the tap.

Cold water splashed into my face and I twisted out of the way, blinking my eyes open and spluttering snot and water. It took me a second to catch my breath and see clearly. Rachel wasn't in the room – where had she gone?

The water was filling the tub around me, making it even harder to move. I could probably get out of the bath, but where would I run to? My bedroom? I was torn between fighting back now and saving my energy. Terror paralysed me.

The thunder of Rachel's steps rumbled up the stairs and she reappeared at the door with her hands full. She carefully placed the bottles of vodka and the knife on the bathroom counter – the staging for my suicide – neatly arranging each item.

I thought of the kids – they would never know that I hadn't abandoned them, and Mum – how would she cope, losing me so soon after Amy? And poor Adam, who would blame himself. It was my fault. I should have seen it. The answer had been in front of me all along. And now I hadn't just failed Amy. I'd failed all of them.

I was shivering – I didn't know if it was from the biting cold of the water or terror. Rachel crouched at the side of the bath and removed the lid from the bottle of vodka. With a tenderness that took me by surprise, she slowly peeled off the tape from my mouth. I was aware that it stung, but numb to the pain of it.

'Please Rachel, please don't do this.' I begged. 'Let's work something out...'

'Shh... Just drink,' she said in a soft voice.

She gently tipped my head back and put the bottle to my lips. I clamped my mouth closed shut, the vodka running down my chin. She slapped me again and pinched my nose until I gave in, gasping for air, and shoved the bottle roughly into my mouth.

Vodka had never tasted so bad. It burned like icy fire, every drop scorching my throat, pooling in my stomach like poison. How much would she force me to drink? How much could I hold down?

The pain in my wrist was pulsating and the water was still rising – it was now at my chest and the weight was crushing me, pinning me down. I was powerless, and at that moment, I gave up. This was how I was going to die.

Tears rolled down my cheeks. Exhaustion took over and I closed my eyes, tuning out everything except the sound of the water. *The water, the water. Listen to the water. Focus on your breathing. Take yourself away from here.*

I imagined I was on the beach with Amy, lying on our backs. Sand beneath us. No need to talk to each other – we always knew what the other was thinking anyway. She wasn't disappointed in me, and I hadn't let her down. Amy turned her head towards me and smiled, and I knew that she wasn't far away from me now.

A smash and a scream ripped me back to the moment. Not a scream so much as a war-cry, a guttural howl...

The smash had been the bathroom door slamming open against the wall. Rachel whipped around, but barely had time to register Auntie Sue, howling, her face contorted with rage – or the stone foo dog she was holding high in two hands – before Auntie Sue slammed the ornament down hard against Rachel's head.

I saw a glimmer of confusion on Rachel's face as she fell backwards from her crouch, and Auntie Sue's shock as she looked down at her own hands, violently trembling, still tightly clutching the foo dog. She took in the set-up on the dresser and looked at me, her eyes wide, the colour drained from her. Her expression was of sheer terror.

Rachel gave a low growl like a wild animal, shaking off the blow. She gripped the edge of the bath to steady herself as she slowly got back to her feet.

'Auntie Sue!' I screamed. 'Do something!'

Just then, Mum crashed through the door behind her, barging past Auntie Sue. She charged shoulder-first into Rachel, throwing her entire weight against her and sending the pair of them hurtling backwards towards the window.

There was a splintering as the ancient wooden frame cracked and the glass panes shattered into infinite shards. They seemed to teeter there for a moment, fighting against the pull of gravity and the long drop down, before Auntie Sue grabbed the back of Mum's kaftan, clutching a fistful of fabric and yanking her sister away from the precipice.

Rachel's arms flailed wildly and desperately, grasping for something to save her from the fall, but there was nothing except the night. She toppled backwards, plummeting sound-lessly through the darkness, down towards the harbour far below.

Silence.

The curtains billowed in the breeze and the bathroom was filled with cold, briny air. Auntie Sue shuffled to the window and peered down.

'Isabelle!' Mum rushed to me, looping her arms around me and slowly raised me out of the bath, my body wracked by uncontrollable shivers. She turned the tap off and wrapped a towel around me, rubbing my back, then took the knife from the dressing table. With steady hands, she cut the plastic ties from my wrists. Cooing a soft lullaby, she started to peel off my wet clothes.

Adam appeared at the door.

'Izzy! Oh, dear god. We came as soon as we realised! I just got off the phone, the police are on their way. I'm so sorry, I should have...'

'Don't, honestly – I'm OK. Is Rachel...?'

Auntie Sue shook her head.

'How did you know I was in trouble?' I said through chattering teeth.

'The message you sent – well, the message that was sent from your phone. I could tell right away it wasn't you,' said Adam. 'You would never not be there for the kids. Also, it was signed it off with "xxx". That's how Rachel signs off.'

'You weren't yourself at all, I just *knew* something wasn't right. I should have realised sooner.' Auntie Sue was fighting back tears. 'It was weird, the way Rachel had followed you out.

Mike broke down when I asked him if there was anything he wasn't telling us. I'll never forgive him for this.'

Mum said nothing. She hummed her lullaby as she rubbed my back, rocking me gently, and I melted into her, surrendering myself to her care. The distant wail of a siren grew louder, and soon the bathroom walls were lit up by flashing blue light.

Chapter Twenty-Six

Quick! She's coming on now!'

We were crowded into the living room at Amy's – I still thought of it as Amy's – and gathered around the television.

'Quiet, everyone!' I shushed the excited chatter as the presenter introduced the next guest.

'Many of us have experienced the pain of losing a loved one, but few have managed to turn that into a positive thing. One person who has done that very successfully is Hannah Sanders from Northumberland, who created a platform for teenagers to access mental health support after she lost her mum in a road accident. And we're very pleased to have Hannah with us today.'

We collectively gasped as the camera panned out, revealing Hannah sitting on the iconic red sofa. Her long blond hair had been blow-dried and she was wearing the outfit we had chosen together – her leather jacket over a printed tea-dress and Amy's old shell necklace.

'Hannah, tell us – where did the idea for MySelfHan come from?'

'Well, after my mum died, it was very hard to talk about my feelings...' I mouthed the words with her as she said them. '...

And I found that it was easier to communicate with my friends through social media. I supposed it's because young people like me, we've grown up with everything being online, and we're sometimes more comfortable with that.'

She smiled. *That's good, Han – remember to smile.*

'It began with posting how I was feeling, and the strategies I was using to cope. At first it was just my friends, and it sort of just grew from there. Then I realised that what I was going through could help other teenagers who were facing a tough time, so I started to share more widely.'

The screen cut to show images from Hannah's Instagram, then of Hannah speaking at an event.

'It's a fantastic story, Hannah,' the presenter smiled, 'and once again we see how powerful social media can be. And yours in particular – I understand you've been nominated for an award?'

Hannah squirmed in her seat and blushed. She still wasn't used to being the centre of attention. 'I have, yes – I've been nominated for a Gleam Award. And while it's lovely to be recognised, there are lots of really amazing people up for prizes, and I'm just happy to be part of it.'

The presenter beamed at her. Hannah seemed to have this effect on everyone these days – people found it impossible not to like her. Amy would have burst with pride.

'Hannah Sanders – thank you very much for joining us.'

We cheered and applauded as the show cut to the next segment. I let out a sigh of relief – it had gone so well.

It was all part of the plan that Adam had put together for her – his vision was that Hannah would be an early pioneer of a new generation of influencers with more depth. She had content pillars, editorial calendars, and a weekly call with Adam to go over the engagement analytics. For Hannah, it was all about helping people who needed it. A fitting tribute to her mum.

I worried that it was too much pressure, but she had assured me she would stop if ever it got to the point that it was no longer fun – and promised us that schoolwork would always come first. I would be glad when she got home tonight. At least in Seahouses, she could melt back into her normal life and be a regular teenager – not an online celebrity with sixty thousand followers. Mike and I had even created a new rule – phone-free time – to make sure she was getting enough time away from the screen.

Mike and I had eventually made up, although it had been hard work to get to that point. I didn't want to hold what had happened against him – I could have, but I chose not to. It sounded like something Mum would say – to make a conscious decision to not be angry – but I didn't want to live with the negative energy. Anger and resentment were bitter seeds – I couldn't let them take hold. If I did, they would grow fast and spread like weeds, poisoning the soil.

Mike had been devastated to learn about Rachel – we all were – and blamed himself for what had happened to Amy. Everyone had misjudged her, it seemed – she'd even had Amy fooled. Mike's remorse and the guilt he felt that I'd almost become Rachel's third victim was enough for me to forgive him, in the end.

It had taken months of therapy to get Mike back on his feet. We paid off his business debts when I received my final bonus from the bank, and his work had taken a backseat for now, leaving him to concentrate on enjoying time with the children. This time it had been his turn to accompany Hannah to London. I hoped they were enjoying some father-daughter bonding time.

I'd resisted therapy, but the trauma had left its scars and it had been a long time before I could finally sleep in my own bed again. Mum and I had spent weeks cleansing the energy at Puffin Cottage. It had taken a complete crystal purification and multiple smudging ceremonies before I'd felt at home again in the cottage.

Instead of using booze to numb my pain, I'd taken up long-distance running. It turned out there was nothing like almost being killed by a deranged maniac to put you off the taste of vodka, and I now had some of my best creative ideas while pounding out miles along the sand. I still avoided Southend Rock, even long after the police divers had recovered Phil's body, choosing instead the stretch of golden sand in the direction of Bamburgh.

Auntie Sue beamed at me excitedly from her seat on the small sofa next to Emily. After that night with Rachel, she'd decided that life was too short to live with regrets. It hadn't taken her long to track Emily down, and it had been an emotional reunion.

Emily was beautiful, with skin like porcelain and hazel eyes, and she hung on Auntie Sue's every word. They went for long beach walks and I would often watch them making their way back up the dune path, hand in hand, their faces gleaming with exhilaration and the salty air. The only time they weren't laughing was when they did the crossword together – that was serious business.

Auntie Sue was almost unrecognisable. The way she walked and the way she laughed – I had never seen this side of her before. She was younger, lighter, freer. I saw now that all the years she had spent with us – ever since she came back to Seahouses – she had been a tightly-coiled spring. Solid, sturdy, but tense – and now she had been released. She and Emily had missed out on so much time and they were determined to make the most of their second chance.

Now that Mum was much more 'steady on her feet', as we all liked to say, Auntie Sue felt that she could finally leave her for a couple of weeks. She and Emily were flying to Santorini on Saturday, a place that they had planned on visiting before Dad had died. It would be Auntie Sue's first holiday in twenty-five years.

Mum no longer seemed to have her bad days. At Diana Wheeler's suggestion, she had joined the RNLI committee and become involved in some of Amy's community groups. She had even started hosting meditation, yoga and mindfulness sessions at the village hall. It had taken a while for the classes to take off – meditation just wasn't a thing in Seahouses yet – but people were gradually warming to the idea.

After Rachel was killed, we were worried that Mum could face charges. The police had been talking about whether her use of force had been necessary and proportionate for self-defence. I wanted to ask what level of force was appropriate for a psycho killer who had murdered one of your daughters and was trying to kill the other, but Mum was very zen about it. DCI Bell wasn't assigned to the case at first, but as soon as she got involved, Mum was given the all-clear.

Izzy Morton Interiors was hard work, but it was slowly taking off – we were even considering taking on another member of staff. Most of it came through word-of-mouth – guests at The Stables frequently commented on the wonderful ambience of the hotel, and Jennifer never hesitated to recommend us. We had just wrapped up a project on a luxury hotel in Newcastle and were about to land a second contract with the same chain.

Although I put our success down to good fortune, Mum had other ideas – citing everything from karma, positive intention-setting, and the spirits of Amy and Dad watching over us. I didn't argue with her, just in case Dad and Amy were listening.

Smiling at the thought of this, I padded into the kitchen to check up on Lucas. He was still working on perfecting Amy's recipes and putting them together in a book. Each of us was dealing with the loss in our own way, and this was how Lucas wanted to honour his mother's memory. It meant that we often ate the same dish three nights a week, but only Betsy complained.

Jake was watching him cook. It hadn't taken much for Jake to go from solicitor to friend to boyfriend. He came to see me in hospital the night that Rachel tried to kill me and officially asked me out. I joked that he'd taken advantage when I was vulnerable and had a possible concussion, but ten months later, we were still going strong. He'd even asked me to move in with him, but I'd told him it was too soon. I was still finding the right balance in my new life, and I didn't want to put the kids through more upheaval. But he'd wait. Jake was a keeper.

I still talked about Amy all the time with the kids. They had so many questions about her, and I often spent the hours when I wasn't with them trying to remember stories or morsels of information that I could pass on.

Mike and I had to tell the children the full story of how she died. They would have found out sooner or later, and it was better that they heard it from us. We told them everything in one painful session, and it was cathartic to lay all our misjudgements and misgivings and mistakes out in the open.

There were no more secrets.

The children grieved for Rachel, too. The memory of the Rachel they'd thought they knew. I suppose we all grieved for her, in a strange way. I found I couldn't be angry with her – it would require more emotional energy than I possessed.

Grief was like the sea. It was always there. Some days it was still, reflecting a bright blue sky punctuated by clouds of happy memories. Other times it was grey, deep, endless. And on the worst days, it raged, dark and angry. It could change at a moment's notice, catching even the most seasoned sailor off-guard. All I could do was stay afloat, waiting for the storm to pass and the blue sky to return.

I saw Amy every day.

In the kids' acts of kindness – the big gestures, but also the small things that they did for me, for their grandmother and great-aunt, and for each other. In their mannerisms and their expressions.

Betsy's laughter was like having Amy in the room – it still occasionally startled me. I heard Amy in her sarcasm and sass. When Hannah was reading, I couldn't take my eyes off her – sometimes she looked up and caught me staring, and I was afraid to tell her that it was as if her mum was just there. The way Lucas sat at the window and watched the birds in the garden, how he poked his tongue out of the side of his mouth when he was concentrating, and the delight he got from nourishing the people he loved – he was Amy, through and through.

I saw her in me, too. She was always with me, and we'll never truly be apart.

Acknowledgements

Sincere and profound thanks to you, dear reader, for accompanying me on this journey (and making it to the end). I hope you enjoyed reading Salt Sisters as much as I enjoyed writing it. Please join the other readers who have left ratings and reviews on Amazon and Goodreads, and help more people discover it. Reviews make a huge difference to new authors, and it's the best way you can support the book.

Writing a novel is something I have wanted to do for a very long time. Thank you to everyone who said I should, and those of you who convinced me I could.

And above all thanks to Igor, for helping me finally believe that I would. You were there from the start and kept me going until the end – and beyond. Thank you for giving me the support, encouragement, and the time I needed to achieve this, and for your endless patience, generosity, and love. Every day, I thank the universe that our stars collided.

Writing a book is not a solo effort – it takes an entire village. To my early readers, I give a heartfelt thank you. My dear friends Paul Johnson, Helen Seymour, and Bernadette McGee showed great enthusiasm for an early draft that was just the boost I needed to get me to the finishing line. It's not easy to cast a critical eye and it takes a true friend to be honest. Thank you to my wonderful mum Brenda Clelland, who read not one but TWO drafts of Salt Sisters, and my incredible aunt Anne Simms (I don't have an Auntie Sue - I have an Auntie Anne, and she happens to be a literary genius). Without all of your ideas and support, Salt Sisters would not be as good as it is. To give your time and energy to this, particularly when you were each navigating the nightmare of a pandemic and everything that 2020 entailed, is a generosity I cherish.

I owe a debt of gratitude to my editors, Nicole Frail and Gabrielle Chant. Thanks for all the advice, for keeping my fragile writer's ego intact, and for polishing a rough diamond. I also wish to thank Joanna Penn of The Creative Penn podcast, and all the other authors who have taken the time and energy to share wisdom and experience with budding writers. Particularly the authors I'm privileged to know personally – Howard Mutti-Mewse and Syd Goldsmith – thank you both for your advice and encouragement, and Yvonne Iwaniuk, who I'm fortunate to count as a mentor and friend.

A shout-out to my sister, Beth Edwards, with whom I share more than a lifetime's worth of memories. A sister truly is a best friend forever, and I'm so grateful that I got such a good one. That's what this story is about, really – it's a love letter to sisters everywhere, and our unique, unbreakable bonds.

I also want to thank Beth for her contribution to my roster of seven nieces and nephews; Tammy, Nieve, Jasmine, Dylan, Isabelle, Grace, and Jack, who have collectively taught me that being an auntie is the most important job I will ever have. I love you all.

Thank you to Johanna Harston, Terri Rae, Cathy Dowse, and my Taipei bookclub girls (Best F*ckin Book Club Ever), who lent moral support and enthusiasm throughout this process.

Huge thanks too to Brenda Smyth for showing me around Hong Kong, to Ahmet Sammali for his advice on cars, and to the many other friends who gave perspectives and ideas for Salt Sisters, even if you didn't know you were doing so at the time.

There were many days when reaching 'the end' felt like an impossible mountain to climb. Thanks to all of you who gave me the encouragement to keep going - you made the difference.

Seahouses is a real village in Northumberland, and I was lucky to spend many weekends there as a child. However, I used some artistic license in my descriptions of the village in this book, which I hope you will forgive me for. It is a beautiful part of the world, with kind and friendly people, and I urge you to visit. Have a pint and stay overnight in The Olde Ship Inn, when you do.

The idea for Salt Sisters came following a conversation one night with my friend Richard Forster and his wife Beckee. Over dinner in Singapore, we started discussing the moral (and lifestyle) implications of 'inheriting' custody of children after the death of a sibling - one of those crazy 'what if' conversations, and it got me thinking. It is not based on real-life experience - neither mine, nor that of anybody I know. It is a work of fiction.

Will there be a follow-up to Salt Sisters? I hope so.

Visit my website KatherineGraham-author.com and sign up to be the first to hear any news.

Thank you for reading. And before you go, please don't forget that review.

About the Author

Katherine Graham

I'm never not reading. Growing up, we had a rule in our house that my mother frequently had to enforce: no books at the dinner table. What can I say – stories are simply delicious.

I built a career as a professional storyteller without even realising it. I started out as a trainee journalist and ended up in communications and PR. I've spent 15 years helping some of the world's biggest brands craft their narratives and find the right words to tell them. Stories are, and have always been, what I do.

But it took a while for me to find the confidence, time and commitment to write a story of my own. I began writing fiction back in 2008, maybe even earlier. My debut novel Salt Sisters was eventually published in 2021. That's a long draft.

I'm originally from the North East of England and today I live in Taipei with my partner. I love 90s RnB, Cadbury's chocolate buttons, spin classes and bubble baths.

Visit my website to learn more about me, get exclusive book club content, and find out what inspired Salt Sisters. You can also sign up to my mailing list and be the first to hear about future books.

You can connect with me on:
🜨 https://www.katherinegraham-author.com
🖉 https://www.instagram.com/dame_graham

Subscribe to my newsletter:
✉ https://landing.mailerlite.com/webforms/landing/c7k1y7

Made in the USA
Middletown, DE
27 May 2021